THE JACK PEOPLE

BY

JAMES REIMER

This book is dedicated to my wife Judy, whose patience and encouragement was appreciated in writing and marketing *THE JACK PEOPLE* and *ARDMORE*.

To the memory of my lifelong friend, Russ Inbody.

My thanks go out to a good friend and fellow author, Dick Jacobsen, for his direction and support!

PREFACE

The Jack People is the second book of a three-part series that exposes more possible episodes of Nebraska's hidden history. The main character, Jake Young, is again drawn into a strange series of events that transpire during a week in December of 2013. Part One is a history of events that took place back in 1959 and lead up to Part Two.

Jake and five other men find themselves battling aliens and alien abductions, uncovering jackrabbit-sized little creatures, exposed to unexplained cattle mutilations, and discovering a murder. The main setting for the story is once again Scottsbluff, NE, located in the western panhandle of the state.

The author sometimes intertwines Scottsbluff and Gering. The two cities are just across the Platte River from one another and it's difficult to include one without the other. I hope I don't confuse too many readers!

I'd like to give a brief background of each of these phenomena individually and shed some light on their credibility. This is information that you, the reader, may be unfamiliar with.

Aliens and alien sightings have become commonplace around the world. About half of the world's population believes they do exist.

There have been many documented sightings in Nebraska, many of which are listed on the UFO Chronicles website.

As a matter of fact, the first recorded flying saucer crash occurred in the little town of Max, Nebraska in the very southwest corner of the state on June 6, 1884. A rancher by the name of John Ellis and three hired hands witnessed the crash and reported it. The story was told in the Nebraska State Journal.

The crash took place well before the Wright Brothers first recorded flight in 1903 and the Roswell Incident in 1947. The story is recreated on page 42.

Did the incident actually happen, or was it fabricated? Credible sources at the time say it did. Can you, the reader, say with certainty that it didn't?

Cattle mutilations have become readily identified with this part of the country. Numerous Nebraska ranchers have reported these strange events over the years. Experts have yet to be able to come up with a logical explanation. No reported arrests have ever been made in connection with a cattle mutilation.

You can read numerous accounts on various websites listed under the search "Nebraska cattle mutilations" to get more information.

The real uncle Hank characterized in *The Jack People* was a District Court Judge in O'Neill, Nebraska. Uncle Hank told his nephew, the author, in detail of an incident he'd witnessed while traveling in this desolate part of the state.

Hank was visiting with a local sheriff one day back in the early 1980's when the law officer was summoned to a nearby ranch. He asked Hank to come along. The two men were taken out to a pasture where a mutilated cow had been discovered. Hank told of the harrowing experience in great detail and was truly shaken by the incident.

The last and strangest phenomenon is not as widely recognized as the first two, but an actual photograph and documentation now make it just as conceivable.

This involves the Wee People of eastern Wyoming. These mythological creatures reportedly roamed the Pedro Mountains, which is approximately 200 miles from Hemingford, Nebraska, where they reappear in *The Jack People*.

In 1932, two miners discovered the mummified remains of a Wee that stood no more than fourteen to twenty inches tall. They took their find to Casper, Wyoming where scientists from around the country were called in to examine the find. Believing it was a hoax, the remains were x-rayed. The results showed the perfectly formed skeleton of a man believed to be around sixty-five years of age. He had been brutally beaten to death. Skeptics say they were the remains of a malformed child.

The mummy was displayed in numerous sideshows over the years before disappearing. Its whereabouts are unknown, but the story remains. Again, you can research the story by researching "Wyoming Legends," "Little People" or "the Pedro Mountain Mummy" online.

My first book in the series, entitled *Ardmore*, is created partly on factual Nebraska history based on the early stories of from people of both European and Native American descent from the eighteen hundreds. The truth is mixed with some supernatural stories that took place in the western panhandle during the mass immigration west. The latter events have been brought back to life through various articles surfacing on related websites and are interspersed with real events throughout this thrilling book.

Unbelievable accounts such the ghost ships of the Platte River, the witch's grave in Aurora and others merge with true historical accounts of the Ghost Dancer Movement, the Civil War, the Homestead Act, Wounded Knee, Ft. Robinson and the Oregon/Mormon trails. They are told through the eyes of this fictitious main character and their relationship to the demise of the real ghost town of Ardmore, South Dakota is explained.

Jake Young is a casket salesman who travels this part of the country calling on area funeral homes. He gets caught up in the real and the imagined and *Ardmore* is his story of both.

Ghosts, ghost tales and some real documented atrocities relevant to the time dominate *Ardmore*. This book tells an eerie tale of western Nebraska's history and follows a subplot including a myriad of fictional horror stories that led to the demise of this authentic, abandoned ghost town located two miles across the state line.

The author, a fourth generation Nebraska native, is intrigued by the state's interesting documented history. He took great pleasure in combining it with some of the more controversial tales and drawing them together in the first two books of his trilogy.

James' purpose is not to try and convince his readers of their validity, but to raise the question, "Could this be more fact than fiction?" He hopes you'll enjoy *The Jack People* and again, wants to let you draw your own conclusions.

Both books are available through Amazon, Nook and Kindle.

Connect with Jim:

Blog: JamesReimerAuthor.com
Facebook: Facebook.com/jamesreimerauthor
Twitter: Twitter.com/jamesreimer6

CONTENTS

PART ONE - 1959

PART TWO - 2013

PART ONE

1959

SCOTTSBLUFF, NEBRASKA

RURAL RANCH COUNTRY

CHAPTER ONE
DOC MINO

"Ok, I've got her. You can release now. Great job!"

"Pull slow and steady now Ray, be careful not to yank!"

"Ok, good, keep pulling until I say stop!"

"Easy, easy."

Ray let go of the rope and heaved a big sigh of relief. With careful guidance and an experienced hand, Doc Mino delivered another baby calf into the world. For this strong country vet, it was just another day at the office.

Ray Tickner, the proud owner of the new calf, thanked Doc as the two took off their elbow-length, heavy black rubber gloves. By this time, the calf was unsteadily standing on all fours and being groomed by momma. Both were doing amazingly well, all things considered. Ray was no stranger to helping all of his livestock give birth to their babies. He didn't need a veterinarian to help deliver the roughly 75 new calves brought into the world on his western Nebraska ranch every spring. This particular calf, however, had turned and the umbilical cord had wound around the calf so tight that Ray couldn't free it to pull down the birth canal. The mother was having a hard time, as was Ray. It was in situations like this that he called Doc Mino. He knew the doctor would get there as fast as he possibly could. He'd counted on the vet in such emergencies and his success rate of saving Ray's livestock was commendable.

Ron Mino, Doctor of Veterinary Medicine, graduated from the University of Nebraska's College of Veterinary Medicine in 1955. He had the opportunity to take over an established practice in Scottsbluff, Nebraska shortly after graduation due to an untimely death and an immediate need. Ron couldn't have been happier with the chance to move back to his roots.

The young veterinarian was raised in Crawford, Nebraska. Ron had done his undergraduate studies at nearby Chadron State College, about a half hour drive from where he was raised. His grandfather was an immigrant from Italy and had homesteaded the original 160 acres. Over the years, he acquired over 1,600 acres of surrounding land. Ron's father continued the family business and had owned the ranch in the Crawford area for more than forty years until his death in 1980. Ron was raised around livestock and had acquired an early desire to become a vet by watching his dad and granddad tend to the animals over the years.

Dr. Ray Kassis had served the ranching community of western Nebraska for over thirty years before suffering a fatal heart attack a year earlier. Dr. Kassis was returning to town from a late night emergency call and was found dead in his Jeep station wagon by a passing motorist the next morning.

Doc Mino knew every rancher and pet owner within a fifty mile radius of Scottsbluff. He'd tended to their animals for the last four years. Ranchers depended on the doctor to treat their sick or injured cattle, horses and dogs that were the mainstays on any working ranch. From time to time hogs, sheep, goats, cats and birds would also be added to his repertoire. He was the go-to guy if there was any animal in need of a good veterinarian. Sometimes his salves and remedies also worked well on two-legged patients who occasionally requested them during his visit.

Doc and his wife Janet purchased a large, white, wooden two story home across the road from their clinic when they moved to Scottsbluff back in July of 1955. The couple had two young daughters: Margaret, four, and Maureen, two.

The small clinic was surrounded by five acres of pasture and holding stalls for the sick animals. The building housed a reception area, an office, a locked storage room for all of his pharmaceuticals and an examination/operating room. Just south of the clinic was a two story white barn that was primarily used for feed storage. Doc enjoyed racing sulkies as a hobby and kept several of his trotting carts and horses in the barn. He enjoyed loading up one of the horses and his cart into a modified horse trailer and heading off to race at a county fair somewhere in Nebraska when his schedule allowed.

If he wasn't in the office, which was often, he had his full time receptionist, Anita, handle the phone, manage the daily scheduling and take care of the billing. Anita had a two-way radio on her desk and when the doctor had to be reached in an emergency, she'd get on the hand-held microphone and call for Doc to pick up. It often took several tries to get through before Ron could answer if he was in the middle of a procedure somewhere out in a barn, corral or pasture. The reception wasn't the best, but the two seemed to understand the majority of the message through the static and squelching that seemed to dominate most of their brief and to-the-point discussions. If a phone was handy, he'd call in for a clearer conversation.

Doc Mino had two Jeep station wagons that he used for work. He and Dr. Kassis combined had put close to 300,000 miles on a 1948 green unit Dr. Kassis had purchased new in Scottsbluff. Ron had replaced the tired old beater two years ago with a new 1957 wagon. He kept his old one for emergencies. They weren't the most comfortable vehicles to ride in, but they both had four wheel drive and a sizable storage area to carry all of his needed ropes, syringes, drugs, boots, coats, blankets, halters, radio equipment, chains, a shovel and various other specialized instruments of the trade. The four wheel drive was invaluable in the terrain he was required to cover. Most of Doc's time was spent on the dirt back roads of western Nebraska sliding, plowing or splashing through the mud- and snow-covered rutted roads to get to his destination. Many people would easily get lost or stuck trying to maneuver in this desolate prairie-scape, but Doc always seemed to find his way. He couldn't use a map to help plot his course because many of the roads and paths he traversed weren't shown. He depended on his keen sense of direction and gut instincts to get him to where he needed to go.

3

You could always spot Doc at the monthly livestock sales with his white coveralls, rubber boots and trademark cigar. Years of wrestling with stubborn horses and cattle had given him broad, muscular shoulders and strong arms and legs on his 5'10" frame. His thinning black hair was usually covered with a ballcap given to him by one of the livestock feed or drug company reps. He'd lost half of his left middle finger and the tip of his ring finger to a horse and rope several years ago, but that didn't hamper his capabilities in the least. He was still very good at getting a rope around any animal in range.

Doc Mino made a point to get to know his clientele and understand their needs. He knew their family histories, how long they'd been ranching on their land, their relatives, how many acres they owned, how many head of livestock they owned, what their brands were, where their property boundaries were and their political and religious beliefs. He was a welcomed member of their undeclared fraternity and they depended on Doc to keep them informed of the latest news.

Television reception in rural western Nebraska in the 50's was very limited. Even with rabbit ears, the best black and white picture was blurred with so-called snow and lots of loud, irritating static. For the few that had invested in this frivolous piece of furniture, it was hardly worth the effort to turn it on.

Scottsbluff had one local radio station that mostly played music from seven o'clock in the morning until six at night when signing off. They would have the local, state and world news on at eight, noon and five as well as the stock market and futures reports. Noon was the best time for everyone to hear the news, because that was when all the family and ranch hands would gather at the main house for lunch when convenient. The weekly newspaper also provided news, but it seemed that Doc was usually more knowledgeable of the unprinted details.

Doc Mino usually started his mornings early. He'd be out of the house by 6:30 and grab breakfast with the locals at the Whistle Stop Cafe before getting into the clinic by 7:15. He'd open the building, feed any of the animals he was caring for and head to the barn to feed his own three horses, two dogs and four cats.

When there was any roundup work to be done on the schedule, Doc would count on Buddy, his trusted three-year-old border collie to do all the legwork. The dog loved to corral the catch of the day in a timely fashion that always won his master's praise and the rousing approval of their client. Buddy was a welcomed travel companion on Doc's daily rounds, proudly riding shotgun in the passenger seat. If there were any mean barnyard dogs on the route, Buddy stayed in the jeep.

Anita would be in shortly before eight and the two would sit down and go over the daily plan that she'd booked for him as his time demanded. She'd usually try and arrange scheduled rounds in a certain direction from town so the doctor wasn't wasting time backtracking all over the countryside. Unless it was an emergency, Doc tried to stick to the schedule. She tried to allow ample time in the day for her boss to chew the breeze and get caught up on the daily happenings over a glass of lemonade or piece of pie.

There was a lot of windshield time in his Jeep. It might easily take over an hour between calls just driving from one ranch to the next, a n d that was on a good day. If the weather was bad and the roads were rough, it would take him even longer. Doc always tried to finish his last call by four and allow an hour for the long trek back to town. He'd end the day sometime around five o'clock back at the clinic and do his chores again before walking over to the house.

The girls looked forward to seeing their daddy's Jeep pull up in front of the clinic. That was their signal to find Mom to walk them across the street to the office and help Dad. They looked forward to seeing new animals and how they were cared for. After a shower and a cold bottle of Budweiser, the family would sit down to dinner. Doc and his three girls normally didn't eat their evening meal until around seven.

5

Doc would oftentimes come home with some gifts he'd acquired during his daily travels. Jams, bread, sweet corn, apples, watermelons, cookies, pies or cakes seemed to be a popular token of appreciation extended to him by the ranch wives. It was always fun to surprise Janet with the goods. Over the years of receiving these neighborly gestures, Janet could often guess where he'd been that day just by the tantalizing aroma of a freshly baked cherry pie or a dish of apple strudel. Dessert was the course of the meal they looked forward to. Doc would welcome the opportunity to thank the parties responsible for their kind generosity on his next visit and tell them how much his family enjoyed whatever they had bestowed upon him on his previous visit. That warm token of appreciation and thanks would in turn usually yield another round of goodies. And so the cycle went. Just one of the small perks of being a country vet.

Janet was kept very busy for most of her waking hours caring for her two young daughters. She and her husband would find a little quiet time together at the end of their day after the girls went to bed around eight-thirty. Doc was glad to listen to her varied topics of conversation and enjoy another beer after a long and hectic day. He'd share some of his daily highlights, but Janet usually wasn't interested in the details of making a difficult calf delivery, castrating young bulls, vaccinating a corral full of yearlings or treating a lame horse that managed to get tangled up in some barbed wire. She enjoyed having a conversation with an adult and told her stories with unbelievable detail to her husband while Doc spoke in generalities. The girls' activities usually dominated much of their conversation.

To get away from the girls and spend a little time to themselves, they would make a point to hire a sitter and attend the Sons of Italy banquets held the first Monday of the month at their local lodge located in the downtown area. Janet enjoyed spending the afternoon fraternizing with a number of her girlfriends, preparing the spaghetti and tossing the salad. Ron thought it was great therapy for Janet to get a break from her motherly responsibilities and made his schedule available to pick the girls up from school and entertain them until the sitter came around six.

The routine seemed to work well for the Minos, and it had kept them happily married for the last eight years. Tonight their nightly routine would be different. Doc had seen something several days ago that he'd never seen or heard of before. He hadn't shared this bizarre story with anyone other than the few people involved. Most people wouldn't believe him anyway on this particular case. They'd think that Doc Mino was losing his marbles with his upcoming thirty-third birthday next month.

He usually didn't bring work home with him, but Janet sensed something was bothering her husband recently. Doc was exceptionally quiet and distant throughout their meals. He wasn't his usual jovial self around the girls. Tonight, after a quiet dinner, he brought an unfinished bottle of wine into the living room and settled into his lounge c h a i r next to Janet. He figured they both could use an extra glass after what he was about to share with her. Tomorrow morning he had another meeting at the sheriff's office at nine and they would again discuss this troubling subject in depth. Until then, Doc needed to get this horrific story off his chest and confide in his trusted mate. Doc slowly filled the two glasses and sat down to tell a story he'd never told before.

CHAPTER TWO
LANKILA'S PASTURE

Doc had been called out on an emergency call first thing Friday morning, April 27, 1959. Henry Lankila's family had ranched in the area for over seventy years. Henry and his wife Susie had twin boys, Zack and AJ. They ranched 2,000 acres of prime grassland about twenty-five miles east of Scottsbluff. Dr. Mino knew the family well. The Lankilas were hardworking, honest people and well respected in their community.

Doc arrived at the ranch house at 8:30 and was greeted by Henry and his seventeen- year-old fraternal twin sons. Minutes later, Sheriff Joe Suske arrived. The men wanted both experts to see what they'd found out in the south pasture earlier in the morning.

The men climbed into the twins' pickups and made their way along the narrow cattle trail that led back into the river country that bordered the nearby Platte. They could see a dead cow lying on its side as their trucks approached. Nothing else out of the ordinary was noticed in their immediate sight range.

Suske poked Doc and chuckled, "We both come running out here to see a dead cow?"

Zack led the men over for a closer look at this Black Angus heifer that weighed close to 1,100 pounds and was in otherwise good health. She had been seen by the boys just a couple of days ago and appeared to be doing fine.

Griff, their yellow lab, inexplicably wouldn't leave the cab. He cowered on the passenger floor and wouldn't budge even with the twins' friendly encouragement. That was very unlike the normally frisky one-year-old pup. The dog usually went everywhere with them, but today the whimpering pet refused to budge.

As the men bent down over the cow, they were immediately overwhelmed by what they were witnessing. Nothing in the many number of years shared between these professionals came close to anything like what was before them. One thing the men noticed right away and soon commented on was the total lack of any foul smell. Usually when an animal or person has been filleted open like this and left for any time, the i n t e r n a l organs would give off a very distinct, nauseous odor. Normally the stench would be a deterrent in approaching a dead animal but the telltale scent of death was not present here. It may be understandable if this was a below zero day in February and the carcass was frozen, but that was not the case. It was Doc's best guess that the cow had been laying in the pasture for at least three days.

There were no telltale maggots or flies to be found on the dead animal. Even scavengers like coyotes or vultures normally would have torn the carcass apart, but it literally hadn't been touched.

The immediate physical observations were so numerous they initially didn't know where to begin. Doc suggested they cover one area at a time. He would make detailed notes as they carefully examined the animal hoof to hoof, starting from the rear up.

Their eyes focused immediately on the tail. The tail was gone, as was the anal core, sex organ and one teat. What was even more astonishing was the fact there was no blood! There were no tire tracks or footprints of any kind including the dead animal. The parts had been removed with what they considered to be surgical precision. T h e very sharp and defined cuts were clean and exact. A faint purplish gel lightly coated each incision line. The head was severely traumatized. The left eye ball, nose, lips and ear were missing. The tongue had been cut out at the very back of the throat. The flesh on the left jaw bone had been removed down to the mandible, exposing the teeth.

The level of skill required would be nearly impossible to execute in the dark in the middle of a cow pasture. The

9

temperature dropped down into the forties over the last three nights after a cloudy, cool, drizzling and unpredictable late fall weather pattern passed through western Nebraska. The elements definitely hadn't cooperated with these perpetrator(s) and the heinous act they dealt this poor, unsuspecting animal.

Doc Mino instructed the men to each grab a hoof and roll the animal over on its other side for further inspection. There was a very noticeable crater-like indentation under the animal. If the cow had been killed at this site and simply fallen over, there wouldn't be such an imprint. It looked like the animal had possibly been dropped from a substantial height. With the cow rolled over, Doc Mino felt the downside rib cage. A quick feel to the area indicated that a number of the ribs were broken, which supported his theory. Perhaps the cow had been sliced up elsewhere in a more conducive place to do such precise cutting, all traces of blood washed away and then flown over this remote site by airplane and dropped from the sky. But why? Maybe they had done it to stir up questions like this and get some headlines in the local newspaper and possibly make the national news. This would take a lot of time and effort to do in such a short window of time. How would they remove the animal from the ranch without their vehicle being noticed?

The men got back on their feet and their attention next focused on what or who could have done this. Doc Mino wrote down the immediate possibilities as the men tossed around their ideas. At this point, nothing would be considered off the table. They began their list.

1. **Scavengers**. Maybe it was a single animal like a cougar or a pack of coyotes. Typically when a scavenger feeds off a dead animal, the animal is ripped apart in a very unorthodox fashion. This obviously wasn't the case. Maybe after the initial kill was made, some sort of insect or a smaller predator like a fox or vulture came in and ate neatly around the rough tear marks like a leach on a wound. They come in and do the cleanup. Why weren't any still remaining? Where are the footprints? Where is the blood? Cattle, elk, deer, coyotes and

other larger a n i m a l s are frequently found dead around the area on other ranches. Why haven't they been mutilated in this fashion? They moved on to the next option.

2. **Humans**. Possibly this animal was part of a prank, like a "scavenger party." Maneuvering around this big animal would have left footprints, especially in the light mud. Why would you carve up an animal in this way if the usual purpose of killing the cow was for the meat? The desired edible parts of the animal were left intact. What's the point?

3. **Cults**. Perhaps a strange cult had targeted this animal as some sort of ceremonial sacrifice. Sheriff Suske had heard of these rituals before, but nothing out in this part of the state. Omaha and Lincoln might be the only known cult areas in Nebraska. This area was very distant and remote from any major highway. Navigating these slippery, rutted mud roads and paths to get to this animal would be difficult. This location was not ideal for anyone, including cultists. They would have found much easier targets before they got this far back on the ranch. No signs of their entry were noticed.

4. **Aliens**. The men had heard stories of flying saucers, but no one had seen one, at least among this group. Since they didn't know anything about the subject, and it would be a very, very remote possibility at best, they decided to pass on any unfounded discussions until later. Due to their previous topics, this had to be a consideration, but they needed some input from someone that may know something about the subject, if such a person even existed. This option would be difficult to research, yet it needed to be included on the list.

5. **Government.** Maybe it was some secret operation being done by the state or e v e n the federal government for some undisclosed reason. It would probably be classified information. Perhaps a preliminary phone call or two by Joe Suske would shed some light on this possibility.

11

Doc asked Henry if this was positively their animal. A Black Angus is black! There were no unusual markings to differentiate it from the next. Maybe this heifer wasn't one of the Lankilas', but had been left there to make them think it was. AJ said this was not a possibility, since all of their cattle had gone through an annual brand check. The reason they recently s a w this cow was to do a head count to make sure all of their livestock were accounted for. They did this frequently in the spring during birthing season to k e e p track of their herds. Cattle thieves, poachers, a downed fence and predators were always a threat. These cows were money on the hoof and they are watched very closely. The men rolled the cow over further to check the flank. Sure enough, the well-known Lankila turkey foot brand was visible on the right rear hip of the cow.

Sheriff Suske photographed the crime scene during every step of the initial investigation. Doc Mino took exhaustive notes and documented every detail since they had first gotten out of the trucks and approached the area. The sheriff made sure that the crime scene wasn't disturbed any more than he deemed necessary to do the work. There was no more they could do here in the pasture. Henry asked Joe and Doc what they wanted to do with the dead animal. After a brief discussion, they decided to cover the animal with a tarp to protect it for the next twenty-four hours. Joe would call in a state crime scene investigator from Lincoln to see if they wanted to do an inspection. Doc thought that if this was the case, they might want to bring the carcass in to his clinic and do a thorough autopsy and perhaps get more detailed information that might offer a clue. Things would clear up quickly if they could uncover an overlooked bullet entry. The men would make the necessary phone calls and contact Henry within the next day to fill him in on what the next course of action would be. Until then, this was not to be discussed with anyone.

CHAPTER THREE
OUTSIDE EXPERTISE

Sheriff Suske went back to his office and closed the door. He didn't want to be disturbed for the next hour. He immediately got on the phone with the Nebraska State Crime Laboratory in Lincoln. He knew one of the lead investigators in the department, Nick Jensen, from numerous meetings held around the state. They'd worked before several years ago on a major cattle rustling case in the Scottsbluff area.

After exchanging a few pleasantries, Joe quickly got to the point of his call. He explained what he'd just seen in detail. Although it wasn't a homicide, it was strange enough that Nick should be aware of it. What he did with the information would be entirely up to him. After hearing Sheriff Suske's story, Nick didn't hesitate. He would fly out to Scottsbluff on one of the state planes first thing the next morning. Two of his associates would accompany him. He'd never heard of such a story in Nebraska. Nick would call around to several neighboring states to see if anything like this had surfaced elsewhere. Joe offered to pick the men up at the airport at nine the next morning. Doc Mino would meet them in the pasture around nine-forty and he'd transport the animal back to the clinic for an autopsy in his horse trailer.

The small Cessna 172 arrived on time. Nick Jensen had brought along the State Veterinarian, Dr. Ken Knighten. Knighten's primary responsibilities dealt with stockyard health control issues, slaughter house sanitation, animal cruelty cases, animal epidemics and control, veterinarian licensing, regulations and enforcement. Jensen wanted Dr. Knighten as an expert witness. His observations and contacts would be critical to the investigation. Dr. Knighten had known Doc Mino for five years and they respected each other's reputation. The men would work well together, even though the state doctor was some twenty years Doc Mino's senior. Sometimes during an investigation like this, competing egos could get involved and one party wants to control and dominate the case with title and seniority. This was true in the medical field, like any other profession. Fortunately, this wasn't the case with any of the men involved. They would work together to try and get to the bottom of this unsolved mutilation.

Doc Mino brought his trailer and portable hoist. Sometimes when an animal couldn't get up, Doc would use the hoist to lift the creature to its feet. He and the Lankilas were already at the scene awaiting the Sheriff and his small entourage.

AJ and Zack pulled the canvas back to expose the carcass. The three new men at the scene were repulsed, just like the others had been yesterday. Nothing like this had been seen before. To move things along, Doc suggested that they again start at the rear of the animal and work toward the head. As they moved up the cadaver, Doc would read from his notes and highlight with a stick what the men were focusing on. Nick Jensen got out his camera to take additional pictures and had their assistant record Dr. Mino's assessments before the examination proceeded.

The first thing that Dr. Knighten noticed was the total lack of smell, as was noted yesterday. The dead animal had had another day to decay yet there was still no odor! That in itself was very strange.

As Doc Mino continued his findings, he pointed out the faint traces of the light purple gel coating that lined the cuts. Dr. Knighten removed his glove and made a swipe across the substance with his forefinger.

He instinctively pulled back his hand and let out a loud, "Shit! That stuff is hot!"

The surface area on his finger had immediately turned bright red and was covered with a small blister. AJ quickly handed him his handkerchief to wipe his hands. Maybe those precision cuts were made with some sort of acid or chemical.

14

After the examination, the men gathered by Doc's trailer to determine their next move. Nick Jensen commented that it was also peculiar that this dead animal had been left out in the pasture overnight for a second time and there were no obvious traces of any predators disrupting the body. Even with the canvas cover thrown over the body, this would not be much of a deterrent for a hungry coyote. Usually the coyotes or crows would have already made a feast of the remains. There wasn't even a single fly! Flies and maggots would surely be swarming over a dead animal by now. Very strange. Not even a footprint to show the presence of any scavengers during the night.

The men followed Dr. Mino's loaded trailer into Scottsbluff and made their way to the clinic. Doc had a covered, close fenced concrete slab with a drain located just outside the south end of the building designated specifically for such events. He backed the trailer up and positioned the dead heifer squarely in the middle of the slab.

Before beginning, the men decided to get something to eat. It was close to noon so they chose the Steel Grill across the Platte River in Gering, which divided the town from Scottsbluff on the other side. The small group arranged to sit in a separate dining area at the front of the bar where they might talk in privacy.

After placing their orders with the waitress and closing the door, the trio from Lincoln all concurred. This was indeed a very strange scenario that they'd never seen or heard of, at least not in the Cornhusker State. Nick had made a few calls yesterday afternoon to neighboring state crime departments. He'd called South Dakota, Iowa, Wyoming, Colorado and Kansas. Nothing in those states to report. He'd expand his calls to North Dakota, Montana, Oklahoma, Texas and New Mexico this afternoon. That would pretty much cover the major cattle ranching areas of the United States.

Because of its rarity, this would be considered a criminal case. Ordinarily, if any animal was found dead due to foul play, it would

15

be reported to the local authorities and they'd determine how to proceed with an investigation. The unique mutilation of Henry Lankila's Angus was a first for all of them and it deserved special attention. This unexplained occurrence would rank as a top priority.

After lunch, the men anxiously proceeded back to Doc Mino's clinic. Dr. Knighten wanted to make a quick stop first to the local meat locker or butcher shop. He needed to purchase a fifty pound block of dry ice. They'd use it to get any specimens back to Lincoln for further observation in the state crime lab. He purchased two dozen large, heavy-duty Hefty bags and a dozen five gallon buckets. They would be perfect to put their samples in.

Among the obvious samples, Dr. Knighten wanted to make sure the hoofs were taken back to Lincoln intact. Where the animal stepped or what it stepped in might be of significant importance. The head would also be of value.

Upon their arrival, they looked for the obvious first. Doc grabbed several large magnifying glasses from his examination room.

"Let's examine the hide closely to see if there are any immediate causes of death, like a bullet hole, burn mark or puncture wound."

Doc began cutting off the coarse black coat with his electric shearers.

During this thorough inspection process, Dr. Knighten pointed out a small indentation beneath the exposed hide. It was not deep enough to penetrate through the hide, but had exerted enough force to leave a mark. It was surrounded by a small bruise. He placed a piece of yellow tape on the area. Several more of the marks were found, and again covered with tape. After completing the inspection of the hide surface, a distinct pattern was outlined where the yellow tape had been placed. Four equally spaced indentations were on both the left and right side of the animal, just on the lower rib cage above the belly. The pattern looked like

16

something mechanical had been used to possibly lift the animal from its feet and maneuver it. Nick's assistant kept busy taking thorough notes and detailed pictures of their activity.

The next thing the men noticed was that the purple gel that burned Dr. Knighten had completely vanished. After Hunter first touched the gel, Doc noticed that the color had faded. It was much lighter than it was during his initial observation yesterday. That was also peculiar.

The two veterinarians took particular notice of the precision cuts made on all parts of the animal. If someone or something used a knife or saw, there would be some sort of telltale blade mark or rough serrated sawing pattern made with each stroke. There was nothing. These incisions appeared to have been made with one single, steadily applied motion. Since there were no signs of blade marks, perhaps the gel may have burned the precise lines. Further examination of the hair and hide right next to the cut indicated an absence of burn marks. If something hot had been exposed to this area, there should have been a trace of some type of cauterization left on the remaining side of the incision. There would also be a distinct burnt flesh odor, of which there was none.

No bullet holes or burn marks were found. Immediately behind the remaining right ear, the two veterinarians could see a very small puncture wound that appeared to be deep.

Penetration in this area of the skull was possible since there was no bone directly behind the ear. There are soft spots in a cow's skull, just like in a human skull's temporal area which allows the outer ear to connect through the skull to the inner ear. This thrust, close to the brain, could cause immediate death. The mark had the two experts puzzled. It was impossible to know if it had any connection to what initially brought the large animal to the ground or what object could have made this small but potentially lethal wound. They would note this finding in their report.

The two veterinarians tried to piece together why the specific body parts and organs were removed and others left. Neither could come up with a logical explanation for the randomness of the missing parts. Since all blood and bodily fluids had been mysteriously drained from the animal, the remaining internal organs were now shriveled up and looked as if they'd been freeze-dried.

Dr. Knighten wanted to open up the stomach to see if the contents might offer any clues. Maybe the cow was fed something that either killed or tranquilized it somehow. Doc put on his elbow-length rubber gloves and gently reached up inside the cow's belly with a pair of snips. He freed the stomach from the body cavity and slowly pulled it out intact. The two vets decided to take it to the stainless steel operating room table and take a closer look under the surgical light. The withered digestive organ was carefully placed on a large tray and transported into the surgery room.

Dr. Knighten grabbed one of the plastic bags and buckets he'd purchased and began to slice off some stomach lining samples to analyze at the lab. If there were any traces of a drug, a gas chronometer might still pick them up. The contents were scattered on the cold, shiny table and carefully picked through with a scalpel. A cow's stomach is pretty easy to examine: there should be nothing but grass, hay and bile. Samples would be taken back to the state lab to see if the contents held any clues. The remnants of the stomach and its contents were scooped into two of the buckets. Doc had a large incinerator behind the barn and they'd be disposed of there.

While the vets proceeded with their task, the two law enforcement officers were busy making calls. Suske and Jensen divided up the remaining states on their list. The last call made was to New Mexico. The Sheriff was put into contact with their State Crime Division. The department head on the other end listened to the officer's brief story to see if anything similar had happened down in the Southwest.

"Why yes, as a matter of fact. We investigated a similar incident over by Cloudcroft just about a month ago," said the law enforcement agent on the other end of the line.

The two men were very eager to continue on the subject. First, Joe wanted to get Nick Jensen on the line and join in the conversation.

Captain Ernie Mandere, New Mexico State Crime Division, told them a similar story. A cow had been found in a remote area of the Roger Estey ranch about 10 miles southwest of Cloudcroft up in the foothills. He was called in on the investigation team.

Their findings were very similar. The captain didn't recall the indentation pattern on the underside of their carcass, but everything else right down to the purplish slime seemed to match up identically. This was their first experience with such a mutilation and they were also at a loss in trying to solve the case. This incident left them all completely baffled.

Captain Mandere would be glad to share any information they had, but couldn't give them any clues to finding an answer. Since there were now two incidents, perhaps these state authorities should set up a network with the listed states and let them know what had transpired in Nebraska and New Mexico. That way any future activity could be m o n i t o r e d and shared. Maybe after the word got out amongst law enforcement, ranchers and veterinarians, someone might be able to provide some needed clues or even an answer. Until then, Captain Mandere didn't know what direction to take next. Nick w o u l d be doing some extensive forensic work back in the state lab tomorrow and he'd be in touch if anything of significance surfaced.

Suske and Jensen met up with the vets back in the barn. Nick shared the information from New Mexico. It was getting close to three P.M. and the entourage from Lincoln determined it was time to head home. Dr. Knighten would get started in the morning and examine the samples they were now packing with dry ice. Hair samples, soft tissue, bone sections, hoofs, teeth and several large hide areas that had been meticulously cut would be taken back for inspection. The two teams would exchange pictures once developed and their typed notes when they were completed over the next couple of days.

CHAPTER FOUR
JAN GRADERT

Mrs. Jan Gradert had taught elementary school for the past seven years in the small town of Hemingford, Nebraska. She and her husband Dave lived in Scottsbluff. Dave owned a successful automotive repair business and relocation for him was not an option. Jan had been offered several teaching positions closer to home, but the eight hundred residents of Hemingford were like family to her and she couldn't imagine ever teaching elsewhere.

Most of the time she didn't mind the sixty mile drive. In the morning it gave her time to collect her thoughts and plan for the day ahead. After a long work day, the commute gave her the opportunity to unwind a little before she got home. Jan would push the radio station buttons in the dash to satisfy her mood. If the weather conditions were ever a threat, she could stay with one of her fellow teacher friends that resided in the little town. They were a close-knit group who gladly looked out for each other.

Dave insisted that her car always be in tip-top condition. A breakdown could sit for hours on those barren stretches of road along Highway 71, which saw very little traffic. If Jan experienced car trouble, it could be a long time before help might arrive. He had purchased a mint, low mileage 1958 Chevrolet Impala from the dealer in Scottsbluff just last summer. It had been the owner's demo car for the past six months. They picked that car because it was Jan's favorite color: powder blue with a white interior.

Dave put an extra gas can, blanket, chains, jumper cables, shovel, a .22 rifle, gloves, a heavy water resistant coat, a small tool kit, bottled water, a small assortment of canned food and a transistor radio in a large wooden box in the trunk just in case there was ever an emergency. He was an old Boy Scout and always prepared.

Jan enjoyed the panoramic views her commute had to offer. She'd witnessed some of the most beautiful sunrises, sunsets, cloud patterns and rainbows imaginable in this remote part of Nebraska. Occasionally she'd see a thunder storm off in the distance. She was amazed to see the massive clouds billowing magnificently so high up in the sky. It was a true gift from the heavens to watch the lightning dance amongst those clouds and hear their distant booms. It surely was a sight to behold. Seeing such beauty strengthened her belief in God, for surely only the Creator could provide such shows of beauty.

She witnessed the ranchers herding their cattle to winter pasture. She'd seen more deer and antelope than she could count. There were beautiful stretches of flat prairie that went on for miles, as far as the eye could see. When the highway made the bend east towards Hemingford about twenty miles outside of town, the terrain turned into some pretty rolling hills covered by beautiful rock formations and pine trees. This had once been Sioux country and sometimes she'd have to slow down and take a second look up on some of the nearby buttes. Her vivid imagination and keen eyes would sometimes play tricks on her during this stretch of the drive. She swore she'd seen numerous proud young braves sitting stoically on their painted ponies, looking down on her from their vantage point high above on one the hilltops, observing the thousands of grazing buffalo right here in this same locale.

Other times she imagined wagon trains winding their way west right before her very eyes. She knew her visions weren't real, but her imagination enjoyed envisioning them nonetheless when she approached the hill country.

Numerous jackrabbits seemed to spring out of nowhere in the late afternoon or early evening and dart across the road in front of her. She seldom saw large numbers of them at once. They seemed to range from one to six or eight at a time. She'd never hit one, although she'd come dangerously close on numerous occasions. It seemed like maybe the rabbits were playing a game with her and her big blue Chevy. They'd flirt with the front tires without being run over. It probably scared her worse than it did them. These rabbits livened up their otherwise dull evening with their sporting game of chicken.

The crushed bodies of the losers made an excellent roadkill snack for the many scavengers that roamed the area. It wasn't uncommon to see their scattered remains lying on the side of the road.

Sometimes in the winter months she wouldn't get home until after the sun went down at five o'clock. It would be even later if there was a teacher's meeting, a sporting event or parent-teacher meetings. Driving in the dark seemed to bring them out even more. The darkness gave the jackrabbits additional cover to unexpectedly spring into action and play their daring game. They'd go unseen until the approaching headlights gave them away at the last second. By that time, they seemed to be on top of Jan. It was amazing to watch them zig and zag at their lightning pace. They could change their direction on a dime. Jan marveled at their speed, agility and fearlessness.

The jackrabbits and Jan were the only living creatures on this deserted road for miles, and they seemed to enjoy each other's brief company.

There were very few ranch houses visible from the blacktop road. Most sat off in the distance. Usually the only time Jan even noticed them was in the winter months when she could see smoke rising from their distant chimneys or when the numerous large shade trees were barren and left the buildings standing naked and exposed. Many of the simple two story ranch homes were second and third generation homes built back in the early 1900s. They were kept up over the years, but lacked many of the frills found in the newer city homes. Air conditioning was limited to the wall units placed in the window. The outer walls were constructed of wood and the inner walls were made from lath and plaster. A thin layer of newspaper was put in the middle for insulation. Clear, single pane glass windows would frost up during a cold night to the point of being opaque. Wood or coal oil stoves provided the heat. You could tell how a home was heated the minute you walked in, simply because of the smell. Both were pleasant, but completely different from each other. The aroma added to the character of the house.

Ranchers were often considered to be land rich but cash poor. Fancy houses gave way to necessities like a tractor, cattle feed, livestock, a dependable truck and maybe an older used car for the wife and kids to take to town occasionally and for church. The family homestead was a tradition and their multi-generation owners were proud to keep the old house up. It was like a beacon that shone brightly over their land and family. The house was truly the shelter from the storm during the harsh weather often experienced in rural Nebraska. Hail, severe rain, floods, tornadoes, blizzards, lightning, dust storms, grasshoppers, wind, ice, sleet and snow could wreak havoc on man and animal alike if caught out in the elements.

One of the few homes close to the highway was the Bosworth place just 10 miles south of Hemingford. Jan had taught all four of the Bosworth girls, Laurie, Susie, Sharlene and Jenny during her tenure. It had been several years since she'd talked to any of the family. She'd wave every now and then if they were out doing chores or getting the mail from the box by the road.

Like most rural folks, they didn't socialize much and kept to a hard work regimen that required their full attention. There were few days off and fewer vacations for a ranch family. Something always needed to be fixed or tended. Livestock needed to be fed daily. Ranching was the only life these simple, upstanding people knew and they all felt blessed to live it. These Christian families would come together on Sunday and attend church services at two of the community churches. There was a Catholic and a Methodist church in Hemingford.

A handful of old deserted homes lined the two lane highway between Hemingford and Scottsbluff. They'd been abandoned for years. Their former occupants more than likely purchased the land right before the Great Depression hit in the late '20s and wound up losing it. Others just left their ranch when the Dust Bowl struck the rural Midwest back in the mid ' 30s. Each of these two calamities took their toll individually, but when they hit back to back, the combination took a crushing toll on the land owners, banks and businesses that made up the backbone of these small communities. People had no choice but to pack up and leave.

Others unknowingly bought their land on good faith, only to find that there was no adequate water source. Either the wells had run dry or the water was too acidic and unfit for consumption. Without a good dependable water source, their land was worthless. Riverboat gamblers had nothing over the farmers and ranchers of Nebraska. Sometimes you won, sometimes you lost. Losing carried severe consequences. Those families caught on the downside would sometimes try and sell the land for pennies on the dollar to anyone who might be buying. More often, however, they'd simply load their few belongings into the family truck and drive away.

Those that survived knew the value of a dollar and how hard they had to work to earn it. The saying went that Tough Times was every rancher's middle name. Material things held little value unless they could be put to good use on the ranch. The word frivolous was not in their vocabulary.

A handshake was a man's word. If someone needed a helping hand, they could count on their neighbor. If you did happen to get stuck in bad weather, you could count on their help to pull you out or offer shelter. It was a simple life with simple rules. *Do unto others as you would have them do unto you.* It was the law of survival, and rural Nebraskans knew it well. Lives depended on this philosophy and besides, it was the neighborly, Christian thing to do.

Occasionally, after the years of living in the same small community, there would be some bad blood between families for one reason or another. Someone couldn't pay off a loan. There might be some discrepancy over the ownership of livestock or property lines. Water rights created hard feelings between those who had it and those who needed it. Perhaps there was a bad or failed marriage thrown in the mix. There would be family squabbles over the usual things families fight about. Alcohol and abuse reared its ugly head and ruined lives. The differences rarely ended in bloodshed between the parties; they simply avoided each other and held a longstanding grudge.

Anyone in the surrounding area with any long roots probably had to side with one or the other when friends or family got involved. *Go along to get along* always prevailed over the *eye for an eye* philosophy, at least in this neck of the woods.

City slickers seemed to have their own set of rules and all bets were off when dealing with those folks. They'd end up getting lawyers involved, and the attorneys were the only ones to make any money out of the lawsuit at the end of the case. It was best to avoid the lawyers.

There were people in town who held respected positions. The ministers usually held the top spot, and they were followed by the judge, the banker, teachers and the funeral director. They were the stalwarts. The drunks, the bar owner, the garbage collector and most lawyers rounded out the bottom of the barrel. Everyone else struggled to find their rightful pecking order somewhere in the middle, always striving towards the top.

Jan Gradert was a respected woman in the little community of Hemingford even though she didn't live there. She was responsible for the children's education and that was a position that was not taken lightly. The teacher was well liked by her students, t h e i r parents and her peers. She started her teaching career right after graduating from K e a r n e y State Teacher's College. Her family was from the Scottsbluff area and she g r e w up on a ranch herself. She was welcomed as one of them. She knew most every family between Hemingford and Scottsbluff either through her position, her church or her volunteer work. You could usually depend on Jan to spearhead a community fundraiser or sit on the school board. You could take her word to the bank. It was gold.

Mrs. Gradert was also responsible for putting on the annual Christmas Talent Show. Students from all grades would audition for a spot in the highlight event of the school year. Jan would start the auditions right after Thanksgiving break and select the acts to use in the performance. There would be singers, ropers, dancers, baton twirlers, jugglers, magicians, dog tricks and an occasional comedian. It seemed to her that the entire school was full of comedians, but only the truly outstanding ones ever auditioned, much to her delight. The school pep band would play at scheduled intervals between the skits. The senior class would elect candidates for the titles of Christmas King and Queen and the winners would be announced during the intermission. Winning the crown was a big honor.

The community came out in full support of the function. Parents, grandparents, aunts, uncles, brothers, sisters, cousins, friends and neighbors would attend. A small fee of a quarter was charged and used towards the prom expenses in the spring. The school council members would host a small concession stand outside the auditorium in the lobby for additional revenue. The smell of nickel bags of buttered popcorn permeated through the foyer and served as a powerful enticement to the crowd as they filtered in.

The teacher would never forget the late evening hours of December 10, 1959. After the night's last performance, she turned off all the lights in the auditorium and locked the side door as she exited. A light flurry of snow driven by a sharp, cold north wind immediately greeted her as she headed for her car. She was headed for Scottsbluff shortly after nine o'clock.

The falling snow hit the lights and her windshield as she navigated through the pitch black evening. Highway 71 was barren except for the 1958 Chevy Impala. She turned on the radio to keep her entertained and to avoid the hypnotic spell of what people in these parts called snow blindness. The white falling snow reflecting off the headlights and hitting the windshield mesmerizes a person into a trance-like state. Instead of focusing on the road, the driver's mind is teased into watching the bright flashes of constant white being beamed in front of their eyes like a rapidly flashing strobe light. Driving skills are diminished when the driver's eye coordination isn't in sync with their hand and foot reflexes.

Jan turned the car radio up louder. It was better to keep her concentration on the music instead of the annoying light show being forced on her. At this time of night KOMA out of Oklahoma City was the only clear reception she could receive on her AM dial. That was fine with her. They usually played a lot of her favorite rock n' roll music, but tonight the playlist was mixed with Christmas music. Bing Crosby's "White Christmas" was starting to play. She began to sing along.

From out of nowhere about a dozen extremely large jackrabbits started running on the road ten yards in front of her headlights. She'd seen plenty of these critters in her years of commuting, but these were very different in size. To her astonishment, something on the back of the rabbits would intermittently turn its head to look back at her. They had noticeably large black eyes and a very tiny, frail human form. These strange creatures were actually riding on the backs of the rabbits! Approximately ten seconds later, they darted off the road and headed up the approaching embankment on the shoulder.

What the hell was that?! she thought. She frantically tried to regain control of her car as it suddenly veered off the road.

"Oh shit!!" blurted out of her terrified, trembling lips. She slid down the slight embankment that paralleled the highway and abruptly stopped with a solid thud.

Jan lost consciousness momentarily when her head hit the wheel. Luckily she was only going about 40 miles an hour in the limited visibility. The car had died. Still shaking, she put it in park and turned the key. The car took a little coaxing, but after several attempts the engine turned over and she hurriedly put it in drive. The whirring tires spun in the snow-covered small ravine where the car had careened. She tried reverse. The rear of the car refused to budge. She was stuck.

"Dammit!!" she screamed.

As she got out of her car to evaluate the situation, she reached up to adjust her scarf and coat collar. She noticed blood on her glove. The light on the opened door gave her enough visibility to check her throbbing head in the exterior rear view mirror. Her hair was matted in fresh red blood. She couldn't determine the source of the bleeding, but seeing the blood made her nauseous. She quickly walked around the car and as she suspected, her rear end was slammed tightly down in the ditch. There was no way she could possibly rock her way out. She'd need help and soon. The temperature was dropping, it was getting very late and her headache was making her dizzy.

As the evening hours brought more blustery weather, the already limited travelers were now off the roads. Who knew how long she'd have to wait in the car for help. With the way she was bleeding and the way her head was pounding, Jan suspected she'd suffered a concussion. She didn't want to wait in the car all night and pass out from her injury. She might not wake up. She needed to find help.

Jan grabbed the keys from the ignition and began to walk down the middle of the abandoned, snow-packed road. As the snow began to accumulate, she made sure she stayed on the road and didn't wander off course. She'd traveled this stretch of road countless times and knew her best bet was the Bosworth ranch. She remembered passing it shortly before the accident. It shouldn't be more than two or three miles.

CHAPTER FIVE
THE JACK PEOPLE

We-Ota-Wichasha, meaning rabbit boy in Sioux, grasped the ears tightly down at the base of the skull of his large jackrabbit and brought the big buck to a crouching stop. The firm grip on these large and sensitive organs controlled its every move. Pull to the right and the rabbit goes right. Pull left, the rabbit goes left. Pull back and he stops. A gentle but firm nudge with the foot to the hind quarters could accelerate the rabbit to a full gait in seconds.

The eleven other members of his scouting party did the same. They would let up just enough for their lightning fast mounts to inch their way slowly toward the Sioux teepees nestled in the pines high on the butte overlooking the endless prairie below. When the desired stopping point was reached, several gentle strokes on the head signified a deserved rest.

A nearby band of nomadic Native Americans made camp in the last hour of w a n i n g daylight on the frigid February night. Cold winds howled through the grove of cedar trees and offered them limited shelter. The fires in their buffalo hide lodges were stoked by the occasional gusts that forced their way under the hides of the staked teepees. It was the winter of 1747 in the panhandle of the land the Indians called Nebrathka, meaning "flat water," for the major rivers that ran through it.

The Jack People of this remote panhandle area had lived here for centuries, although nothing could be found of their civilization in the history books. This small band of a scarce and unique species was much different than their Native American counterparts with whom they shared the land. This culture did not compete for food or territory with any of the various tribes. They were seldom enemies. Their superior intellect was never outdone. They rarely ever even made contact with the others.

However, the Sioux, Crow, Pawnee, Arapahoe and Cheyenne greatly feared the Jack People. They were bad omens. I f n e e d b e , the Jacks could inflict great physical and emotional pain on their victims. These tribes prayed to the great spirits for protection from the evil and misfortune that could be cast upon them seemingly at will.

Other civilizations around the world had similar mythical legends ranging from leprechauns, elves, gremlins, pixies, fairies, gnomes, trolls, Sasquatch, vampires, unicorns and werewolves, just to name a few. These mysterious beings weren't created by any one individual and spun into a legendary being; they were conceived after many rare but real sightings in multiple settings by a broad range of people throughout humanity's existence on earth. Such creatures lurked in the shadows of man's fear of the unknown and were hidden there, never to be showcased except in story. The reality of their existence would be too much for most to fathom. Widespread fear can create pandemonium that is very hard to control amongst the masses once it's released.

It's much easier to be a skeptic than a believer. The odds are always stacked in the skeptic's favor. Unless one sees them personally, they simply don't exist. If someone should happen to make real contact, they'd still be viewed with tremendous skepticism regardless of how honest and believable they might be. It's human nature. The old adage of *out of sight, out of mind* applies here.

Although the region they occupied in western Nebraska was relatively small in size, the Jack People were legendary to the Plains Indians that had the misfortune of passing through their land. After having felt the wrath of these small creatures for several hundred years, the native tribes avoided this twenty-five mile strip of prairie surrounding the tall buttes and pine trees that highlighted this otherwise flat stretch of Jack territory. Fear of starvation was the only thing that would draw the warriors into this ominous region to pursue the mighty buffalo. Starvation is a great motivator.

These creatures were also very different in their appearance. Their height averaged only fourteen to twenty-two inches. Their life span, however, could range up to two hundred years. Large, bulging black eyes, drooping eyelids and slanted foreheads accentuated their strange features. Their teeth were pointed and extremely sharp and they could easily penetrate human flesh if the occasion ever presented itself. Their small bodies were hairless with pale gray, wrinkled skin. Facial features included a small, flat nose and a little rounded mouth with thin lips. The little people were very quick and agile despite their diminutive stature.

Initially, these small beings had only one purpose. A limited number of subordinates were put on Earth centuries earlier to mine uranium found in this area for their distant relatives on the slave ships that shuttled their needed precious commodities to the larger Mother ships roaming the universe. These two related species depended on each other for their survival. One needed the valuable fuel to continue exploration of the universe. The other depended on the many unearthly benefits available from this higher source. Providing the uranium to their extraterrestrial second cousins was their primary obligation, second only to taking care of their sacred rabbits.

The Jack People, a name given to them centuries ago by the native people that also inhabited the region, were very adept in eking out a life in the grassy plains and their complete dominance of the ever present jackrabbit.

This plan had been devised millenniums ago when this planet was first visited by these galaxy hoppers. The plan didn't require a great number of aliens to be left on Earth. It just needed a hearty, strategically placed clan tough enough to survive the sometimes harsh elements and stick with their one imperative objective.

The twenty-eight members of the Jack People were all responsible for hunting, gathering and protecting. Most of the male members spent time in their mining operations. Not only did they live in this range of bluffs, but they also carried out major excavations deep in the surrounding hillsides to pull out their prize. Tons of ore were stored below the surface in the numerous caverns that riddled their limited but uranium rich territory. The Jacks had been mining the material for centuries, and to them it was priceless, although it held no value to anyone else at the time.

The need to reproduce and increase their numbers was irrelevant to this clan. The goal was never to try and compete numerically with the human race. The Jack elders h a d   determined centuries ago that twenty-eight was a good, workable number. They inhabited a relatively small territory and there was no reason to expand that land to accommodate more Jacks. They could adequately take care of their responsibilities with this set number. They'd seen the devastation caused by overpopulation.

Since they had such longevity, the need to constantly reproduce was eliminated. Casual sex was never in the equation. When one of the clan died, the body would be buried on the selected narrow, raised ledges that ran through the quarry tunnels. In the old days, at the appropriate time after losing a member, the others would vote on who should mate with whom in order to provide the best qualities possible in the offspring. After all, the new arrival would be around for a couple hundred years and there weren't that many newborn Jacks produced. When a new member was in order, they strove for the best.

The gestation period for a newborn was relatively short. Four months after mating, the infant would be born and, like most animals, the offspring hit the ground running. There wasn't much of an infancy stage for the new members. The need for survival trumped the need to pamper and coddle. If they survived the harsh elements, they'd reach full maturity in less than six months.

In this short period of time they spent time in the mines learning the high-tech m e t h o d s the others had bestowed on them. Their small, frail frames weren't built to s w i n g a pick or a shovel. The young ones were taught to ride a jackrabbit, care, feed and protect their assigned mount and hunt from its back. These lessons were paramount for their survival. Without the jackrabbits, they were sitting ducks for any number of predators. The jack's lightning reflexes and breakneck speed put them at a big advantage in avoiding danger. By learning to feed their rabbits, they learned to feed themselves.

Food, much like sex, was not considered to be something they craved. A plump Jack who stressed the limits of his ride might find himself without transportation, and that would mean certain death in the rugged environment. All members of the clan ate and bred out of the survival instinct and never for the pleasure of it. They could go for days with little sustenance, but they did enjoy the opportunity to gorge themselves when i t presented itself. They grazed throughout their waking hours, scouring for food while carrying out the daily activities. In the wintertime this became m o r e of a challenge when their sources were covered in snow. This was particularly troublesome when they were occasionally forced out of their comfort zone. In the harsh, cold months that blanketed their plains in snow, the Jacks preferred to stay close to home.

Another valuable lesson that they mastered on this short learning curve was weaponry. The new offspring learned how to protect themselves and the others by perfecting the ability to accurately place the correctly sized dart with the right toxic tip and hit their target at full gait from the back of their mount with a blow gun.

Both skills were critical components in their survival.

Jacks didn't pair off as couples, but instead they were devoted to the clan as a whole. There was no jealousy, envy, deceit, betrayal, lies, ill-will, hard feelings or contempt among any of the members, ever. They were bound by their equally profound respect and love for each other. This small band of Jacks had an inseparable bond that could never be broken. Loyalty ran deep among the family over their extended lifetime.

All of their daily responsibilities were assigned according to ability. Males were more proficient at certain tasks. Their focus was on mining, protection and their valued rabbits. The females spent their time gathering food and preparing lavish feasts of fresh rat, prairie dog, snake, nuts, apples, choke cherries, rhubarb, carrots and whatever else might present itself in the daily preparation. Every edible thing on the planet was fair game, but they would never, never eat their sacred rabbit.

On rare occasions, they might sit down and feast on a human adversary as a token of victory. It was more of a celebratory meal than a desired staple. If someone was brazen enough to relentlessly pursue the Jacks to cause them harm, they were likely candidates. And yes, there were always those stupid enough to put themselves in that select category.

Each member was skilled at self-defense and would ruthlessly fight to the death with any man or beast, regardless of size. Surrendering and being taken as a hostage was n e v e r an option. Since they hunted in packs, if one member was in danger, the others would automatically come to the rescue. They were skilled masters at unleashing their torment on their unsuspecting opponents. They were most feared in the darkness because of their stealth, cunning and superior eyesight.

If one of the Jacks was killed in combat, by a car or some other unforeseen accident, the dead was never left at the scene. It was of the utmost priority by the others to retrieve their dead and return them to the tribe for a proper ceremony and burial.

The little people were totally dependent on the sacred jackrabbit for clothing and transportation. Ornate, hooded rabbit robes and boots made them blend in perfectly with their mount, so well that they would mostly go undetected. Unless you saw one face-to-face or a portion of an exposed leg draping out from under the robe and nestled in the rabbit's rear flank, you wouldn't see their extremely delicate, pale gray skin. The Earth's seasonal elements were always hard on them. The fur garments were worn year-round.

Jackrabbits were the perfect animal to domesticate for these creatures. First of all, they were numerous on the plains. Secondly, these small aliens were never a threat to the rabbits. They treated them extremely well, much like humans do their horses or dogs. Thirdly, antelope and other fast animals were too big and dangerous to catch and tame. And lastly, but most importantly, coyotes, wolves or mountain lions, although very swift and agile, would eat a Jack for lunch and look for more.

Because of their speed and agility the jackrabbit had a limited number of predators other than man. The Jack handlers took extra precautions in protecting their herds and would kill to protect them from anything that was perceived as a threat.

The Jacks were very selective about their mounts. The rabbits had to be young, strong and large bucks. Over the centuries, the Jack People had domesticated their rabbit herds and bred them for these desired features. A few select clan members were assigned this major responsibility. It was a very important task and those who were chosen were held in the highest esteem. Without the rabbit, the Jack People could not survive, so it was critical that the rabbit herds were tended to accordingly. The rabbits graciously accepted the terms of this amicable arrangement. They showed no fear towards the creatures and even sought their companionship.

These small caretakers were very adept in their ability to breed and train an adequate number of desired jackrabbit mounts to suit their needs. The large rabbits were trained to carry these small creatures on their back at lightning speeds of up to 45 miles an hour. A good rabbit could match the agility and short distance speed of any horse. The jackrabbit is the seventh fastest animal on the planet, compared to the horse's tenth place rating.

The Jack People laid horizontally on the back of the rabbit instead of upright like a man riding a horse. Since they both measured roughly the same length, they could distribute their light weight evenly over their mount and only negligibly impair a young buck's speed by fractions of a second. The Jacks had no need for a saddle. It would be too cumbersome to carry around and weigh the rabbit down. A thin strip of laced rawhide with small hoops on each end offered the rider proper balance. The Jack People would drape it over the muscular rear haunches and insert their feet in the hoops sewn into their moccasins, tucking the riding strap in a small side pocket for easy access. The crucial strip was never lost and was always ready for immediate use. The Jacks would ride the rabbit much like a jockey rides a Thoroughbred racehorse. When not directing the mount by the ear, their small hands gripped the skin around the neck for frontal balance. Their fully balanced body weight was evenly distributed on the back of the mount and they seemed to float effortlessly on the animal at full gait. Their weight was seldom felt d u r i n g the course of a chase. When hunched down over the length of the rabbit, they were extremely hard to see and aerodynamically streamlined for maximum speed over a great distance.

Their weapons of choice were small blow guns made from horsetail reeds found a l o n g the river banks. Sections would be cut to size depending on their use and hollowed out to varying dimensions depending on the number of darts to be used. The Jacks would tease the numerous porcupines found in the area and harvest their 30,000 sharp, barbed quills and easily modify them into aerodynamic darts. These quills have hundreds of minute barbs on the shaft that run in the opposite direction of the point and draw the quill deeper into the flesh of their target. The shaft of a typical four inch quill might easily break off, yet the portion of the quill remaining deep in the tissue flares out and snags the soft tissue. Left untreated, the wound can fester and cause heart and brain damage to the victim. Wolves, coyotes and mountain lions have died trying to attack a porcupine.

Porcupines don't throw their quills, as once thought. If an animal attacks, the quills, acting much like a pin cushion, will penetrate into the aggressor's paw or face, causing a very painful injury. If a quill is propelled through a forceful blow at high velocity, the results are far more catastrophic, especially when dipped in a special concoction of selected venoms, natural drugs and poisons.

A carefully placed dart could easily penetrate the unsuspecting victim and render them harmless or even kill them. It depended on the desired result at that given moment.

Each dart would be meticulously labeled by intricate carvings on the shaft for easy identification of who made the hit. Each successful strike would be counted and the responsible Jack would earn another prized notch on his quiver. The Jacks took a lot of pride in their own unique shaft design and the respect garnered from their hunting skills.

Select blow guns were made by tying several reeds together which could hold multiple darts that could be shot individually or be released all at once. To them it was like p l a y i n g a harmonica. You could play a single note or a chord. These strange looking little creatures could sneak up on any prey with ease and inflict a great range of injuries at will, depending on the need.

Smaller blowguns and darts were used for short range while the longer range targets would require a much longer blow gun and dart. The longer the reed, the better the accuracy. Both sizes were just as lethal. The blow gun could be used with one hand while the other hand controlled the velocity and direction of their mount with a firm grasp of their mount's ear.

The jackrabbit originally had few natural enemies, as did the Jacks. Their speed, agility and cunning would usually keep them out of harm's way, except for the recent new threat of the automobile or a newly imposed bounty. An occasional mountain lion, wolf or coyote might be able to kill one, but not when mounted with a rider. The fearless Jack People were highly skilled at killing these larger predators and protecting their rabbits by unleashing their dart of choice in one powerful blow. The poison barbs would penetrate the hide and within seconds the animal would feel the paralyzing effects. In less than a minute, with the right lethal compound, it would be dead.

If they chose not to kill their victim but instead just create pain or render them harmless, they would use a less potent concoction.

Sometimes just a river pebble out of the blow gun would inflict great discomfort to the groin or head. Most of the time they just needed to momentarily immobilize or temporarily paralyze their target and escape to safety.

The assorted blow guns and darts were carried in a leather quiver strapped to the back and segregated in small designated sections by sinew strapping. Each compartment determined the capabilities to inflict the desired result. These prized quivers were carefully and skillfully decorated by the females with intricate, ornate symbols that identified the owner by his status based on age. An elder's quiver would have a shiny, smooth, dark brown texture weathered by time and the elements and be highly decorated with honors, hits and ranks he'd earned over the years, like a gunslinger's notch on his revolver handle.

All the Jacks carried small flint knives and bolas made from hemp rope. These weapons were stored in a side pocket sewn on the inside of their robe and readily available. The strong, relatively short strand of rope had weighted rocks tied on each end. With a skillful toss, the weapon would wind around the animals legs and easily trip a deer, antelope, horse, buffalo or man running at full speed. They were very skilled and relentless in taking down their targets.

The Jack People made their home in the small caves hidden in the bluffs, buttes and hills that dominated their territorial habitat. The inner caverns were easily accessed through narrow tunnels and numerous rabbit burrows on the surface. These caves had been their permanent homes since their arrival in western Nebrathka over six hundred years prior. They were very content to stay within their desired twenty-five mile range but were quite adept, when the elements cooperated, in venturing outside of their comfort zone if the need presented itself.

Vindication and retaliation of some sort seemed to be the two major reasons for the Jacks to leave their protected territory. They had a keen sense of direction and over the centuries had learned the landscape of their surroundings within a several hundred mile radius.

Some tunnels were more desirable than others in the different seasons and elements. The lower openings seemed cooler in the summer, especially those under the tree cover. They offered immediate refuge in storms or from danger. The lower tunnels also led to the mine shafts, but they were also very susceptible to flooding or unwanted enemies like rattlesnakes. Select areas of the ledges carved out of the sides of the lower tunnels held the remains of the dead and these were considered to be sacred places. Special hieroglyphics adorned these chamber walls, telling a story of each of the honored fallen.

The upper caves kept them dry from the rain and snow. They also served as vantage points that allowed utmost visibility for security. Guards were always posted in the high tunnels to protect the clan. All tunnels had ample food and water supplies stored in strategic locales. There was no need to move around following their food sources while in their territorial zone. A wide variety of food and fresh water was always abundant.

The small exterior surface openings each led to three different arteries serving a specific purpose. One tunnel would lead to the lower mines. Another would lead to a massive main den area where the tribe lived with their select rabbit herds. The third tunnel was for emergencies. If the need presented itself, the Jacks could escape through this shaft to another connected tunnel opening located far away from the immediate threat.

When the large herds of migrating buffalo entered their restricted territory, they would provide them protection. They hated to see these majestic animals slaughtered. They had great admiration for the gentle giants and envied their size and brute strength. Never o n c e had a buffalo ever intentionally harmed a Jack or his mount. Outside of their sacred rabbit, the buffalo was the only other animal that the Jacks openly exposed themselves to. A mutual respect was shared by both species.

There was, however, a more sinister side to the Jack People when provoked. When witnessing these vicious buffalo attacks anywhere in their region, they would hop on their desired buck and join in the hunt and quickly turn the perpetrator into the victim instead of the aggressor.

The Jack soldiers would chase down a galloping Indian pony and run behind the rear wheels, unnoticed by the rider. They'd whip out their special bola rope that was designed to trip a running animal. With a simple toss, the horse and rider would go down, head first, into the grass and dirt and slide or roll to a painful, screeching halt.

Other times they might ride parallel to a hunter and shoot a non-poisonous quill into a leg. The end result was that the rider would pull up his horse, wincing in excruciating pain. Either method would save the life of a buffalo friend.

The Jacks understood there was a fine line in running this interference. They only provided protection within their realm. Outside of this, the buffalo were fair game. The limited number of Jacks certainly couldn't protect the millions of buffalo that roamed the vast territory outside of their boundaries. The Indians depended on the buffalo for food and clothing. Native Americans were doomed without the buffalo, and the Jacks acknowledged their situation. For that reason, the natives were never intentionally killed in the hunt by a Jack. The buffalo was to the Indian as the rabbit was to the Jack. The Jacks were, however, unmerciful to the white buffalo hunters who later appeared to simply slaughter for sport, money or hide. They had no qualms about using their deadlier darts on this new breed of murderers.

Native Americans who dared to pass through their lands were especially susceptible to their pranks. Although the Indians posed a dominant physical threat, size-wise, to a full grown Jack, they were no contest mentally. The Jacks were feared by the tribal people for their stealth, cunning, relentlessness, and overall ability to ruin their day when their paths crossed. It was considered

41

extremely bad luck for a brave to meet a Jack face to face. They were looked on as evil spirits and were to be avoided by all means.

On the other hand, Jack People enjoyed playing their tricks on any human who passed through their domain and considered them fair game. It was true that the Jacks could unleash extreme pain and even death on a human if they had to, but since the humans posed no serious threat to them and actually avoided the Jacks, there was really no reason to harm them other than to occasionally reinforce some diminished respect. The Jacks held the upper hand with fear, and they intended to keep it. If that meant the untimely demise of a tribe member, the message must be sent. Always keep them guessing and fearful. Fear has a powerful upper hand over might.

Over the years, when challenged by aggressive behavior from man or animal, the Jacks could unleash deadly havoc on their unexpected victims. Usually, however, they just wanted to have some fun at the other creature's expense. Their primary reason to kill was for food. The second was in self-defense. Since humans weren't a major part of the food chain and seldom posed an intentional physical threat, they were usually spared. Not so much with their pride.

We-Ota-Wichasha was the veteran leader of the Jack People. Tonight he and his small group of hunters would have some fun when they stumbled across the Sioux. The Jacks hunkered down in the tall grass that surrounded the temporary camp and patiently waited until most of the camp was asleep. The several braves posted as lookouts could easily be fooled or avoided. It depended on We-Ota-Wichasha's mood.

He or any one of his soldiers could simply distract the guard away from his post by mimicking a desirable, available female member of the tribe. The Jacks were highly proficient in their methods of communicating when interacting with man or animal. Their superior intelligence allowed them to master a multitude of desired languages and sounds over the years. The members of the clan took great pride in their ability to mimic both males and females according to the proper need. They sometimes entered into contests to make the challenge even more enjoyable. Outstanding mimicry could warrant a special notch on the quiver. The Jacks preferred to interact with each other, however, without saying a word. They could communicate easily over any distance simply by using their extraordinary mind power.

The Jacks, being very astute with their ventriloquist abilities, would successfully entice any lookout by impersonating an eligible member of the opposite sex. For the Jacks it simply meant a fun challenge to see how far away from camp they could lead their subject before he would get frustrated and retreat, embarrassed, back to his post.

In the meantime, the rest of the Jacks would stealthily sneak under the tent canopies and play their mischievous pranks on those unsuspecting victims deep in sleep. They'd take moccasins, robes or other personal clothing items and place them inside the other neighboring teepees. In the morning, it was fun to watch the commotion when things were missing and later found in an adjacent tent. Jealous fits and accusations were always great entertainment. How did that happen? The attempted explanations were priceless.

Jack soldiers often stuck fresh rabbit pellets in an ear or on a forehead and then tickle the spot with some soft rabbit fur while the others anxiously watched from underneath the buffalo skin teepee covering, harmlessly hiding out of sight. It was hilarious when the sleeping dupe would take a swipe at his or her head only to be rudely awakened with a handful of fresh rabbit crap.

Oftentimes the braves would return to camp late in the day reminiscing over the hunt. For those unlucky braves who took a nose dive on a tripped horse at full gallop, had been hit in the leg with a porcupine quill that would soon have to be cut out with a red hot knife or had taken a direct hit to the nuts with a pea sized river rock and had to continue bouncing up and down bareback on a pony for the next ten miles, it was not a good day. Their various injuries were painful reminders of who they were dealing with.

43

Those unfortunate few would try and rationalize with the others and seek a little sympathy for the fact that they were random victims of the hunt by blaming little men riding rabbits for their woes. The teasing and ridicule would be merciless, but it provided all with a loud, wholesome laugh on the long ride back to camp. These stories would once again be shared when the braves returned and the good hearted laughter and teasing would start all over again and could go on for weeks. Special stories would take on legendary status and be told for years. Days like this were character builders and it seemed that at one time or another, most of the men had suffered similar consequences. It was a rite of passage.   The leery braves became paranoid of the seldom seen Jack People and were constantly looking over their shoulder to make sure they weren't being lined up as the next target.

One of the Jacks' favorite pranks was to gently and delicately weave two sleeping heads of hair together and watch what happened when the couple awoke and tried to get up. They'd lie hidden in the prairie grass cover and anxiously watch as the couple inevitably stumbled clumsily out of their tent, most of the time naked, with their heads tied together and plead for assistance.

These knots were tied close to the scalp and could never be untied. Their long black locks would eventually have to be cut. The victims carried their unenviable ugly new haircuts around the village for months, gathering renewed snickers wherever they ventured as an unpleasant reminder. It didn't take much to amuse these miniature pranksters. They'd leave their clueless dolts wondering what the heck had just happened while they were asleep, minding their own business.

It didn't take long for the hapless victims to figure out who had violated them, but they wisely chose to ignore any thoughts of pursuit or revenge. It would always end badly and therefore was never an option. The old saying *grin and bear it* seemed the best course of action in such cases. The other members of the tribe found great humor in these follies and laughed heartily, as long as they weren't the brunt of the tomfoolery. The Native American

44

people were luckily known to have a keen fondness for laughter and a good sense of humor, for which the Jacks gladly provided much of their material.

Although seldom used, a similar but more serious sign of their presence would raise its ugly head. Intricate, unrecognizable patterns like those written on the burial walls would inexplicably be found permanently woven into a horse tail. These strange weaves and braids could never be untied and also had to be cut out. This was a very bad omen that someone in the tribe would inexplicably perish, which they inevitably did, usually within a forty-eight hour window. It might be at an enemy's hand, a sudden but deadly illness, an unexpected choking, a snake bite, falling from a horse or any number of maladies the natives faced in their daily lives.

The stark reality of an imminent death would cast its ugly shadow over the tribe and leave them nervously wondering who was going to pay the price for the Jack People's lesson in fear. The tribe prayed to their gods to break the chain and spare them the impending pain the evil sign brought, but to no avail. This was bad ju-ju.

To the Native Indians, these Jack People were more of a vision than a physical being. The little people were mostly unrecognizable to their naked eyes and when seen on a fleeting rabbit, they were simply mistaken for a very plump one. The Jacks were more than a figment of their imagination when they were in their presence, however. Something bad usually happened and they wanted no part of the little demons.

CHAPTER SIX
JAN'S STORY

The cold Nebraska wind continued to swirl the light snow across the deserted highway in front of Jan Gradert as she began her hike back to the Bosworth Ranch. Some of the assorted supplies that Dave packed in the trunk were finally being put to good use.

By now the bleeding had stopped, but she still could feel her head throbbing under the burgundy wool cap that one of her students had knit for her several years ago. The flashlight beam made a dull circular pattern on the blacktop surface, like misplaced halos searching in the dark for a new soul to adorn.

This stretch of the road was bordering the hill country. She began ascending the steeper pitch in the highway towards the crest. Jan had a better view from top and she scoured the barren darkness for any sign of life. She could see a faint light a short distance to the right of the highway, just over the next ridge. The teacher didn't know if it was the Bosworth Ranch house, but it would be her best bet for immediate help.

The light was coming from just below some large rock formations about a quarter of a mile from the main highway. It certainly wasn't the Bosworth ranch. She saw a dull patch of blue light hanging just to the south of a grove of pine trees. She couldn't see the s o u r c e of the light and decided to investigate. Surely there would be someone there who could help her. She was certain they were vehicle lights. Maybe the person could assist her in getting out of the ditch, or if need be, take her back to Hemingford or even into Scottsbluff. Just the thought of a warm, functioning vehicle gave her encouragement.   Jan just wanted some help and to get back to civilization. It was extremely dark and cold, she was hurt and getting very wary of her predicament.

The young teacher noticed a cattle gate about thirty yards up the road. A narrow path led through it and disappeared up into the trees. That would be ideal if she could follow a trail back to the light rather than traipsing through the snow-packed pasture. She spread the barbed wire open wide enough to crawl through and began the moderate ascent along the tree-lined trail.

Several minutes later, she reached the crest of the ridge and looked down upon the light source. To her astonishment, she saw a large saucer-shaped object hovering just a few feet above the ground. Strange little creatures were standing upright and wore what seemed to be rabbit pelts. Nearby, a large number of jackrabbits anxiously pilfered through the snow, looking for prairie grass roots to graze on since food sources were limited this time of year.

The dull light she'd seen from the road flooded the small work area below her. It seemed to originate from whatever it was hovering directly below her. There appeared to be a very rapidly moving assembly line that stretched from the small hill opening up to the unknown object. Close to twenty or thirty of these very small, frail and manlike creatures stood in the background and watched as eight somewhat larger, bulkier silver-robed bodies floated containers of rocks above one pair of cradled hands over to the next. Their movements were very coordinated and precise. There was no physical effort to move this large quantity of rock in a short period of time. The rocks seemed to levitate over their hands without so much as a slight touch. The ore containers moved effortlessly, much like the vessel, into a massive bucket attached to the inner wall of the craft. Each creature worked in unison to complete the task at hand.

A constant chatter could be heard in the frigid air and Jan tried hard to make sense of any of the strange noises that she was hearing. It certainly wasn't a language that vaguely resembled anything from the human dialect. It sounded more like a constant low hum, like what is heard around power lines. Whatever it was seemed to flow in some sort of unison.

47

Within minutes, the organized movement suddenly ended. The eight larger forms disappeared into the floating object which slowly rose above the surface and shot outward into the pitch black Nebraska sky, disappearing within seconds. The shorter creatures wearing the rabbit pelts retreated back into the tunnel and pulled a final rock over the opening before disappearing.

The woman couldn't imagine in her wildest dreams witnessing what transpired less than fifty yards from her. Maybe she was hallucinating from her head wound and simply slipped out of consciousness for a brief time. There was no apparent logic to what she'd seen. The helpless teacher would have plenty of time to think about it later, but now the realization of her dire situation immediately set in again. Jan needed to find aid before she passed out and froze to death.

Mrs. Gradert frantically turned the flashlight back on and carefully made her way down the hillside and back out to the highway. From her new vantage point at the top of the hill she could now see the yard light from the Bosworth house in the distance. Jan crossed the small bridge that spread over the ravine that separated the Bosworth ranch from neighboring Mike Robinson's Bar X spread. She anxiously picked up her pace and thought of a warm stove and hot drink to give her some immediate comfort once she reached her destination. Fear of the dark and any other unknown surprises made it easier to maintain her new hurried tempo. She was scared to death and needed help.

For a brief moment the thought of no one being home ran a shiver of added fear through her already overly chilled body. The panic-driven adrenaline rush now propelled her feet into a slow jog.

They've got be home on a night like this, she thought as her heart pounded in rhythm with her rubber boots squishing through the newly fallen snow. If they weren't, she'd break into the house and suffer any consequences later. This was life or death. Jan needed help *now*.

As the teacher approached the yard light she had seen from the highway, a parked vehicle in the yard and lights emanating from the house came into view. Jan grabbed the handle on the front door screen and rapidly banged it loudly against the door frame.

Robb and Shar Bosworth were present at the door when it swung open. They immediately saw that the woman standing before them was in trouble. Robb grabbed her arm and helped her into the living room where he sat her down in a chair next to the wood stove. They immediately recognized Jan as she took off her wet hat and unraveled her scarf from around her coat collar. They also saw caked blood eerily matted in her damp hair.

"Are you all right Mrs. Gradert? Can you tell us what happened?" asked Robb in a concerned voice.

Jan was still in total disbelief about what she'd just experienced. Her ever-present senses of logic and alacrity were obviously not working coherently. She did manage to softly participate in some limited and strained conversation.

"Thank God I found you home! I need help. My car got stuck in the ditch up the road and I was stranded. I knew you were the nearest farm house," was her frightened, barely audible response.

Robb could see the fear in her eyes and her lower lip quivering from the cold. "Would you like some hot tea?"

Jan nodded her head as she bent over to take off her boots. Her toes were numb and she wanted to get them closer to the fire. "Yes, please."

It was apparent to the Bosworths that Jan was not herself. The woman was very sullen and withdrawn in addition to being extremely cold. She was very much relieved to have found physical shelter, but no one could help her current disoriented mental state. It was hard for her to come up with any logical explanation and she knew that no one else on Earth would be able to help. The confused teacher decided to wait to tell her incredible

49

story until her husband arrived. Jan was scared and wanted Dave there with her. Maybe her blow to the head was more serious than she thought and might lead to losing her grip on reality.

Shar helped her out of her coat and rushed back to the bedroom to grab a quilt from the bed. "Here Mrs. Gradert, put this on."

Jan asked Robb if he would please call her husband in Scottsbluff. It was now past ten thirty and he must be very worried. Robb dialed the number with his index finger in the one piece, stand up rotary phone sitting on a nearby table. Once Dave answered the phone, he handed it to Jan.

"I've been in a minor accident, honey. I hit my head, but other than that I think I'm okay. The car is in the ditch and I'm safe at the Bosworth ranch. Could you drive out and get me? Please hurry!"

After answering a few short questions from Dave, Jan gave the hand piece back to Robb to give her husband directions. "He'll be here as soon as he can. Thank you for letting me use the phone."

While they waited for Dave Gradert, Shar warmed up some left over pot roast and potatoes in the oven. Jan huddled in the warm quilt and sat silently in the living room rocker as she slowly began to warm up. Once again she could feel her fingers as the stinging and tingling subsided. Shar got a large bowl of warm, soapy water and a towel to tend to her head wound. She gently washed her hair of the dried blood and pulled the wet hair away from the small gash now visible in her scalp.

Having tended to four daughters, a husband, hired hands and countless animals during her years of living on a ranch, Shar considered herself to be somewhat of an expert when evaluating the severity of injuries. "It's just a small cut. Head wounds have a tendency to bleed a lot. I think it looks worse than it actually is.

Here, take these two aspirin and you'll be fine. I don't think the cut warrants stitches, although you may have suffered a concussion."

Shortly after Jan finished her meal, headlight beams lit up the frosted kitchen window. It was Dave. Robb greeted him at the door and quickly invited him in out of the blistering cold. After a brief introduction and a heartfelt thank you from Dave, the men joined Jan and Shar back in the living room.

His immediate concern was his wife. He wanted to know what happened. He'd noticed the Impala on the side of the road about three miles south of the ranch. They wouldn't worry about the car tonight. Robb volunteered to help get the car in the m o r n i n g with his tractor. Dave joined his wife on the couch and she snuggled close to him.   Shar made a fresh pot of hot coffee and they all settled comfortably in their seats to hear the details of Jan's strange and inexplicable ordeal. The Bosworths thought a lot of the story didn't make sense and blamed the head wound for much of the confusion. When Jan finished, she and her husband were led to the small guest bedroom where they'd spend the night.

CHAPTER SEVEN
FLYING SAUCERS AND MUTILATED COWS

Although seven months apart, dozens of convoluted yarns soon began to spread around the Nebraska panhandle after Jan Gradert and Doc Mino had their stories printed in the Scottsbluff Star Herald. Even though both were respected members of the community and their word was impeccable, the people of western Nebraska found their recollection of events rather unbelievable. They could even be called skeptics.

"Doc Mino must have been bitten by a mad cow. It's made him delirious!" or "The school teacher must have hit her head pretty bad to come up with that whopper!" were the more popular comments that were buzzing around the area.

"Why would anyone believe such foolishness, regardless of who's telling it? It's total nonsense! They've got to be doing it for the publicity!" echoed others.

Eventually they all began repeating the quote "Well, you know you can't always believe everything you read in the papers."

Now they seemed to think that the newspaper was in cahoots with the two and embellishing an otherwise uneventful story to gain readers. It was all a big conspiracy and the poor, honest citizens of western Nebraska were being duped.

Both Doc Mino and Jan Gradert took their fair share of razzing from outside their inner circle of family and work associates. So did the Bosworth and Lankila families, along with Sheriff Suske. They'd also been included in the scrutiny. After months of teasing, all of them would just excuse themselves from the conversation if it came up or change the subject. They knew what they had seen and other people's ridicule was certainly not going to change that fact. It was really of no benefit to them to argue the point. The original doubters were by now hard core skeptics.

Gavin Aldama, a writer for the Omaha World Herald, wrote a three part series on cattle mutilations, flying saucers and evidence of "Jack People" in the summer of 1960. The timing was right. Much of what Aldama had to say supposedly had been witnessed in various parts of the panhandle. His series simply added some credence to what these western Nebraskans had been writing off as pure poppycock. Gee, now it seems that a growing number of fellow Nebraskans have witnessed similar events since 1884 everywhere from Omaha to Lincoln to Hastings to North Platte to Scottsbluff and b e y o n d . Aldama pulled stories from the library archives that cast some truth on what D o c and Jan had been trying to tell the locals for the last several months. They were not alone. Altogether there were more than 100 sightings across the state over the years. Aldama figured for every sighting reported, there were probably four more that went unreported. And that was just Nebraska. Similar stories were surfacing all around the country and the world.

One story of a saucer crash back in 1884 up around O'Neill, Nebraska surfaced in his article that was actually well before what had been documented in the now infamous Roswell incident that had taken place much later, in 1947. A local rancher by the name of Stan Lundahl was out riding his fences with a hired man when they came across what appeared to be some sort of crash out in his pasture. The only thing they could compare i t to size-wise was a locomotive engine. Whatever it was had apparently fallen out of the sky, and this was nineteen years before the first airplane would be flown by the Wright Brothers in 1903. There were no wagon tracks pressed firmly in the prairie grass to suggest otherwise.

The wreckage consisted of various sized sheets of shiny, lightweight material strewn over a quarter mile of his pasture. Unlike a current day airplane crash, this outer skin wasn't crumbled. It retained its smooth surface. It had been torn, but not one piece was mangled. Numerous larger objects that resembled instrument clusters, gears and wiring harnesses were also found. Although these massive pieces appeared to be very heavy, the two men easily picked several of them up and placed them in the wagon.

Three small, badly charred bodies of some sort were found at the site. They were burned beyond recognition, but their size and the odd shape of their skeletal features (what little remained) indicated that the bodies were not human.

Lundahl and his hired hand loaded up a limited variety of pieces of the wreckage, along with the bodies, into their wagon and took them into O'Neill. He showed them to Sheriff Rick Harrison Smith and Dr. Guy Piche for them to examine in the corral behind the sheriff's office. Lundahl showed the men the lightness and durability of this exterior skin material by crumbling up a large piece in his hand like a gum wrapper and throwing it on the ground. Within seconds, it would magically revert back to its original shape!

Both men documented their observations in their own separate journals, which appeared in the local Holt County Independent newspaper two days later.

The grass never did grow back at the crash site, and for that matter, neither did anything else.

Because of the remoteness of the crash and the lack of any modern communication network, the story went untold outside of the immediate area. The wreckage site was somewhat of a local novelty and people living in the area visited the remote site to get a piece of the strange material as a souvenir. Over the years, all was forgotten and any remnants of the crash eventually disappeared. The only remaining documentation was the small story printed in the Independent, and over the years even that got buried in the archives until Gavin stumbled upon it.

Similar stories from around the state were recorded over the coming years. Credible people living in their communities went on record having witnessed low flying, saucer- shaped objects that appeared out of nowhere and would hover above them before s h o o t i n g off into the night sky. Several even claimed to have been literally picked up and pulled into these strange flying vessels. They would be released with very little detailed memory of their experience, but they would be sporting strange markings and small cuts or puncture wounds on their bodies. Some even claimed to have miniscule implants of some sort placed in various locations on their bodies that somehow altered their memories and personalities.

There were many theories about flying saucers based primarily on where they came from and why they would visit the planet Earth, but one struck close to home with Aldama. O f all the places to visit, why would they pick a desolate prairie landscape void of any major human population like Nebraska? Why not visit New York, Chicago or Los Angeles? Perhaps take in the World Fair or visit Disneyland. Maybe they didn't want to expose themselves to the masses and create a major panic. Maybe they preferred Nebraska because it might offer a badly needed source of nuclear fuel like uranium.

Nebraska is the eighth largest provider in the United States for mining o f this metallic chemical element and the surrounding states of Colorado, South Dakota and Wyoming are all in the top twenty. New York, Illinois and California aren't listed. Perhaps they aren't coming to observe humans on Earth, but for a fuel source. When you're galaxy hopping over light years of time, even aliens might need an occasional tank of fuel. Coal, oil or steam probably didn't fit the bill.

The solar system is infinite. Our solar system as we know it is only a small pebble on the beach. Are we Earthlings so naive to think that Earth is the only planet out of m i l l i o n s or maybe even billions that can sustain life? The odds aren't in our favor to hold such a limited and selfish notion. There have been a lot of very smart scientists over the years who argue the existence of life, man's evolution and how we humans have grown from the stone age to the space age and how or if we're capable of evolving even further in the progression chain.

Numerous obstacles could stand in our way. Will we run out of energy sources and disappear? Will we be hit with a giant meteor and cease to exist? Will we simply blow ourselves up with a massive nuclear war? T h e r e a r e so many staggering questions and not enough simple answers. There are countless mysteries surrounding life that go unanswered, yet some believe wholeheartedly that we're alone in the universe. Everyone has their own beliefs, but shouldn't visitors from other planets remain at least a possibility? Most have to see it to believe it themselves. They simply can't take the word of another, no matter how credible he might be. They might be called skeptics.

Gavin Aldama had interviewed both Doc Mino and Jan Gradert along with roughly two dozen other Nebraskans who claimed to have witnessed these three odd phenomena that made up the bulk of his extraordinary feature story. He had planned on just writing a single article about saucer sightings around the state, but Doc and Jan expanded his horizons. Newspaper articles and film clips about flying saucers had been around for years and he certainly wasn't the first journalist to write on the subject.

Cattle mutilations and little people riding rabbits certainly got his attention and expanded his options. These topics had never been exposed through the printed media. This was new ground for the young writer, and it might make his story a feature series in newspapers or even a magazine that could be sold around the world, and that got Gavin excited.

He was fascinated by Doc Mino's pictures and notes. He contacted Scottsbluff Sheriff Joe Suske, Nick Jensen from the State Crime Lab and Dr. Knighten, the state veterinarian, for their input on the mutilations. All four of the men welcomed the opportunity to have their story exposed to the press by a professional newsman that would tell their story the way it happened rather than slant it to make them look foolish, which was often the case with such unbelievable events and hack reporting.

Nick Jensen shared the New Mexico mutilation and the fact that other agencies were now part of a network of professionals monitoring any similar activity in their respective states. Nick was the man spearheading the program. The pictures and reports that

Nick was sharing with these people was the same he was sharing with Gavin. Jensen could now comment about saucer sightings, since they also came through his office. Much like the mutilations, the saucer reports went into a special file section in the cabinet. They certainly offered no conclusive evidence and any comments contained in them lacked any hard facts. Skepticism again prevailed.

These guys are all experts in their respective fields and if they're involved with such an outlandish account of what they'd found out on the Lankila Ranch, then there must be something to it, Gavin thought. It was up to Gavin Aldama to relay their story to the reading audience, wherever they may be. Pictures don't lie and nothing like these photos had ever been published before. He was indeed breaking new ground!

Jan Gradert was a totally different story. She was the only eyewitness to her odd testimonial. Several days after her experience, a local Scottsbluff newspaper reporter got a lead and did a small one column story based on a short interview he did with her. Of course it garnered a lot of local attention, but the coverage was not kind to this otherwise very credible member of the community. It basically was her word alone, and without backup witnesses, she was ostracized by most everyone who read or heard her outlandish tale.

While Doc Mino and Sheriff Suske both had identical notes regarding their whopper, Jan was hung out to dry. Her account of this totally unbelievable event would certainly be a major challenge for Gavin to try and convince his readers. The flying saucer part might have a small chance of offering credibility when coupled with the main feature article, but the little men riding rabbits was going to be very difficult to sell to his readers. At least until he stumbled on an eighty-eight year old Sioux Indian by the name of Joe Yellow Bear.

CHAPTER EIGHT
JOE YELLOW BEAR

For years Joe told stories to his tribe of his youth and the elders. He was now in his eighties and living with his daughter in Alliance. While doing the stories on Doc Mino and Jan Gradert, Gavin Aldama heard about the old man and his amazing stories. Gavin decided to interview Joe and hear his tales. Segments of the interview were used in Aldama's newspaper article.

Joe Yellow Bear was born in May of 1872 on the plains of the panhandle near Alliance, Nebraska. He and his family were proud members of the Lakota Sioux tribe that inhabited parts of western Nebraska, eastern Wyoming and southwestern South Dakota.

The expansion westward by the White Man created many hardships on the tribe. Their buffalo were being slaughtered needlessly for their robes. The many trees that g r e w in the hills were being cut down for new building frames that made up the new little communities springing up across their lands. These unwelcome intruders also competed with the Indian for elk, deer and antelope. There was much turmoil and uncertainty about their survival. His people were constantly being forced to move to more confined lands d e void of the few necessities they needed to survive.

Joe's early memories were filled with a lot of sadness. Death, disease, famine and the elements were not kind to his people. More despised than these calamities, however, was the hated White Man. His father and grandfather would often lament to young Joe about the days before the White Man and the way life used to be. The men of the tribe would often sit around their fire at night and reminisce about the good times they once shared.

When Joe reached puberty, he was asked to join in and listen to his elders share their stories. Several stood out to the young man and he could never hear them often enough. He would ask his elders to explain these strange stories in detail. It was hard for him to understand without experiencing them, like these men he admired greatly had once done. The lad relished them. They were his most prized possessions in his otherwise meager childhood. These ancestral stories were something the White Man could never take away from him.

Several stories that Joe especially liked revolved around what the elders called Jack People. They sort of resembled a man, but were very short and had strange looking heads and facial features. They had only been seen from a distance, because to the Sioux they were bad omens and they would certainly never challenge them. The old men had s e e n them in action from a distance though, as they would sometimes be seen during the buffalo hunts riding on large jackrabbit bucks. The Jacks could inflict great pain to e i t h e r the horse or rider and sometimes both. The only proof they left on such incidents would be the small, sharp quill that would have to be cut from the victim. It was always barbed on the point, making it difficult and painful to remove and would have intricate yet unrecognizable markings carved on the small shaft. The injury would always result in a painfully festered leg. If any infection set in, the wound would have to be cauterized by a hot knife to cleanse the area which, again, was very painful and took a long time to heal.

That was about the least pain they could inflict and the braves would feel somewhat fortunate if that was all they had to endure from these very elusive and seldom seen little adversaries. Other stories told of the pain the warriors might endure due to a tripped galloping horse or a strategically placed river pebble from a blow gun to the groin.

One of grandfather's favorite stories told of when his father was just a young warrior and he joined a small band from their tribe to scout for Crow warriors. The elders warned the men that the hills where the enemy was seen belonged to the Jack People and were bad medicine. Stay out! The five braves were hungry and they didn't listen to the advice. They split up to look for food. One of the warriors saw a jackrabbit and silently drew his bow and arrow. With a direct hit, the rabbit fell dead. As he ran to claim his prize, he suddenly grabbed his neck in excruciating pain.

It took the others about an hour to realize their friend was missing. Half a day of exhaustive searching yielded few results. They found the missing brave's pony. The tail had been braided in a very strange and meticulous pattern unknown to any of the tribe.

Braided hair was very common among both men and women but this particular braid was like nothing they'd ever seen. The pattern resembled a strange combination of various sized circles and what appeared to be stars. The men decided to leave the tail alone and show the strange braid to the others upon their return to the village.

The only other clue was the lifeless rabbit found nearby with the lost brave's arrow still protruding through the neck.

The last faint glimmer of sunlight slowly faded over the western horizon as they wearily sat and pondered their next move around their campfire. Suddenly a large, bright, shiny flying object seemingly appeared out of nowhere and hung directly above them, about one hundred yards above in the dimly lit evening sky. Within seconds, they heard a sickening, dull thud in the nearby prairie grass as the object shot out of sight over the eastern horizon. The terrified braves found their friend in the prairie grass, about twenty yards from where he had been dropped.

The men were mortified. They had never seen anything like this before. This was bad medicine to the extreme. They wasted no time wrapping the dead brave in a blanket and started a hasty retreat back to the village some twenty miles away.

They reached the village the next morning and immediately told their story to the elders in their tribal teepee away from the others. Several of the older men proceeded to the area where the dead brave had been hidden. His heart had been removed along with his testicles, scrotum, one eye, an ear and several fingers and toes. Six of his front teeth and both of his lips were also gone. There was not a drop of blood anywhere on the body. The incisions used to remove the body parts were very clean and precise, like nothing they'd ever seen before. There was no odor. The men did notice a thin line of purplish goo that seemed to follow along the outline of the cuts.

The men were aghast at what lay before them. The council adjourned to a sweat lodge fabricated from buffalo hides draped over poles. Water was poured over hot coals and t h e instant burst of steam released a loud hiss.

Once the men were comfortably settled, the discussion began very awkwardly. No one knew where to start. After a few minutes of trivial conversation, the tribal elder raised his hand for silence. Hearing of the dead rabbit and the location of the incident, Chief Little Duck began to unravel the mystery. This was the work of the Jack People. The young braves had encroached on their marked land and paid the price.

Joe Yellow Bear was always reminded of that incident and was very careful when walking through the woods. The Jacks were silent and deadly adversaries that could strike at very close range. From that day on, Joe never killed another rabbit. He'd heard of the deadly consequences firsthand.

A second story the elders told was of a seventeen-year-old girl of their tribe who went missing. Two days after her disappearance, the girl's pony returned to camp. J u s t t h e d a y b e f o r e , m e m b e r s o f the tribe had inexplicably found a very ornate decoration braided into another pinto's tail. The design was unknown to any of the tribe. One of the women tried to undo the intricate braiding from the tail, but found the task impossible. Several young braves were assigned the delicate task of cutting it out with their hunting knives.

Apparently she had ridden her pony down to the river directly below the bluffs to bathe just before sundown and never returned to camp. A search party found the girl's body early the next morning upon a ridge looking down over the river, about fifty yards up the rocky hillside. A small rabbit skin robe was hanging from a nearby branch.

At first glance, it was apparent that she had been brutally raped. The dead girl was found naked and spread eagled near the river bank. The soft skin around her breasts was deeply bruised and her groin area was a bloody mess. The body was covered by small bite marks and scratches.

Was this some type of coming of age ritual killing that a warring tribe might have performed? Maybe this was a new strategy of psychological warfare where the enemy would try to instill great fear into their tribe by performing this cruel and brutal act. As a rule, warring tribes would generally never mutilate women or children. There were no other footprints found around the body, which upheld that belief.

The only similarity between the two bizarre killings was the intricate horse tail weaves left at both scenes. Both horses had inexplicably ornate patterns braided into their tails. The master weavers studied the detail in the unrecognizable patterns and tried to replicate them. To give them a clue, they tried to untie the tails and follow the pattern to the beginning and then copy the pattern. To their astonishment, the braids could not be unraveled. The weave was so tight and interwoven that it could not be undone or copied. The women drew the designs on some stretched leather and presented their findings to the tribal elders.

Joe Yellow Bear relayed his tales to the young reporter. In turn, he wanted to hear Gavin's stories. Gavin began to share the unbelievable stories of the Jack People riding jackrabbits, cattle mutilations and flying saucers with the old man. Joe had carried stories of what he couldn't understand with him all of his life. At his age, he didn't need to add to the heavy burden. After a few minutes, he raised his hand, got up from his chair and simply said "Enough."

CHAPTER NINE
SEVERE FEAR

We-Ota-Wichasha had started his reign as the leader of his Jack People back in 1837 and had led his clan for over 120 years. His father had given his son this name in honor of the Sioux, who greatly feared but respected the Jack People. Their interpretation meant "rabbit boy." This crafty and fearless Pygmalion-like creature took the leadership role at the spry young age of fifty. His father had been the leader of the Jacks for over 165 y e a r s before being accidentally trampled to death by a Sioux pony while trying to protect their beloved buffalo. The Jack warriors were all very skilled riders, but an occasional stray arrow, unexpected trampling or a tripping ride could bring down even t h e best Jack in the course of a raging stampede.

Although his people were feared by the Plains Indians over the centuries, they too had never crossed paths with the White Man. The new breed of invaders to their land had no respect. The trespassers scarred up the river banks with their wagons. Their livestock devastated the thousands of acres of buffalo grass along the many trails that now crossed the land and made their buffalo look for new pastures, which were rapidly declining. The rare trees along the riverbanks were being cut down for firewood and beams for their newly built living quarters. They always seemed to take and never give back.

The new intruders to the land had a bad habit of killing off the Jack People's beloved buffalo. The Indians did it for survival and only took what they needed. They wasted nothing. We-Ota-Wichasha and his people realized this fact and also knew that even though these red men killed the buffalo, they too considered the animal sacred and showed it great respect.

The new breed the Indians called the White Men were different. Not only did they destroy the land, they actually hunted the buffalo for sport. Hundreds of thousands of these majestic creatures would be shot down, skinned of their hides and left to rot on the prairie. Worse yet, the unwelcome invaders loved a pot of rabbit stew. This rude and offensive behavior was deplorable and certainly not to be tolerated.

Over the past century of the White Man's dominance of this land, We-Ota-Wichasha and his people had openly waged war against them. They needed a serious lesson in humility. It was just a different strategy than what the enemy was used to. Before, when the invaders were attacked by the Indians, they would bring their cannons and rifles to a knife and bow-and-arrow fight. No contest. Even We-Ota-Wichasha could see that. Since his people stood less than two feet tall and could muster no more than a large poisoned porcupine quill shot through a reed or perhaps throw a spear similar in size to a modern day golf club a measly fifteen yards, their method of warfare had to take a different approach in order to survive and conquer.

No Indian ever called a Jack stupid. Quite the contrary. It was as if they had superhuman intelligence. They might be little and pose no physical threat to their opponent, but they were unmatched when it came to their cunning and stealth. When angered, their justice could be just as swift and deadly.

We-Ota-Wichasha led his people during this mass migration across the prairies. He'd seen the White Man conquer the Indians, hunt down all God's creatures, spread steel rails and wire across the prairie, build strange tall structures out of wood and brick, group them in major clusters across the land from coast to coast and steal the shiny, valuable metal they called gold from Mother Earth, leaving gaping holes in the ground.

Now this strange breed of humans was driving strange, colorful shiny metal objects up and down these hard, black trails that were now named and numbered with ugly metal signs.

As the planet evolved, the world as they'd known it for centuries was changing almost daily. The invention of the automobile was their Waterloo. A jackrabbit could outrun many things, but they met their match when up against a new, deadly and unconquerable enemy called a car. It was no contest and easy to predict their long term future.

It was time for We-Ota-Wichasha to change gears on his strategy when dealing with these obnoxious intruders. He'd earned a lot of respect from the Red Man over the centuries, but these crude and disrespectful White Men were oblivious to the Jacks and what they were capable of.

For some reason, about this same time humans began to think of the rabbit as an invasive critter, much like the coyote or prairie dog. Seems like they didn't take kindly to sharing the vegetables they'd plant back behind their wooden shelters. Bounties would be placed on their ears and fur. It was a sport that appealed to a large number of humans, especially the young ones just learning to kill. Hunters would needlessly slaughter them for twenty-five cents an ear and fifty cents for the pelt. Hundreds of thousands of jackrabbits were slaughtered every year and the losses were taking a toll on the species' survival. They were truly a dying breed.

Rabbit feet were made into key chains and sold in every dime store across the country back in the fifties and early sixties in a variety of ugly dyed shades of greens, blues, pinks and purples. They were considered good luck charms if you rubbed them. They went faster than a rabbit in heat.

Since the jackrabbit was vanishing at an astonishing rate, the Jack People were put at a distinct disadvantage for their survival as well. This upset the apple cart for both the Jacks and their alien allies. If the Jacks perished, so would their ability to provide the n e c e s s a r y fuel they had been put on the planet to mine. The two leaders from each civilization decided to try the concept of crossbreeding with humans. This was a totally new direction for them to take, but due to the rapid changes that surrounded them, it was determined it was a necessity for their combined survival. The

Jack People would soon no longer survive in the White Man's land. If they could successfully mate and start a new strain of human species the aliens could control, the playing field could be somewhat leveled. In order for their species to survive, they'd have to mate with the dominant form of life. This proved very difficult, and they relied on their only allies when the opportunity to breed with a human presented itself. As Chief, We-Ota-Wichasha took on the responsibility personally.

The midget to a midget had to act fast. He and his small, aging band of followers were the last of a dying breed and now with the Red Man fighting for survival in the White Man's world, totally forgotten. This new breed of White Man hadn't even a small clue about their existence. There would be no more. They were the last of an endangered species. Their lands, homes and food supplies were all being devoured by these new intruders. Even their prized uranium was now of value to the White Man, and they were competing for their energy supply. If they were going by the way of the buffalo, they'd at least go down fighting.

Back in the early days, We-Ota-Wichasha and his clan could disable or kill both man and beast with a skillfully placed poison dart. They could go completely undetected in the night on the backs of their cherished rabbits and poison the food and water supplies that were critical for survival. It became insulting, because so much of their detailed planning and devastation would go completely unnoticed and unappreciated. Wagon trains and even small communities would be devastated with an epidemic and automatically it would be blamed on cholera or the flu. Little did they know that it was a carefully placed poisonous concoction that went undetected. These events became very monotonous but very effective in killing the enemy. A correct tincture of Jack poison could bring down armies.

Not to diminish their desire for entertainment in the process, a skillfully placed piece of undergarments in the right locale would cause these strange people to actually kill each other! For some inexplicable reason, in that aspect they were no different than the Indians that had preceded them centuries earlier. This time-honored sport brought back to life in a new form was truly amusing and the Jacks relished every opportunity to witness such hanky-panky.

In the early days of the automobile, these silly people in their new contraptions actually made the sport easier by coming out to the Jacks. They were playing *their* game on *their* home field! They would drive out on these deserted roads in the middle of nowhere, shed their clothing and become easily distracted right there in the Jack's back yard! All a skilled Jack had to do now was to grab those garments and hightail it back to the weeds that lined those gravel paths. It wasn't long before the entertainment began. These two humiliated humans would cautiously get out of the car, search the area, swearing and blaming each other for their carelessness and then discuss their devious plans on returning to town.....naked! When they pulled this crafty maneuver, they usually could count on never seeing that same contraption or human ever again.

With their uncanny ability to mimic sounds and voices, the Jacks reveled in the chance to call out a bad name or insult to one of these strange beings, especially when they'd been drinking, and sit back and watch the repercussions. Talk about cheap, instantaneous entertainment!

Jacks would throw out a loud, "Hey mister, your wife's so ugly her face could stop a clock!" The outcome was predictably always the same.

It became a matter of numbers, however. The Jacks could only do so much. The White Man continued to come. Now that the buffalo and Indians were gone, the Jacks needed to pool their efforts with another plan to try and delay their pending demise.

Something that the White Man seemed to fear. Something unseen and mysterious. Fear works wonders. It always has and it always will. One just needs to understand it, be able to control it and unleash it at will when the occasion presents itself. Since the late forties and now into the late fifties, the time to call on old, higher connections was just right.

Many centuries ago, We-Ota-Wichasha's people were dropped to Earth at this precise locale to begin a great working relationship with their inter galactic shirttail relatives. The Jack People's mining abilities in small, confined spaces offered them their crucial uranium to fuel their exploits. In return they were given superior knowledge, longer life expectancy, resistance to diseases, keen senses, strange healing powers to the injured, a superior sense of dialect and the ability to request special favors when the need presented itself. There was an unbreakable bond formed by a long friendship and loyalty interlocking the two.

This partnership had existed completely unnoticed for hundreds of years. White M a n ' s modern technology had changed the rules. Up until fifty years ago, mankind had literally existed unchanged. Horses were the accepted means of transportation. Light c a m e from a fire, not a bulb. You could never imagine communicating with someone outside of your voice range. Now there are strange noises and voices coming from a box or the inside of these strange moving contraptions being called the automobile. The only things that could previously fly were the three B's.......birds, bugs and bullets. You had to fetch food for yourself or you and your family would starve. Now these men go into a building and wheel out carts of whatever they want to eat and they don't have to chase it down and kill it. Things that were hot in the summer were suddenly hot in the winter and vice versa. Now these humans have some sort of box that can show pictures as proof and also actually speak to the people at the same time. It pressed the known bounds of logic. This breed of humans was smoking and drinking strange things and wearing less clothing. Life was becoming more of a challenge to the Jack People and We-Ota-Wichasha had thought long and hard to find a solution. In order to pass on a simulation of a new generation of Jacks, they would have to carry out the plan to mate with these humans and control them through fear.

One night back in the late 1840s, while refueling one of the saucers, a young group of white people showed up unexpectedly up at one of their mines on an obscure butte. The band of seven rowdies came roaring over the hill on their horses out of nowhere. They were drinking from a big brown jug and boom, there they were. It was an innocent standoff; neither party knew what to do next. Suddenly these idiots tore off across the countryside to where they'd come from, screaming and hollering. It appeared they were in state of severe fear. We-Ota-Wichasha had found the solution long ago and it was now time to re-instill that sense of fear.

To prove his theory, he asked his friendly heavenly visitors to occasionally fly over one of these new-fangled clusters of humans and see what happened. It worked every time. People would yell and scream. Many covered their eyes, fainted, or even worse, died right there on the spot. Others might even spring a leak. Panic would prevail over those directly involved, but it didn't seem to scare the masses. Nobody or nothing ever got hurt or died, like back in the old days.

Only an accidental reading of Orson Well's *War of the Worlds* over the radio one Halloween night re-created the desired chaos.

After a decade, the whole flying saucer thing became passé. Even his alien counterparts became bored with the game. Whoopee, let's outrun another bi-plane or t w o . A few B grade alien movies and Buck Rogers. Where's the challenge there? These strange beings longed to use their superb intellect and technology to help these Stone Age mental midgets build more ancient pyramids or another Easter Island. The nifty pieces of craftsmanship have stumped the humans for several thousand years.

What if? What if we put the old fear factor back in a new package? It had been tried many years ago, back in the late 1840s, on humans. It worked then; why not try it again now?

"We'll experiment. Let's pick 'em up in a saucer and put 'em back down. They'll tell their story firsthand with more gusto than we could ever imagine. Instead of just seeing a flying saucer, now humans are being picked up by them! Let's put that talking picture box to our use and become more visible. Hover, jet away and let them chase us again in their new jet airplanes. Come in groups. Whatever it takes to get the image captured in this gadget that speaks. Whatever we do will be embellished ten-fold! We'll start a couple of new phenomena to invoke even more fear. Let's expose some crop circles worldwide and do some animal mutilations simultaneously. The aliens don't have to go out of their way to do this. They can do it right here while fueling, where cows, corn crops and wheat fields are plentiful. Wait until the first crossbred baby comes out of the womb and is shown in the picture box.... that should really create some real severe fear!

CHAPTER TEN
PORCUPINE QUILLS AND BOLAS

Nick Jensen from the State Crime Lab called Dr. Ken Knighten over to the lab several days after their trip to Scottsbluff.

"I've got something that may be of interest, how soon can you be here?"

It was a ten minute drive from Dr. Knighten's capital building office out to the lab off of Cornhusker Highway. Ken was soon on his way.

Dr. Knighten anxiously entered the lab's east side door and headed directly to Nick's front corner office. After a few minutes of polite conversation, Nick led the doctor down the hall to the lab.

"Ken, take a look at this and tell me what you think," he said as he flicked on the high- intensity light hanging over one of the autopsy tables.

One of the buckets used to transport the marked body parts back to the lab sat on the floor. He bent over the severed left rear hoof that was now shaven clean for closer examination.

Dr. Knighten immediately noticed a dark bruise ring that wound around the entire hoof. "Let's check the others and see if we find any similarities," he murmured quizzically.

After examining the other three, the right rear hoof revealed a similar pattern but at a slight angle, higher up toward the lower leg joint.

"It looks like a very small rope, less than the diameter of a pencil, made these marks, but how?" asked the doctor.

Nick paused in silence for a brief time and then slowly and carefully posed a question to a question.

"Since they're around the feet, maybe the animal was tripped somehow. Hey Ken, did you ever study Argentina in any of your junior high school geography classes? Can you recall the Gauchos? They're Argentinean cowboys who use bolas to trip the animal to take it down. Are you familiar with them?"

"Yeah, but I don't see the connection. This is like bringing a pea shooter to a gun fight. The tool doesn't fit the purpose. There's better ways to bring a large animal down other than with a piece of cord and a sharp stick."

"One thing we didn't check is what we might have found *in* that ear wound. Maybe the animal was brought down in the very primitive manner of tripping, but was stabbed with something like a small spear. We assumed the depth went to the brain, but we never proved it."

"Good idea. I'll have one of my staff do a head post this afternoon and I'll give you a call," said Nick as he looked down at his watch.

Ken quickly replied. "Got a soccer match I've got to go to. My daughter plays for the Lincoln High team. So far they're undefeated. I think coach Inbody might take these girls all the way to the state championship this year."

Around ten o'clock the next morning, Dr. Knighten received the call.

"Ken, we have proof the puncture wound never penetrated into the brain. One of my assistants did find a tiny fractured splinter deep in the wound that must have been broken off when the animal hit the ground. We're not sure of the splinter's origin yet. The remaining fragment is very small. Maybe there was some sort of drug or poison on it to help bring the animal down or initially kill it, but there's no way we can test for that now. If I find anything else, you'll be the first to hear."

"Thanks for the update, Nick. We have some answers, but we've created more questions. I'm glad this isn't a murder investigation. We might be looking for some real little midgets from outer space that decided to kill a cow! Go figure. It just doesn't make sense. I'll call Doc Mino and Joe Suske after lunch and let them know what we're up against. Since this isn't a murder, maybe the only thing we can do now is to share the information with the other state authorities, send them some pictures and forget about it. At least till it happens again somewhere out-of-state and we can get more help. Thanks again Nick. I'll talk to you later."

Dr. Knighten hung up the phone and sat at his desk for a few minutes to try and comprehend the conversation he'd just been involved in.

"It just doesn't make sense! Out of all the veterinarians in the world, why me?" he silently grumbled to himself.

After grabbing a cheese frenchie at King's Restaurant, Dr. Knighten made the calls to Doc Mino and the sheriff. He thought about contacting Gavin Aldama with the information, but decided against it. People around the state already thought this investigation was bizarre. Rather than waste his time now trying to put the pieces together by himself, he'd file them away and deal with them again at a later time if the need ever presented itself. It was Friday afternoon and he was looking forward to a nice weekend playing golf.

CHAPTER ELEVEN

RAINING CORPSES FROM THE SKY

Doc Mino was busy vaccinating about 100 hogs on the Earl Bydalek Ranch about thirty-five miles southwest of Gering when he received a call on his Jeep radio from Anita. The man sprang over to the vehicle parked about ten yards away and grabbed the mic.

"Doc, I just received a call from Kevin Piper and he's got something that needs your immediate attention. He didn't say what it was, but asked if you could please hurry. What should I tell him?"

"I'll be done here in about an hour. It'll take another forty-five minutes to get there. Tell him I'll be there around three. Thanks Anita."

Doc placed the handset back in the cradle mounted on the Jeep dashboard and went back to the pen to finish his shots.

As promised, Doc arrived at the Pipers' right at three. Doc pulled his Jeep into the yard and was met by Kevin, waiting in his pickup.

"Glad you came, Doc. You won't believe what I found out in the pasture around noon. Hop in and I'll show you. Just so you know, Sheriff Suske is already out there."

The two men drove about four miles back to the southwest corner of the ranch. Sure enough, there was the sheriff.

"Well Doc, looks like we got another one. What's it been now, about eight months or thereabouts? Pretty much the same scenario, just a different pasture."

Doc and Kevin approached the dead cow. Doc gave the Angus carcass a brief once over and replied back to Joe.

"Six months is more like it Joe. You're right, we've seen this before. Pretty much just like the other one. Have you searched the immediate area? The ground will be dry this time of year compared to the muddy ground we had to deal with late last spring."

Joe hadn't scoured the area. All of his focus had fallen on the dead cow.

"Nah Doc. You wanna take a look around? I'm gonna call them Lincoln boys to see what they want to do with this one. You two young, good lookin' guys go ahead and I'll catch up with ya in a few minutes."

Doc started to weigh his options. There was a draw about one hundred yards away, and he headed in that direction. The rest of the surrounding area was flat. He'd take a look down in the grove of trees that couldn't be seen from his current vantage point.

"Hey Joe, we'll meet you over there in a few minutes," he said as he pointed in the direction he was heading.

Doc made his way west with Kevin close behind. When the two men reached the bottom of the draw, they noticed a shallow, narrow creek flowing through the tree-lined gully. There were plenty of cattle tracks in the mud, indicating this was one of their watering holes. Nothing out of the ordinary. They walked another sixty yards before Kevin spotted something partially hidden high up in the overhead tree cover.

"Look Doc! Doesn't that look like a body up there!" yelled Kevin.

Doc Mino quickly eyed the torn red and black one piece swimsuit the corpse was wearing, high up in the branches.

"Joe, damn it! Get down here now!" Doc frantically yelled.

A few minutes later, the three men focused on the body of what appeared to be a young girl caught in the tree about thirty feet up.

"Holy Christ! I'm calling those Lincoln boys back and have them out here pronto. Nick Jensen needs to get involved with this one. This is no coincidence. We've not only got another mutilation, we've got a dead body! Don't touch anything. Let's go back to the car and radio into Lincoln and see what them State suits have to say about this," ordered the sheriff.

Nick Jensen called the hangar and reserved a state plane for a five P.M. flight to Scottsbluff. He'd bring Dr. Ken Knighten along. They'd be there before dark. Nick suggested he get some of the portable lights out to the crime scene and stay put so nothing disturbs the area. One of Suske's deputies would meet the plane and drive the two men out to the ranch.

As planned, the two men showed up around dusk. Sheriff Suske instructed his deputy to bring out the generator powered lights to the scene and then head back into the airport. Suske had cordoned off the immediate vicinity beneath the tree in case there might be some incriminating footprints in the mud.

Following a brief overview of the body positioning, the men determined that the body could not have been dragged up the tree by a human. Maybe it was a powerful mountain lion that forcefully carried the girl up into the trees for safekeeping from ground predators like coyotes. If that was the case, there would be cat tracks somewhere around the tree. No prints were found. There was no trace of blood. That ruled out that possibility. At this point they had to assume the body had been dropped from above and landed in the tree. There was little they could do at this point but to get the body down as carefully as possible and continue their investigation in the morning. In the meantime, the fire and rescue team could make the removal and take the corpse to the local funeral home.

Sheriff Suske called his forensic photographer, Lilli Brouillard, out to the scene to take pictures of every step of the process. Her main job was taking pictures for the local newspaper, but she'd moonlight for the sheriff since his department couldn't justify a full- time photographer.

The mutilated cow was the least of their worries. The men did do another visual examination on the Angus while they were all assembled again. Just like Doc had said, they'd seen this before and it was a repeat performance. Now that the men knew what they were looking for and where to look, the cow could remain in the field, at least temporarily.

Nick Jensen had brought his Chief Forensic Pathologist, Dr. Kathy Davis, to perform the autopsy. She would try to coordinate an autopsy early the next morning.

Minutes later, about eight PM, Nick put out an APB throughout his state network of law enforcement officers, asking them if any girl around 15 years of age had been missing from their communities.

Later that night Nick received a call at his motel room from the Hastings, Nebraska Chief of Police, Dick Tews. The dead girl might be a fourteen year old who had gone missing from his city of 25,000 people a little over eight months ago. A young girl found dead in a similar or identical swimsuit sparked the Chief's interest. Ron had several pictures of the girl and a detailed description of the suit he'd obtained from the family during his investigation. He would drive out to Scottsbluff first thing the next morning to make a connection to his unsolved disappearance. Maybe this was the break both parties were looking for. He'd meet them at the Steel Grill in Gering at noon.

Nick Jensen, Dr. Kathy Davis, Lilli Brouillard and Joe Suske would be present for the autopsy scheduled at the hospital morgue at nine that morning.

The two veterinarians decided to go back out to Piper's pasture and take a closer look at the mutilated cow to see if Dr. Knighten could again find the telltale signs found on their last mutilated Angus. They'd all meet again over at the designated spot for lunch and review their findings with Chief Tews when he arrived.

Sheriff Suske called and reserved the private room. They weren't to be disturbed. His small office at the police station wouldn't accommodate the number of people and the required room everyone would need. This private room would be their rendezvous spot while these officials remained in town as a group for the next day or two. The room would be locked at night to keep any restaurant staff or curious customers out.

As planned, the group met promptly at noon and were escorted to the private dining area by the host. Their first concern was to put a name with the body and get a positive ID. Nick decided to let the Police Chief from Hastings open the briefing to see if their number one goal could be achieved.

Police Chief Tews spread his pictures out on several of the open tables in the room and began to address his colleagues.

"This case has gone unsolved for the past eight months without much to go on until now. The dead girl could be Leah Krzycki. She was a sophomore at Hastings High School. She was born and raised in Hastings in 1943 and would have turned seventeen this coming August. The investigation regarding her disappearance has been the strangest I've experienced in my twenty-two years in law enforcement. To avoid widespread fear from the public as well as harsh criticism of the findings, I have disclosed very little surrounding the case. What I am about to share with you has not been shared with anyone else."

Dick took a drink of iced tea and continued. "Leah was enjoying the day with her two best friends. It was a Saturday and they were going to have a sleepover down at the family fishing hole. Bill and Nancy Krzycki owned 480 acres about ten miles southeast of Hastings. The three girls were tubing and swimming by themselves at the pond located on the farm about a quarter mile from the farmhouse. The trio was spending the night at the pond and had set up their tent and sleeping bags about fifteen yards back from the water. It was getting near dusk and the two guests were out of the water stirring the coals of the campfire they'd started about an hour earlier. It was time to cook some hot dogs and wash them down with the fresh lemonade Leah's mother made that afternoon.

Leah was slowly paddling her inner tube to land. Within the blink of an eye, a bright beam of light instantly shot down from the low cloud cover and entirely encased Leah. The teenager started to fight and scream as this intense energy methodically lifted her up through the night sky. Her panicked friends were helpless to assist the girl since she was still about thirty feet out in the deeper part of the pond. All the two could do was watch in total shock as Leah was being sucked up into some sort of a hovering craft like their lemonade through a straw. Her helpless, screaming, thrashing body rose up into the heavens in a matter of less than ten seconds.

The two friends stood on the bank screaming until the girl completely disappeared from sight, as did her flying abductor. The two teenagers ran to the farmhouse crying for Leah's parents to come quick.

After a brief, hysterical summary of what just happened, Bill and Nancy frantically jumped into the pickup as the girls quickly hopped in back. The foursome searched the reeds that lined the pond with flashlights and scoured the immediate open pasture with the truck headlights only to confirm their worst fears. Their daughter had vanished without leaving a trace of evidence.

It was probably an hour after her initial disappearance when my office first took the call from the distraught parents. I wasted no time getting to the farm and meeting with the four. I interviewed the two witnesses individually to see if their stories coincided, which they did. I then met with the parents to get a

79

picture for an APB release throughout the region. I did contact the media with details that might help in the search effort, but made no mention of the beam of light that effortlessly lifted her up into space.

I suggested that the two witnesses and the Krzycki family make no statements about what had happened to the press or discuss the omitted details with anyone. It would serve no beneficial purpose and would seriously threaten the investigation. If the public got wind of this bizarre twist, the story would come off as a publicity stunt and hoax."

They all agreed.

"The following morning my deputies and I made a thorough search of the surrounding area. Three search and rescue divers covered every inch of the pond. As expected, nothing was found.

Coincidentally, I did receive a call from Bill Krzycki about two days after her disappearance. I had asked the family before leaving their house to report even the smallest thing that might offer a clue to her abduction. He noticed Leah's pony, Patches, had her tail neatly braided in a very strange, unidentifiable woven pattern. No one in the family had done this and they had no clue as to who might have taken the time to tie the meticulous piece of horse hair together in a fashion that could not be untied. I told Bill I was on my way and not to go near the animal until I arrived. I wanted to take some pictures of the tail before he removed it with his shears."

Dick picked up the picture sitting on the table in front of him and passed it around. "You folks are the first to hear this story. I have absolutely no doubt that the witnesses' testimonies are nothing but the truth. I brought tape recordings of each of the testimonials if you'd like to hear them. Maybe your investigation can put an end to mine. I'll be here as long as this team stays in town to get to the bottom of Leah's death. I'll be glad to assist in any way I can."

After speaking for about an hour, the Chief gathered up the pictures he'd circulated around to his small audience during the presentation and fielded several questions before taking his seat. He placed the photos in his attaché and poured a fresh glass of tea.

After a ten minute break, Joe Suske introduced Lilli Brouillard, his chief photographer, to begin a slide presentation. Lilli luckily was an agile, athletic young woman who had no problem climbing up the tree to take pictures from as many angles as she could of the dead girl before the removal process began. Her camera followed the process all the way though the autopsy. Every detail relevant to the girls' death would be presented on the screen.

Dr. Kathy Davis performed the autopsy as scheduled. A f t e r t h e a u t o p s y, she concluded that the cause of death could be from any number of things. This was a very unique case, though, and her findings would be presented along with the slides from start to finish.   Showing the visuals was the easy part, describing them would be more difficult.

It was obvious that the body had been dropped down into the tree from a distance.   The girl had been impaled in the upper chest region on a large, extended dead branch about twelve feet down from the canopy. Numerous branches had been broken on her descent before the body came to an abrupt halt, resulting in numerous bruises, scrapes and cuts. It appeared to the doctor that the girl may have hit the tree head first. Her skull w a s crushed and the left side of her face had been partially peeled off by the rough bark covering the massive tree limbs she pin-balled off of. Most of her bones were broken. The blunt force of hitting a tree from an undetermined distance would have killed the girl, but Dr. Davis determined the girl was dead before she hit the tree.

The traumatized body made it more difficult to uncover the true cause of death. However, as the autopsy proceeded, the doctor was astonished by her findings. The immediate observation was that the girl may have been missing for eight months, but she'd been alive. The doctor determined that the death took place within twenty-four to thirty-six hours ago. The telltale signs of rotting flesh and the horrendous stench that followed weren't present yet. Remarkably, there was not a trace of blood anywhere on the body.

Severe blunt head trauma was present. The left side of the skull was severely traumatized. There should have been brain matter exposed throughout the remaining cranial area, yet there was none. The girls' brain had been removed prior to the fall. Why? Who would have done this?

The most incredible finding of the autopsy revealed that the young girl was pregnant! The usual signs of a pregnancy were not there. Her stomach and breasts were their normal size. Dr. Davis found an abnormally small fetus, which initially appeared to be severely deformed. The doctor predicted the girl was probably impregnated about two months after her disappearance.

The fetus had, remarkably, remained intact for having gone through such a brutal fall, but upon a thorough autopsy, it became very obvious it was not of human origin. Although it appeared to be fully developed, this baby weighed one pound six ounces! It was extremely small. The detailed features were noticeably different from that of a normal human baby. The thicker gray skin was not the soft pink associated with a newborn baby. The fingers were elongated. The head had a very unusual slant on the front of the skull. The abnormally large eyes had no color; they were totally black. The doctor had never seen a full term fetus with such dehumanized features. The nose and mouth were also out of proportion and very small.

The size, color and design of the swimsuit was the same as in the picture the Chief had brought with him. The hair color matched. The age was that of a young teenage girl. A molar found in the remains of a broken jawbone had a gold filling. Dental records would prove unequivocally that the dead girl was Leah.

An aura of silence filled the room. Although Chief Tews could find some closure in this strange case, the others in the room were shrouded in absolute disbelief as to what the dead girl had just revealed.

As an afterthought, Dr. Knighten spoke briefly before the group adjourned. What would have been an otherwise remarkable story about another mutilated heifer being found out on the remote Nebraska prairie now took second fiddle to a bigger and more personal mystery.

PART TWO

2013

SCOTTSBLUFF, NEBRASKA

CHAPTER TWELVE
JAKE YOUNG REVISITED

Jake Young lifted the lid of his Weber gas grill and turned the four steaks searing above the fire. He took a brief step back as the smoke and flames shot in the air. A long draw from his Macanudo was followed by a sip of single malt scotch. He and his new bride of six months, Judy, were entertaining friends on their patio and watching their Nebraska Cornhusker football team in an early November nail biter against Northwestern in their eighth game of the 2013 season.

Jake recently purchased a 42-inch Sony flat screen TV to hang on the exterior wall of his log patio perched on the bluff overlooking Scottsbluff. His satellite provider installed the specially constructed all-weather TV for such an occasion. The TV could easily be covered with the weatherproof cover that came with his purchase. The accompanying surround sound speakers were hidden under the eaves of their new patio cover in each corner of the structure that Jake built earlier in the summer. Judy purchased a new set of patio furniture that completed their newest addition to the charming old home Jake acquired just two years earlier, when he relocated back to Nebraska from Colorado.

The Youngs were entertaining weekend guests from Ogallala, Nebraska. Steve and Tina Taylor owned the town's only funeral home and lived ten minutes north of the city limits on Lake McConaughy. Steve was one of Jake's casket customers and the two couples had become good personal friends. They tried to get together as often as their busy schedules allowed, which generally ended up alternating several weekends a year in Scottsbluff and at the lakefront home of the Taylors. It was a two hour drive between residences, so when the couples got together, they shared a full weekend of great food, drink and friendship. Being the only funeral director in his community made it difficult for Steve and Tina to get away for the weekend, and they relished the opportunity when the rare occasion presented itself.

Jake took the medium rare rib-eye steaks off the grill and placed them in the center of the patio table. Everyone was focused on the game as the Cornhuskers were up by three with less than four minutes remaining in the fourth quarter. The plates were soon filled with steak, corn-on-the-cob and a baked potato. Judy refreshed everyone's drinks and the four friends settled into a great dinner and an exciting game. Life was good, but it would be much, much better if the Huskers could hold on to clinch the win.

"The Blackshirts need to stop em here!" yelled Judy as the Badgers were faced with a third and eight.

Steve and Jake fidgeted with their cigars until the intense play has finally run. "Yeah, great job defense! They'll have to punt. If the offense can get just one first down and not turn the ball over, we should pull this one out," said Jake as he took another sip of his Scotch and another steady draw off the half burned cigar.

Several minutes later, the game was over and Nebraska held on for the win. After sharing a few celebratory hugs and a victory toast to the Big Red, the couples decided to move inside. The chilling wind had started to pick up and the foursome worked in unison to clear the table and adjourn into the living room.

Tina couldn't help but notice the framed picture of the century old log home hanging on the kitchen wall, taken when the house was first completed in 1900. In front of the home stood the original owner and builder, Ben McIntire.

"Wow! This is too cool! This must be the original house when it was first completed!" exclaimed Tina. "It sure was a lot smaller than it is now!"

"Yes, Jake and I found that picture in a trunk up in the loft of the barn," Judy replied. "Haven't we told you the history of the house? We were fortunate enough to trace its origin through a McIntire family member. This house was kept in the family until

Jake bought it about two years ago. Let's open a bottle of Merlot and we'll tell you two the story."

The two couples made their way into the living room and settled into the comfortable leather sofa and chairs. Jake and Judy proceeded to tell about Ben McIntire and his excursion west on the Oregon Trail with his twin cousins, Elsie and Elisa. He told of their murder along the Platte River and how Ben had transported them by wagon to their final resting place in the church cemetery located just a quarter of a mile north of this house.

Jake excused himself for a minute while Judy told them the story of the McIntire's exceptional musical skills and the violin they'd found in the trunk along with the picture and Ben's diary. About that time, Jake reentered the room with two extremely old v i o l i n s . He gave one to each of the guests. He soon returned with the diary, several more pictures and Ben's guitar.

"If only these instruments could talk! They were made in New York back around 1847."

Jake showed the date and the maker's name found inside the f shaped sound holes on the top of the instruments. Also neatly inscribed on each of the violin necks was the name of their owners, Elsie and Elisa.

"Would you guys like me to read some excerpts from Ben's diary regarding the family history, this house and these very instruments?" It was very obvious that his curious guests couldn't wait to hear more.

Jake started at the beginning of the diary and read the complete story of the three being raised in Hell's Kitchen, New York and growing up in Uncle Fredrick's Tavern, how they each acquired their musical abilities at a very young age and continued to master their craft along the Oregon Trail.

Judy opened the bottle of wine as Jake began the part regarding the tragic murder of the twins and how they were burned at the stake by a religious zealot and a vindictive wagon master. Jake reached in his pocket and showed his guests the dark glasses the girls used to wear to protect their light-sensitive eyes. They'd been worn by one of the girls at the time of her death and Ben had saved them from the fire and placed them in the trunk along with Ben's other cherished mementos.

Jake finished the story about an hour later, ending with Ben starting a business here in the area before Gering was even a town. "If you'd like, we can take a walk over to the cemetery tomorrow and I'll show where the McIntires are buried."

An immediate "Yes!" was the unanimous response.

"Great, we'll even show you the barn where we found the trunk!"

The next morning, Jake made some of his grandma's special pancakes for everyone. Judy rounded the breakfast menu off with some sausage, scrambled eggs and hash browns. While breakfast was in the making, Jake made a pitcher of Bloody Marys.

"Here's to our good friends and another exciting day," he toasted.

After breakfast the four friends headed for the barn. The newest addition to their small family met them at the door. The brother of one of Jake's funeral home accounts in Casper, Wyoming professionally bred and trained German Shepherds. Each litter was highly sought after by both the military and law enforcement for their exceptional bloodlines, temperament and field abilities. Jake had the opportunity to purchase one of the prized shepherds for a fraction of what they usually sold for, and he couldn't turn down the generous offer. Although still just a puppy at six months, Yollie weighed close to sixty pounds. Jake surprised Judy with Yollie for her birthday present and the two bonded immediately. Jake thought it was wise to have a big dog at home for protection since his job demanded considerable travel to cover his territory and required that he be away for days at a time.

Jake swung the barn door open and Yollie excitedly led the way in. The first thing the Taylors noticed was the musky barn aroma. It was a good smell that gave all barns some added character, and this one was no different. Judy pointed up to the loft where Ben had stored his old trunk for years underneath a canvas tarp. Steve was intrigued by some of the old iron tools still hanging above the massive workbench that lined the east wall.

"They sure don't make em like they used to" he quipped as he felt the weight of an antique crescent wrench in his hand.

On their stroll across the outlying five acres of property that lay between their house and the old church and cemetery, Judy briefly told Steve and Tina about their experiences in the old ghost town of Ardmore, South Dakota while visiting Jake's sister and nephews up in Chadron, Nebraska last Thanksgiving. Jake had become totally intrigued by the history of western Nebraska and their ghost town experience was certainly an eye opener to both of them. It was fascinating to be living in an area so rich in American history.

Steve and Tina were again drawn in to another of their hosts' eerie experiences. And now they were heading over to visit a cemetery! Old churchyard cemeteries were their favorite. What a great way to spend the weekend. The two guests were enjoying every minute of it.

The last carload of Sunday morning worshipers was leaving the gravel parking lot of the century-old church as the four approached. It was a simple one room building made of wood with the simple steeple and traditional bell tower. The building was a small structure that could probably hold a congregation of no more than seventy-five people.

Tina was surprised when she pulled on the metal door handle and found it unlocked. "This church is never locked," said Jake. "The integrity of the people that reside in this community and have worshiped here for over one hundred years has never created a need. Walk up front and you'll see what I mean."

Tina and Steve strolled up to the small altar.

"I can't believe this! Not only is the church unlocked, the collection plate is still filled with money! Why, there must be over fifty dollars here!" Tina was amazed.

"You sure couldn't do this in the city. Jake, you certainly have honest neighbors!" The four headed out to the wrought iron gate that led into the cemetery. The out of town guests were amazed to see all of the antiquated grave markers. Most of them were badly weathered white granite, although several simple pine crosses still stood over some of the oldest inhabitants.

"Hey you guys, here is the McIntire family plot over here. There's Ben's marker and the unmarked sunken graves of the twins next to his. I'd like to get two new headstones made for Elsie and Elisa made one of these days. I'll ask one of my monument friends when we're at the State Funeral Convention in Lincoln next summer," Jake added.

"I think Ben and his twin cousins would appreciate that," Steve thoughtfully replied.

Judy walked across the back boundary road and found a grave that was located away from the others.

"Look you guys! This is the grave of Don Sheely! Local legend has it that his sister was accused of murdering her husband because of spousal abuse, but her older brother, Don, took the rap. She had three children to raise and Sheely was a single man. He ended up spending 25 years on death row until the state hung him in the prison yard in 1947.

The body was taken back to his hometown of Gering. The sister made arrangements to have him buried in this cemetery since the family ranch was located about seven miles further down the road. The cemetery board was reluctant to have a convicted killer buried in their church cemetery, feeling it would be in violation of their consecrated grounds.

Before being convicted of this heinous crime, Don Sheely had been helping on the family ranch. He had never been in trouble with the law prior to the murder. Some of the locals at the time of the trial felt that Don might be taking the fall for his sister, but due to the circumstances, no one wanted to speak out and convict a mother of three little children. Many rumors surrounded her spousal abuse and some of the congregation could vividly remember her coming to church with bruises on her face. She always had an alibi, but they seldom held any credence with those aware of her situation at home. If Don was willing to take the fall for his sister and three kids, who were they to say otherwise? She was a victim of circumstance and the real culprit had been taken back to his family cemetery in Cheyenne, Wyoming.

Due to mounting community pressure, the board finally made their decision. He was to be segregated away from the other graves and buried on the outer side of the circular road in an isolated, empty expansion section.

As you can see, the shunned man is the only one buried in this area of the cemetery," Judy explained as she finished her story.

The foursome headed back to the Youngs' quaint old home. Yollie now focused on the two women to toss the ball. "God, if I only had a fifth of that dog's energy!" quipped Tina as she gave the wet, slobbery ball another launch down the dirt road.

It was another beautiful fall day and Jake suggested they cruise into town for an early dinner before the Taylors headed home.

"Great idea," added Judy. "Jake, why don't we take the Ford?"

Jake never turned down the opportunity to get his 1967 Ford LTD out of the garage. The car had previously been owned by his parents and it was basically a one-family car. Jake had owned the car since 1978 and had restored the car back to its pristine condition. The 390 engine ran like a clock. As he backed the car out of the garage, he stepped on the gas just enough to get a deep, throaty roar out of his tailpipes.

"Wow! She sounds as good as she looks!" said an excited Steve as the two women climbed into the back seat of the two-door beauty.

After an enjoyable scenic cruise into Scottsbluff, the foursome dined at the Whiskey Creek Steak House, before returning home.

Thus ended another great weekend. Good weather, a Husker win and the company of two dear friends. Jake leaned over and kissed Judy goodnight as he turned off the lamp. Yollie settled down in her usual spot on the floor at the end of the bed. It had been a full day for all of them and they quickly fell into a wonderful, deep sleep.

CHAPTER THIRTEEN
JAKE'S JACK

Jake pulled into the driveway of their home on the bluff Friday afternoon shortly after three. It had been a long week covering his fifteen funeral homes over in eastern Wyoming. He'd spent the last four nights in a hotel room and was ready to come home. Thanksgiving was next Thursday and he looked forward to having the next ten days to relax. He'd also use some of the much needed break time to get caught up on some filing, finish doing his budget for next year and submit his bi-monthly expense report.

His sister Barb, two dogs Skip and Gunther and cousins Jerome and Dewey were coming next Wednesday and planned on staying at the house until Sunday. In addition, Judy had invited all of her local family. It was going to be a very busy holiday for the Youngs. Judy kept busy preparing the menu, cleaning and shopping all week in anticipation of their guests.

Yollie greeted him as he pulled the car into the garage and shut the garage door. He grabbed his brief case and suitcase out of the trunk and the two proceeded through the breezeway and back door that led into the laundry room.

Judy met him with a warm smile and a big hug. "I'm glad you're home honey! I've missed you!" she whispered into his ear as she gave him a kiss.

Yollie echoed her sentiments with a warm, sloppy lick on Jack's hand.

"I'm glad to be home. I drove in a light snow ever since I left Casper after lunch. The roads are getting slick. I hope it clears up by next week so our out of town guests have good weather for their trip."

Judy asked Jake to open a bottle of Merlot and start the fire in the living room fireplace.

"Great idea...you read my mind. I think I'll go change clothes and get comfortable first," he murmured as he headed for the upstairs master bedroom.

A few minutes later, he was back in the kitchen pouring the wine.

After a short clinking of the glasses toast, Jake asked, "Anything exciting happen while I was away?" as he pulled a chair out from under the kitchen table.

"Not really," she replied. "I met my friends Laurie, Joyce and Jenny for lunch yesterday when I was out doing the shopping. They're all entertaining over the holiday too. We talked about next Friday's last regular season Husker game with Iowa Hawkeyes. All of us are already excited! I can't wait!"

Jake echoed her enthusiasm. "Yeah, it should be a barn burner! Did you get plenty of snacks and beer?"

"Who do you think you're dealing with here, buster....some rookie? Do you really believe I'd forget the Bud Light for you and Fat Tire and Sierra Nevada Pale for Jerome and Dewey? I even stopped to buy you guys a few Punch cigars! Maybe you can enjoy them on the patio and watch part of the game on your new toy. You know the rules about smoking in the house, Jake Young!"

Judy was busy preparing the evening's dinner of spaghetti and Italian sausage with French bread.

"Why don't you take Yollie out for a walk before dinner while there's still a little daylight left while I finish up in here? Dinner won't be ready for another hour."

"Good idea. I could use a little exercise after sitting in the car for the last couple of hours. Come on, Yollie!"

Jake grabbed his sheepskin-lined leather pilot jacket and a flashlight from the laundry room and the two bounded out the back door. Yollie loved it when Jake would go for a walk with her. Judy pretty much just let the dog out into their large fenced backyard when her husband was gone, but Jake liked to go for longer walks up on the mesa. He'd get in at least three miles before dinner and Yollie would probably triple that with all of her running around. They both loved the exercise and cool fresh air.

He opened the backyard gate and the two headed out across the five acre spread that separated the house from the back road behind them. About a mile into their walk, the cold weather was once again starting to drop a light snowfall as the last faint glimmer of light descended in the western sky. Jake pulled out the flashlight and clicked it on.

Yollie immediately found some gratification in chasing the yellow beam of light for a few seconds until something else grabbed her curiosity. There was so much to explore out in the wilderness and she couldn't waste precious time focusing on any one thing for an extended period of time.

Jake and Yollie walked past the church and cemetery then turned south along the county road that threaded through miles and miles of barren prairie. These desolate, quiet surroundings were one of the reasons Jake bought the house. His closest neighbor was well over two miles away. Most of his rancher neighbors were grazing cattle up on the ridge, and the open grassland behind his property went on forever.

The faint full moon was just starting to play hide and seek through the spotty cloud cover that shrouded western Nebraska. It looked like there was a halo circling it that gave off just enough light to highlight the passing clouds. It was a beautiful evening sky despite the cold and the slight flurry of snow.

Jake walked down the center of the road and Yollie ran from side to side, sniffing everything in her path. She was a curious pup, but very well behaved. Jake constantly worked with the young shepherd, and she wanted nothing more than to please her master and earn his praise.

"Good girl Yollie, good girl!"

Usually his companion would scare up a couple of jackrabbits, an occasional p h e a s a n t or a covey of quail somewhere along the journey. She especially loved to chase the rabbits, and Jake was always amazed at how fast and agile both the hunter and its prey were when the chase was on. The dog had amazing reflexes and loved to give t h e rabbits a run for their money. She would occasionally catch up with one and roll it, but the jack would rebound and dart off with a renewed surge of amazing speed. The dog was good for short bursts of energy but was unable to keep up with a big jack for any distance. The jack always had the advantage of speeding under the barbwire fencing that bordered the dirt road. Yollie couldn't go under the bottom wire and would have to miss a few steps in order to clear the leap between the bottom and middle strands.

The rabbits would sometimes just run the fence line, crisscrossing under the wire from side to side, knowing that a dog couldn't be on both sides of the fence at once like it seemed the rabbits could. They knew this crafty little game and played it like a well- tuned fiddle. Poor Yollie wouldn't stand a chance, but she enjoyed the chase nonetheless.

The frisky pup really didn't want to catch the rabbit; she just wanted to play. After she'd had her fill of this effort in futility and conceded the jack was a more agile foe, she would run back to Jake, panting and emitting her radiant smile and warm breath into the cold night air. She was guaranteed to get a nice pat on the head and some well-deserved praise. That was her reward. That's the main reason she played this silly game with the rabbits or other targets. That, plus a good night's sleep back home in front of the warm fireplace with some lovin' from mom and dad, good tunes, a warm bed, candlelight and a fresh bowl of food and water.

Tonight's walk was pretty routine thus far. Jake found a nicely sized stick by the side of the road. Man and dog were enjoying a good game of throw and fetch. This was the big knucklehead's favorite game and she couldn't get enough. No matter how many times Jake would throw the stick, Yollie would chase it down at a full gait and return it to his hand for another long throw.

Yollie was about thirty yards ahead of Jake when she turned her attention to a number of large jacks that had darted off to the dog's left. Forget the stick; the chase was on! Jake knew the usual outcome. Yollie would chase the rabbits until she'd had her fill and return back to Jake in a few minutes.

After ten minutes, he sensed that something about this chase was different. First of all, Jake had never seen that many jacks running together. Secondly, these rabbits seemed to be bigger than he was used to seeing. They were exceptionally large. And lastly, Yollie hadn't returned yet. She was nowhere in sight. He was standing in the middle of the gravel road, all alone in the cold, quiet night wondering where his best buddy had gone.

Jake gave out a loud whistle that Yollie always responded to, no matter where she was or what she was doing. That whistle meant get your butt back to Jake, pronto. Now. She had that order down pat. It was one of the first and most important lessons she'd been taught. Jake whistled again and began shouting her name. There was a sense of urgency in the calls and they became more frequent. Jake began to worry. *Where could that silly mutt be?*

Jake momentarily put the flashlight in his jacket pocket and crawled through the wire fence. He headed in the general direction of where he had last seen the chase while alternating whistles and calls for his missing companion.

After traipsing through the prairie grass for close to sixty yards, he heard a soft yelp coming from his left. Jake stepped up the pace and found Yollie lying on her side. She was glad to see Jake and let out another whimper. The dog made an effort to try and get on her feet, but immediately fell back down. Although she couldn't stand, she didn't seem to have any visible wounds. Granted, Yollie had been in full pursuit of the rabbits, but no more than usual. She should still be panting heavily from the chase, but her breathing seemed more subdued and shallow. Her eyes had a panicked look in them. She made one last feeble attempt to rise to her feet, but couldn't move a muscle.

Something was obviously wrong and Jake wasted no time in picking the sixty pound pup up into his arms and hurriedly headed for home. Once he hit the road, he broke into a slow, uncoordinated jog while trying to comfort the injured animal.

Jake clumsily opened the gate while balancing the dog on his knee and hurried to the back door. He saw Judy through the window and frantically yelled to her for assistance.

"Yollie's hurt! We've got to get her to the vet right now! Go call Dr. Hutton and see if we can meet him at his clinic. I'll put her in the back of the Escalade!"

Judy soon returned and stated the doctor would meet them in ten minutes. She approached Yollie and quickly but gently petted her on the head.

"You'll be okay, girl, you'll be okay. We'll take care of you. You'll be okay. You're a good Yollie!"

By now the dog's breathing was becoming slower and more labored and she was still unable to move. Judy hopped into the passenger seat and the three were off to the clinic.

The waiting doctor opened the back door and instructed Jake to place Yollie down on the first examining table, located in the first room to their left.

"What happened?" the doctor asked as he checked the dog's mouth and eyes.

"I really don't know Doc, we were out on a walk just a half hour ago when Yollie started chasing some jackrabbits through the pasture behind our house. When she didn't come back I went looking for her. I found her lying in the grass, unable to get up. She's obviously hurt, but I really can't tell you much more than that."

The dog's breathing was becoming shallower and her nose was crusty, warm and dry.

After a brief examination by the vet, he calmly reported, "I can't see any visible signs of any injury. Maybe she was bitten by something or she ate something she shouldn't have. It almost looks like she's partially sedated."

Dr. Hutton again ran his hands over the dog, feeling deeper for any clues of a small flesh wound. His trained hand soon stopped on the left hindquarter as the dog yelped in pain. The doctor pulled the hair away from the area and exposed what looked to be a small splinter wound just under the skin. When he tried to pull it out, he felt some resistance. He grabbed a magnifying glass and took a closer look. The small protruding head wasn't a typical wood splinter, or it would have pulled out easily. Because of the difficulty he experienced in extracting it, the object was probably something more like a porcupine quill, with a barbed tip that couldn't be pulled out without causing more damage. It wasn't uncommon for a dog to run into a porcupine, but this one appeared to be somehow different. It was a single quill, which usually wasn't the case. He grabbed a scalpel and a pair of tweezers and gently removed the object for a closer examination later.

"By the looks of Yollie, I think she's been drugged or poisoned. I'm not sure which right now. I'm going to put her on a respirator and oxygen to assist her labored breathing and give her a cholinesterase inhibitor to help with the apparent muscle paralysis. That should stabilize her breathing and neutralize whatever it was that she came into contact with. Let's keep her here overnight. I gave her something for a good night's sleep. She should be better in the morning. I'll give you a call with a progress report. I think she's out of the woods for now."

Jake patted his trusted friend on the head and gave her some encouraging words as Judy gently stroked her soft and thick black coat and offered similar reassurances.

"You'll be okay, girl. Sleep well, we'll see you tomorrow."

Right around seven the next morning, their phone rang. Just as Dr. Hutton had predicted, Yollie was better. She still didn't want to get up, but her bright eyes, cold nose and wet kisses told him that she was much better.

"She should be her old self after the physostigmine wears off," he said reassuringly. "That's great to hear, Doctor. Jake is out for a walk but should be home any minute.

When can we run down and pick her up?" asked Judy.

"Let's give her another hour or two. She'll be just fine here. I'll give you a call when she's ready to come home."

Jake had anxiously arisen at the crack of dawn and decided to take another walk back to where he'd found Yollie lying in the field the night before. He wanted to see if there might be any indication about what might have happened to his dog. He retraced their path and located the vicinity where he'd picked up his four legged buddy. He began to scour the area for any clues. By now the faint pink sunlight was beginning to rise over the gray eastern horizon.

After a few minutes, Jake's eyes were drawn to a bucket sized opening about fifteen f e e t from where he was standing. He walked over to the dirt mound and studied it closely to determine exactly what he was looking at. A miniature object of some sort was partially hidden by snow and tightly wedged into the badger hole.

Badgers are very mean, combative animals that would fight ferociously to defend their den, even with a full grown man. They are one of the most aggressive animal species on earth. Their thick, coarse fur and tough skin are impervious to many traditional weapons like spears and arrows. These mean critters can weigh up to twenty-five pounds.

Whoever dropped the relatively small eight-inch quiver down the hole had been extremely unlucky and was obviously afraid to try and retrieve it at night from the frozen hole, now half covered in snow from the night before. Maybe they'd try finding it in the early morning light when they could assess the situation a little better, figuring out how to get the lodged quiver safely away from the menacing badger entrance without being torn to shreds in the process. Fortunately for Jake, he'd stumbled upon it first. He carefully dislodged the quiver with a nearby stick and pulled it quickly out of the hole.

Jake had a longstanding fear and respect for these savage creatures. One day, many years ago, young Jake and his father, Lou, stopped along a dirt road near the farm to visit with a neighbor. The ten-year-old boy became bored with the conversation and decided t o stroll out into the neighbor's pasture. He'd grabbed a hammer from his dad's toolbox to give him something to throw and retrieve. The boy saw an animal sitting above his burrow about ten yards away. He decided to throw the hammer at it. That was a very b a d decision. He threw and missed. The animal charged at Jake, but before it had the opportunity to catch the screaming boy, the neighbor had grabbed his rifle out of his pickup and dropped the badger with one very fortunate shot. Such an unassuming, innocent walk was just a few feet from becoming disastrous. Jake had never forgotten his badger encounter.

Upon closer observation, the small leather quiver held what looked to be like three miniature blow guns of different lengths, held tightly in place by a tight sinew strap. A large number of porcupine quills with strange markings carved into the shafts were kept neatly organized in the center of the quiver. The ends were stuck into a sponge-like substance that kept them neatly locked in the center of the quiver, and several rose above the others, ready for immediate grasp. All of the darts had a similar barb on the end of them, just like the one Dr. Hutton removed from Yollie's hindquarter.

The quiver and its contents were exceptionally little for human use. Even as a child's toy, it would be tiny. This was certainly not a toy. These were real weapons that could inflict some damage, but who would use them? He took another detailed look. The aged quiver had very distinct markings on it that weren't readily identifiable by Jake. He had no idea what they might represent.

Although it was small, it was very obvious to Jake that there was a lot of skilled craftsmanship that went into making whatever it was he held in his hand. The hard dark brown leather appeared to be very old yet exceptionally well preserved. This quiver didn't have the typical leather lacing or bead designs, so he ruled out his first guess of a local Native American Indian midget. He'd never seen such strange markings before.

The strong early morning winds brought the already cold temperature even lower. Now was not the time or place to examine his find in depth. He placed the piece in his coat pocket and turned back towards the house. It was another cold and dreary day, and at this point he just wanted to be out of the elements.

Judy met him at the back door upon his arrival and told him that Dr. Hutton called. He'd like Jake to give him a call when he got home. Jake immediately went over to the kitchen phone and dialed the number.

Dr. Hutton was glad to hear Jake's voice. He'd been anxiously awaiting his call. There was something that he needed to discuss and was eager to share his findings.

Mark told Jake that last night, before he left the clinic, he'd placed the quill fragment pulled from Yollie into a plastic bag and brought it home with him. He'd had a chance to look at the quill a little closer. In his experience with porcupine-inflicted injuries, it wasn't uncommon for the quills to easily break off at the skin level. Usually the animal would try to pull it out by biting or scratching, and that's all it would take.

This was no ordinary porcupine quill, however. It had very delicate carvings etched all over what remained of the tiny piece of shaft, markings that made no sense to the doctor. He'd put the quill under a microscope and saw that the small markings were made with precision tools that had to be extremely small. They were very smooth and even, probably done in one motion. The depth of the cuts was exactly the same and there were no notches or other defects in the cut. Whoever put them there was a very skilled craftsman with exceptional tools to do such precise workmanship. He'd never seen anything like this quill fragment before. It was a true piece of art that normally would have easily gone unnoticed to the naked eye. He would have loved to see the innate markings on an entire quill.

The only thing he could compare it to was a segment he'd seen on *Sixty Minutes* about a guy in Spain that carves out ornate designs from salt crystals under a microscope. The delicate pieces of art could easily fit on the head of a pin and be lost forever with a misdirected sneeze. The artist could neither read nor write. He had, however, recently sold his entire collection of one hundred microscopic pieces for twenty million dollars!

Jake listened to the doctor very carefully. Although he hadn't really checked the quills and blow gun in the aged leather tube, he was impressed with the workmanship on the miniature leather quiver.

As the doctor spoke, Jake pulled a magnifying glass from the middle drawer next to the phone and put the quiver on the countertop. He carefully pulled out one of the quills and closely examined it. It was amazing! The same delicately carved markings that Dr. Hutton was describing were also on the quills he held in his hand.

"Doc, I've got something I'd like to share with you that you'll be very interested in. Can I drive over in a few minutes and show it to you?"

"Sounds like a plan, Jake. I'll see you soon."

Dr. Hutton was absolutely astonished with Jake's find. Upon further observation under surgical lighting and a microscope, both men were dumbfounded. Whoever possessed these quills had hit Yollie with one of them. The question at hand was, *what was on the sending end of the quill?*

After removing the obvious contents of the quiver on the table, the doctor checked out the inner lining of the quiver. Located on the upper portion of the interior rim were three thimble size, cone shaped containers that appeared to be made of baked clay. They were spread equally around the small circumference and attached to a wood rim with a fine strand of sinew for easy access. The three variously sized blowguns were tightly positioned between each of the tiny pots with the darts positioned in the center. The contents appeared to be some sort of paste with a heavy consistency that wouldn't spill. Moist, but not too moist like the consistency of a firm pumpkin pie. Each pot was marked in three distinct colors of bright red, blue and yellow so they could be easily differentiated for a specific use.

Dr. Hutton was suspicious of the contents and any traces of poisons or drugs that might be on the tips. He suggested they send Yollie's quill, the quiver and its contents into the state crime lab for testing. If the doctor's hunch was right, they all contained some very strong toxins that might easily bring down a large animal, including a human. Time was of the essence.

Jake concurred while he watched the vet put on his surgical gloves. He began to carefully wrap the quiver and its contents snugly into a small, secure and heavy plastic shipping container with bubble wrap. Pharmaceutical companies used the boxes to ship drugs to his office in the mail. Mark placed a small band of plastic through the tabs, which sealed the container securely. If the band was broken, it would be obvious one of the Federal Express employees assigned to the package was the guilty party.

These reusable boxes would be labeled and sent Next Day Air for added precaution. Dr. Hutton took a minute to call the local Chief of Police to get a name to send it to. He wanted the box and its contents to go right to the top, so he labeled it to the Nebraska Crime Lab Department head, Dr. George Souders.

If the package was not personally delivered to Dr. Souders and signed for, it would be immediately returned to Hutton's local office address.

There was a brief note attached to let Dr. Souders know what he might be dealing with, along with a request to call Dr. Hutton before unpacking the contents. He wanted S o u d e r s to take the necessary precautions. There were bound to be many questions when the container was opened and its contents examined. Hutton wanted to give him a heads up and put a rush on finding out what was on the dogs' quill. After all, Yollie might not be totally out of the woods until they found out exactly what they were dealing with.

After the doctor finished packing and labeling the small shipping tray, he gave Jake instructions for monitoring Yollie's behavior.

"As long as she stays alert and her eyes are bright and clear, she's on the right track. She might want to stay down and that's fine. She will eventually get up, and probably be a little wobbly. If she looks lethargic or her breathing becomes shallow again, give me a call."

After Dr. Hutton opened the door, he helped Jake pick up Yollie's temporary bed containing one large, sleeping dog. The men headed towards the rear hatch of his Cadillac Escalade. Dr. Hutton opened the hatch door and Jake slowly slid the bed in.

"I'll give you a call when I get the results back, Jake. It might take a couple of weeks with the holiday. You and Judy have a great Thanksgiving and we'll be talking soon. By the way, why don't you just call me Mark?"

"Great Mark, thanks for everything! I'll look forward to your call. We certainly appreciate it, especially over the weekend. I hope you and your family enjoy Thanksgiving also," replied Jake.

The two men shook hands and Jake made the short drive home.

Along the way, Jake began to ponder the thought of ownership. He'd found it. It is old. It was one of a kind. It was probably very valuable and there would be many offers. The thought briefly passed his mind.

Or, he could donate the quiver to the Nebraska Historical Museum, if he ever e v e n saw it again. Someone could decide it's evidence and not release it, or someone up the chain could simply make it disappear. Anyway, he had no use for it. It would be selfish to keep such a treasure hidden. He didn't need the money. He certainly didn't need the headaches that would accompany going down that path. The lawyers would get all the money anyway. Jake would do the right thing and donate it to the state. No contest.

CHAPTER FOURTEEN
MAKING PLANS
MONDAY, DAY ONE

Jake received the anticipated call from Dr. Mark Hutton the week after Thanksgiving. As expected, the lab determined that the quill tip was laced with Curare, a centuries-old and extremely potent poison from South America. Curare basically paralyzes the muscles and asphyxiates its victim over time. If the victim is kept breathing, the poison eventually wears off and the victim will survive. The key is to keep the victim breathing.

A derivative is actually used now in modern day anesthesiology. This poison, however, wasn't from a drug vial. It was in its original raw form.

Playing the possible beat the clock game, Dr. Hutton used his best-educated hunch as to what the problem might be. He had euthanized many animals during his career and Yollie showed similar signs. He was extremely lucky to have noticed the similarities and took the correct course by putting the dog on a respirator and oxygen to maintain proper breathing. Yollie was fortunate in receiving the correct diagnosis as early as she did, and even more so that it worked.

Their immediate question had been answered, but it threw the door wide open for a slew of others. How had a centuries-old poison from South America made from a specific species of woody vines and roots that are crushed and boiled down to a thick, gooey black paste resembling a shiny resin suddenly appear in rural Nebraska? Many Spanish conquistadors had met their demise from a Curare laced South American Indian dart. Why would the substance be injected into a local dog, and who did it?

109

Dr. Hutton had more startling news. He'd received a conference call yesterday morning from Dr. George Souders and his colleague Nick Jensen, the former head of the Nebraska State Crime Department in Lincoln. Nick had been with the department for his entire forty-five year career in state law enforcement. He was now in his mid-seventies and happily retired on five acres about twenty miles west of Lincoln.

Nick was called upon from time to time for his expertise in the more baffling cases that ran through the lab. The unexpected box from a Gering veterinarian certainly raised a red flag in the lab and the phone call went out to the seasoned crime lab pro. No one in recent history had seen anything like it. Stumbling on that quiver was a real stroke of luck and could prove invaluable to the pending investigation.

Nick told the veterinarian that he'd run across a similar, very unorthodox porcupine quill method used to bring down a large animal back in the late fifties, right in the same vicinity of Gering. Both men were curious how the doctor had come across this second find.

Upon hearing the details, the three doctors concurred: they must get together and examine the new evidence surrounding the decades-old unsolved mystery.

Nick was ecstatic when he heard about the intact quiver. Nothing new had surfaced over the past fifty years, until now, and he was excited to have another chance at learning more about these bizarre findings. That one unsolved case had haunted him all of his life. The fact that Jake had found an entire quiver that contained an arsenal of these strange little weapons was like the early arrival of an unexpected Christmas present of a lifetime.

The two Lincoln crime lab doctors made a tentative date to meet. They'd drive out to Scottsbluff the first week of December and play detective with the two men. Before hanging up, Nick had one last question for Mark. "Say Doc, you wouldn't happen to know a Dr. Ron Mino, would you?"

"I certainly do! As a matter-of-fact, I took over his practice about twenty years ago. Doc Mino still comes down to my clinic a couple of times a month just to check up on me. He's pushing his mid-eighties, but he's still a pretty active guy. If I ever need a fill in, Doc is always available."

Surprised that Dr. Mino was still alive and in the area, Nick shared his relationship with him on the case they'd worked together many years ago. Since retiring, both men had lost track of each other.

"It was Doc Mino that actually got me involved with the case. Would you have any qualms asking Doc to join us when we come to town? I think he feels just like I do. I'm sure he would be very glad to gain some new insight on a nagging unsolved mystery from his past."

"It would be an honor to invite him Nick. I'll give Doc a call and let him know what's up. I'm sure he'll be glad to join us if he's in town!"

Jake was glad to hear that Dr. Mino was getting involved. Both men were members of their local Lions Club and they had become friends over the last two years. He'd grown quite fond of the elderly veterinarian.

"Doc's expertise and vivid memory should be very beneficial to this investigation," noted Jake.

"We'll need all the help we can get. Fifty years is a long time, and it'll be nice to have two sharp minds bring us up to snuff on what we've got here," Dr. Hutton said in closing.

Doc was glad to get a call from his colleague. He spent the next half hour rehashing the mutilation case he and Nick had worked together back in the late fifties.

111

"It was a strange investigation for sure. One of the first documented cases in the country. Since then, there have been thousands throughout the United States and other parts of the world. Still no answers or arrests on any of them.

Over the past fifty years, mutilations have become more frequent and less publicized. I think that the general consensus now among the medical and law enforcement communities is that alien involvement is a very strong possibility.

The missing link in this whole equation is the lack of drug testing in any of these documented cases. I think it's more a lack of funding, rather than neglect. Running a comprehensive analysis on a dead animal in a remote location that is devoid of necessities, like power for the needed delicate analytical equipment, is very expensive and to my knowledge, hasn't been done.

There have been no visible means of bringing down these very strong animals, like a bullet hole. If a cow is approached, it'll run and few men will catch it. No external perforations have been found on the carcass to indicate how the animal was initially brought down by the perpetrators. If such a mark was found, the mutilations could be linked to man. Any known anesthetic or hypnotic drugs such as Pentothal, Fentanyl or even Curare could again be linked to man. A simple tire track or foot print would definitely point to man.

Since none of these three definitive pieces of evidence have been connected to any of what are now thousands of recorded mutilations, the obvious conclusion would be they are not caused by man. Maybe your recent findings might shed some new light on an old subject. Count me in!"

As planned, Nick Jensen and Dr. George Souders made their trip to western Nebraska on schedule late Monday afternoon. The two men met Mark and Doc Mino briefly at the clinic. Jake had

112

offered an invitation to the group to have dinner in their showcase home on the bluff. The log house was one of the oldest and best preserved homes in the area. Many of the locals, including Mark and Doc, had always admired the house from a distance, but tonight they'd have a chance to see it firsthand. Their city guests would have an opportunity to experience some special panhandle hospitality amongst old and new friends set in a very special, historical surrounding.

The foursome drove to Jake's house on the ridge for dinner around six, and they also planned to watch the Denver Broncos play the San Diego Chargers on Monday Night Football. All five were avid Husker fans, but Denver was unanimously their favorite pro team. They all cheered for a local western Nebraska running back by the name of Danny Woodhead from nearby North Platte, now playing for San Diego.

Judy took their guests on a tour while Jake worked in the kitchen. Upon their return, the men made their way out onto the patio. For this late in the year, the weather had actually been very pleasant over the holiday and the immediate forecast was void of any major snowfall for the upcoming week. Daily temperatures should be in the mid-twenties with night temps falling into the teens. Mother Nature wasn't the total bitch she usually portrayed this time of year in the Midwest. Jake had sliding glass doors installed on the patio to keep out inclement weather, but tonight they wouldn't be needed. It was actually a pleasant, rare and balmy December evening.

The covered patio had two propane burners to take any chill off for the two older guests. The men settled into the comfortably cushioned patio chairs surrounding Jake's custom- built stone fire pit. Doc and Nick, being the seniors of the group, were seated in the heavily cushioned seats closest to the comfortable, warm air. The big screen TV was positioned on the nearby wall so everyone had a great seat. Just like indoors, but out here cigars were allowed. The five men enjoyed their Punch Churchill's and a glass of single malt scotch while Jake kept a careful eye on the rib-eyes, baked potatoes and corn-on- the-cob grilling on the gas grill.

This was to be a welcome party for two old friends and several new ones. Tonight was strictly an opportunity to get re-acquainted for Doc and Nick. They had a lot of catching up to do. Any serious discussions could wait until tomorrow morning.

The Lincoln duo did share their intent to return home on Friday. The men wouldn't have this pleasure to be together if it wasn't for Jake's find. They could tell he had a keen interest in the investigation. It didn't take them long to invite Jake and Dr. Mark to join them in their attempt to tie up some loose ends and maybe close a fifty-year-old book with one strange lingering chapter in Nick and Doc's career. Both men graciously accepted the kind offer.

Jake could easily arrange to take the rest of the week off to join this unofficial investigation. His direct involvement reeled him in hook, line and sinker. The short month between the two major holidays of the year was Jake's slow time as a sales rep, and he wouldn't be missed.

His quiver was a key piece of new evidence and he was very interested to help the two old colleagues shed some light on a possible connection with a fifty-year-old mystery. He was very excited and appreciative for the chance to get involved with the four highly trained and qualified men, even though it was deemed unofficial business. If anyone could get to the bottom of these unanswered questions with the new evidence presented to them, Jake's money was on this team. *They've sure got the brains and experience!*

One of the things the men did want to accomplish was to make a plan for the next three days. They managed to work out the details at half time. These old friends were familiar with the mutilation aspect of the mystery. What they wanted to try and determine was if there was anything that might link the quills to the mutilations and where the quills may have originated. This was going to be a challenge.

Nick asked Doc Mino about Jan Gradert. After all, she'd taken quite a ribbing by the locals about the same time that Doc was taking his. Nick didn't waste the opportunity.

"Say Doc, are you still taking them horse pills? You know....the ones that made you delirious! You were accused of seeing weird things and had to stay here and put up with a lot of grief from them know-it-all locals. On the other hand, I simply got on an airplane back to Lincoln and avoided all the hoopla. Are you sure you wanna go there again?"

After the laughter subsided, Doc quipped back, "You know Nick, now that you're off the state clock, there's no reason why you can't carry the water this time. At my age, I can claim insanity and they'll go easy on me. They've all suspected it now for quite some time anyway. I've already taken my blows with the locals. You're just a young whippersnapper from the city. You're fresh meat!"

Jake, George and Mark got a kick out of the guys' quick wit. The two old friends were having fun getting reacquainted and were more than willing to share their great sense of humor.

"You know Nick, now that you mentioned Jan Gradert, I wonder. At the time, we never drew a connection between her experience and ours. We were too naive at the time to even consider a link in the two rather unbelievable stories. If we were to try and piece them together now, I'm curious about the possible outcome. Jan still lives in the area. While you guys are in town for the next three days, would you like to try and fit a visit with her into our schedule? She might be helpful in connecting the dots."

"Doc, in all seriousness, that's a great idea. I think it would be worth a visit since I'm out here chasing this nagging unsolved crime from our past. Plus if we get her involved and this gets out to our critics, I'll be in for only a third rather than a half of the razzing!"

Doc wanted to know if Dr. Knighten was still alive. He was another strong figure in the investigation at the time.

"Sorry Doc. Ken died about ten years ago. He'd been diagnosed with very early esophageal cancer. Instead of putting him through all the trials of chemo, the best bet was to operate to remove the cancer. He died from an infection after surgery."

"What about Sheriff Joe Suske?" Nick asked in the same breath of air.

"Joe and his wife, Joyce, moved out to the Sacramento, California area after retirement to escape this ungodly cold and be closer to their kids," was the response from Doc.

"Say Nick, speaking of law enforcement, do you still carry your badge in retirement?" Doc asked.

Nick reached into his pocket and pulled out a leather case. "It retired too. Pulled it out of the mothballs just for this occasion though, Doc. Don't wear it, but it's there if I should need it. I probably will with you yahoos! It might just keep us all out of jail."

Doc didn't ask, but he was sure George had his badge with him also. After all, he was the head cop in the state and he was on the clock, even if on a short reprieve.

With a plan for the week in mind, their attention centered on the two very important questions of the night: can Denver overcome a ten point lead by San Diego, and where's a fresh round of drinks? Being the pup of the bunch and a great host, Jake took the empty glasses, put them on a tray and headed for the bar.

"While I'm up, would anyone like another cigar?"

It was a very fun evening so far. It had been years since Doc had enjoyed a good cigar and he didn't want to waste the opportunity to have another. They hadn't killed him yet, so why stop now?

"Why, of course Jake! Bring us another. I've got a feeling this is going to be a good second half," Doc replied.

During one of the commercial breaks and a new round of drinks and cigars, Nick couldn't resist taking another friendly jab at his old friend.

"Do you young guys know who's sitting across from you over there in that chair? Doc Mino was one of the first vets in the country to introduce artificial insemination in livestock! So tell me Doc, did you take that heifer to dinner or kiss her first before sticking your arm up there where the sun don't shine?"

With a spry look on his weathered face, Doc fired right back without missing a beat. "Nick, you shouldn't knock it before you try it! Cows never get headaches and rarely say no. Those bossies enjoy gently swatting their tails in your face and giving you a little tickle in return. I've even had a few wink at me! Why, one time I shared a cigarette with one after we were done!"

Doc was on a roll and had to add another jab to his old buddy.

"You guys know what we used to call this guy when he'd come out to visit? Why, we'd call him No Neck Nick! The guy was as solid as a rock, and his big shoulders swallowed up his neck! That's how he earned that handle."

Nick fired back. "Oh yeah? Anyone want to take a stab at why we called Doc the vivaciously vulgar veteran veterinarian?"

After the laughter and ribbing subsided, it was obvious to all that these two guys worked well together, considering how well they played together. They were close in age and life had been good to them. It was going to be a fun and exciting week.

CHAPTER FIFTEEN

THE LINCOLN COPS MAKE THEIR CASE
TUESDAY, DAY TWO

The five men met at the clinic Tuesday morning at eight o'clock sharp. All were eager to get to work. The first order of business was for Doc Mino to call Jan Gradert and m a k e arrangements to meet up with her if she was willing. It had been ages since they'd last spoken.

"Jeez Doc, it's great to hear your voice! Why in the world are you calling me after all these years? Miss me?" she asked in her flirtatious, elderly voice.

"Yea, Jan, I do miss you. So much, as a matter-of-fact, that I'd like to see you again. Fifty years is too long. It's time we finally get together. How about this afternoon?

Seriously, something extremely important has come up. I've got several colleagues from Lincoln that would like to hear your story of that night you had your unexpected encounter. We have some new evidence that might be able to finally connect your experience and mine. Remember, a young girl was inexplicably killed and it's gone unsolved for years. We really need your help on this one. Would one o'clock work for you? We'll be glad to drive over to the house or we can meet you and your husband at t h e Steel Grill for lunch."

"You guys come over to the house. I'll see you at one."

After a five minute phone call to start the day, Doc hung up and joined the others to share the good news.

"We're set for one o'clock this afternoon."

"Great, Doc. Now if you wouldn't mind, George and I have some lab results we'd like to share with you guys. I think our findings will be of great interest to you and a great place to start," said Nick as he opened his laptop and pulled up his initial set of pictures that filled the hanging projector screen at the front of the room.

As he spoke, he'd push the button for the next photo to be reviewed.

"To begin with, let's determine the age of the leather quiver. The test results show that it is approximately two hundred years old, yet it is extremely well preserved. We haven't been able to identify what the preservative is, but it's damn good stuff. This leather and the wooden frame is still in remarkably good shape for its age.

What we haven't been able to determine yet is the origin of the etchings in the leather and what they represent. We're working on that. Our first hunch is that they're tied to ancient Mayan hieroglyphics. Some of these etchings resemble some of the markings on the great pyramid at Chichen Itza on the Yucatan Peninsula of Mexico. Others likely tie in with the Nazca Lines in Peru. As you recall, the thousands of strange markings were meticulously carved into the top of a mountain centuries ago with great precision from t h e ground, using the crudest of tools, and they can still be seen from space.

It's still a mystery as to how they mapped out the detailed, massive-scale hieroglyphs and geometric patterns, or drawings, of different animals and human-like forms. They have to be seen from above to get the full impact of their relevance, yet at the time that would have been impossible. Some scholars believe it was an ancient alien landing strip. There is no other logical explanation for its existence.

In both cases, much like what we're examining here today, we're dealing with the unknown. The markings on the quiver, blow gun, darts and the small clay pots resemble those found at each of the historical mysteries. One from the Mayan culture in Mexico, and the other from the ancient Inca civilization found in Peru. It makes no sense whatsoever. Some of the same minute patterns that are barely visible to the naked eye sitting here in front of you on this table are also found on two of the largest unexplained construction marvels the world has ever known. How could each of the two extremes be replicated with such great detail and precision? What does it mean? Who made them?

It would be a challenge for today's technology to duplicate these feats. It would make today's engineering capabilities test their limits. We have all the modern earth moving machinery and cranes we'd need, yet we'd be at a total loss to recreate something that was done centuries ago without any of our technology and advanced tools and education. Without a computer or slide rule, our guys are lost.

Let's not kid ourselves here. We're grown men and we can handle the realization of what we're possibly up against. Are we so naive to think that out of billions of solar systems that make up this universe we live in, we're the only planet that can sustain life? Let's assume not and move on. We're not here to debate this subject, we're here to try and come up with some answers.

We've got something in front of us that might offer up some very valuable clues. The quiver and its contents have never been recorded in the documented journals of history. We have some similarities, but nothing of this magnitude has ever been found. Our job is to try and connect the dots. Put on your tinfoil hats and try to stay with me on this.

We've got more. I'll let George take this one, since it's more up his alley as the lab expert."

Dr. Souders pulled the computer over and advanced to the next picture while he cleared his throat and began to speak.

"First of all, gentlemen, let me tell you what we factually know about these items lying here. Nick has gone into great detail telling us what we don't know, so let me start with what we do know. In a few minutes, I'm going to tell you about some local folklore and then you can give me your opinion. But for now, let's start with these three miniature clay pots.

As you can see, they're small, yet they fit perfectly into the quiver. They can easily be removed, but at the same time they're designed to stay in place, locked in this coated balsawood rim when necessary. Since these are primitive yet very effective weapons, they need to be readily accessible and ready to use in the blink of an eye. This quiver has an attached leather cover that protects its contents from the elements and accidental loss. It keeps everything intact and can be released in one simple movement.

All of these weapons are made on a much smaller scale than any found before. For example, if I were to shoot you now with one of these darts at an acceptable range, I would inflict some severe pain. The pain would be even worse when pulling it out. These small barbed points make removal impossible without severely tearing the surrounding skin, which would be painful, although not deadly. This leads us to our next subject.

Before us we have three very small clay pots. One wouldn't think that their storage capabilities would amount to a hill of beans. Let me reassure you that is far from the case.”

George took a quick sip of water and continued his presentation.

“This first pot, the red one, is cone shaped to give it depth and allow its contents to settle to a very precise point. It's approximately three quarters of an inch wide and twice that size in depth. You don't have to screw around scraping the bottom of a flat pot to get all of its contents like you would a soup bowl or an ice cream container. The shape of these pots does that for you. Gravity guarantees that everything in the pot is always where you want it when you need it: at the bottom tip of the cone. Upon a complete lab analysis, I have determined that the contents of this red pot are lethal. Jake, if your dog had been injected with this

121

poison, she wouldn't be alive. Neither would we. What we have here is actually a minute quantity of decayed animal flesh injected with just a trace of poison from a deadly inland taipan snake from Australia. The Aborigines would catch the snakes and place their fangs into the rotting concoction and then milk the venom into the foul meat. They would stir it up in a bowl and dip their arrows into the poisonous mixture. That's basically what we have here. A toxic pot of decayed meat spiced with t h e deadliest land snake venom in the world. Even the smallest of puncture wounds from any of the arrows or darts from this quiver dipped in this pot would spell certain death to the largest of animals within two hours once the poison entered into the bloodstream. That's fact number one.

Fact number two lies here in the yellow pot. The paste is from a mushroom found in Brazil called fly agaric. Although it is seldom fatal, effects of the drug can range from nausea, drowsiness, auditory and visual distortions, euphoria, loss of equilibrium and sleep. The mushrooms are dried and then ground to a fine powder. When mixed with water, it turns to a paste like you see here. The yellow pot's contents aren't meant to kill their target, but they will have the desired outcome on their victim. It will render them harmless for several hours.

You are by now all familiar with the third fact we know. This blue pot contains curare, the same drug that was used on Yollie. Again, the substance in this potency is strictly to temporarily paralyze its victim. It's been around for centuries in South America and has been used on dart tips to stop any enemy with just a minor flesh wound. If you wanted to render an opponent defenseless and get close enough to look him in the eye and goose him, this is the perfect stuff to use. Actually, a derivative of curare is used in modern day anesthesiology during surgery to safely sedate the patient."

George continued with his scientific logic.

"These three small pots provide a range of immediate protection for the user. They have the option of killing the victim, rendering them temporarily harmless or paralyzing them. If they should desire to take prisoners or remove a body part as a trophy, they have that capability. Who knows? There may be more that just weren't in this particular quiver. If several similar quivers contain an assortment of these pots with other potions, the options are off the charts. There could possibly be different shooters for different results.

The question that each pot poses is how did the substances indigenous to South America and Australia find their way to Nebraska? We'll have to assume that there is a worldwide supply chain available to pull from. Whoever shot Yollie with that dart has friends in high places with untold resources."

George concluded the presentation by explaining the porcupine quill darts.

"We do know that the darts are definitely porcupine quills; most likely local. The animals are found in every state. They're not hard to find here in Nebraska if you know where to look and how to retrieve the quills. Porcupines do not throw their quills as once suspected. They act more like a pincushion to protect the animal. The quills do have a barb on the tip, which makes removing them from flesh difficult and painful.

If you look closely, you'll notice that one end of the quill has been flattened and slightly notched. This g i v e s it more stability in flight, which greatly enhances the force of the blow. It works much like the feathers on an arrow work. Unlike an arrow, these quills have to be released at a relatively short distance due to the elements. Any wind velocity would render them useless for long range effectiveness, which they don't need. The Jacks are extremely quick and can safely maneuver into difficult spots in order to get that close up shot. They're very aggressive little critters and we can't take them for granted because of their small, frail stature. They're apparently long term survivors in a very tough world.

Most of the materials used to make the three different sized blowguns and the support rings in the quiver are all native to this area, with the exception of the balsa support ring. T h e r e   i s nothing extraordinary about them other than the bowls. The blowguns seem to be rather old, but very well taken care of.

The notches found on parts of the weapons may indicate the number of hits each user has recorded. Their owner displays the notches like a badge of honor. That's a guess, but historically that has been the case with other native cultures.

The rest of the unidentified carvings could, however, mean something to the contrary. I'm going with my first hunch, however, based on the fact that whoever possessed this quiver lost it. Since this is the only one to have ever been found, it makes it exceedingly rare. The fact that Jake was lucky enough to have retrieved it from a badger hole would justify the find. The odds were definitely against him. The fear factor the badger played in the equation is paramount, although it delayed the inevitable. Whoever lost it would certainly be back to find it at the first morning light. Either there aren't many beings that possess this type of weaponry or they're extremely careful not to lose their weapons. Perhaps the owner inherited the weapons. Maybe he took them from a dead enemy as a trophy or maybe the person that possessed the weapons was seriously wounded himself and dropped the quiver. If that's the case, others may be looking for it. Let's certainly hope that's not the case."

Nick again took the floor and pulled some papers from his briefcase. "Doc, I'm sure you remember these. These are the original files from over 50 years ago, when we were first introduced."

Nick began to space them evenly over the table in front of the men.

"Here are the notes and pictures taken by you at the initial mutilation site. This one contains the autopsy report we wrote when dissecting the cow next to your clinic. Here are the notes on my lab findings.

Remember this one? This is the file on the dead girl from Hastings. There are more. I've had a couple of weeks to review them. Technology has vastly improved. Our attitudes have changed. Society has changed. Time has been our friend in this case.

For example, I was able to pull a DNA sample from the quill fragment we found behind the cow's ear fifty-four years ago and compare it to the current one retrieved from Yollie. They're the same. Unbelievably, they were shot by the same person without a doubt. That's the good news. The bad news is that these strands of DNA vary from human DNA. They're similar, but certainly not the same. They don't match up with any species samples from our worldwide computer bank.

We're dealing with a new and worthy opponent. It uses very primitive weapons, yet i t seems to have the capacity to draw from technology that completely leaves us in the dark ages. We have no explanation why and how these mutilations are performed. How do they possess materials found in distant parts of the world? Could we tie the crop circle mystery into this equation? We've got enough on our plate, so I won't even go there at this point.

I said at that time that if we could link something manmade or an earthly substance, we could affirm that whoever killed the cow is probably human and definitely from this planet. With the recent DNA finding, I stand corrected, at least in this particular case. Other investigations from around the world might prove otherwise. The point is that we still don't know what we're dealing with.

We've got some clues sitting here before us that hopefully can shed some light on the subject. Until then, we've got to approach this investigation very carefully. We know that we're up against a formidable and dangerous foe."

In all seriousness, Nick leaned over the table to make his final statement. "Let's face it gentlemen, we're onto something that's much bigger than we are. Sooner or later, we will have some people who will want to join in the challenge before us and we'll have others who will call us crazy. We've got to be aware of that fact and prepare for both scenarios.

Until that time comes, I suggest we do as much as much as we can before the water gets muddied. You already have the top two cops in the state in on the case. We'll know who to call when we need the help. Until that time, we must keep this investigation and any findings to ourselves. Doc, Mark, Jake: do I have your word?"

They all promised to keep the investigation under wraps.

"I'm looking forward to our meeting with Jan Gradert this afternoon. Her recollection of her story might speak volumes to us now.

Jake, I would like you to take us out to the site where Yollie was shot and where you found the quiver. I find it very interesting that jackrabbits fit into both stories. To expound further on our technological advances, we have found that the DNA samples found on this quiver coincidentally, but quite unequivocally, are connected to a very large source of rabbit DNA!

We can now tie a cattle mutilation that happened over fifty years ago to a dog being shot less than a month ago to the same source. When we add jackrabbits to the equation, Jan's story takes on a whole new meaning. We'll actually have a firsthand witness that can give us a description of our only suspect.

What we can't tie to our new findings is any correlation with Leah Krzycki's murder. Her file indicates she was dropped from a substantial height. The second mutilated cow, found approximately one hundred yards away from her, was also dropped from the air at about the same time from approximately the same height. I find that an unlikely coincidence. Hopefully we can kill two birds with one stone on this one."

126

Nick picked up the files and put them back in his case. Both men now stood at the front of the room while the laptop showed one last picture upon the screen. It portrayed two images of a mummified skeleton that was reportedly found in Casper, Wyoming back in the 1930s. One photo was a frontal view of the little man sitting with his legs and arms crossed. If the man was standing, his height was estimated to be around fourteen inches tall. The second was an x-ray taken of the man, showing a complete skeletal image. This indicated that the man was indeed real and not a hoax like many had originally thought when experts from around the world were brought in to examine the find.

George spoke with genuine concern to his small group.

"Guys, in conclusion, I'd like to introduce you to who we're likely dealing with. This is a picture of a Nimeragir. According to folklore, this clan of little people lived in Eastern Wyoming many centuries ago, but their existence has never been proven. This picture is the closest proof we have to their being.

They live in American Indian folklore as being very mean and aggressive little critters that were admirable foes, given their size. Since few have considered them to be real, other than the tribes that called Eastern Wyoming and Western Nebraska home, we have very little knowledge of them. According to the Indians, they should be avoided at all costs.

It would appear, in all likelihood that these creatures do exist and they ride jackrabbits, thus the appropriate name *Jack People* that an old Indian by the name of Joe Yellow Bear aptly referred to them over fifty years ago in Gavin Aldama's article. These are the weapons they use. This is what we're up against gentlemen. Take a good look, because we might be meeting them and their alien allies face to face soon."

Nick solemnly ended the presentation. "Gentlemen, are there any questions?"

The men sat in total silence. The two seasoned Lincoln cops left the room speechless.

CHAPTER SIXTEEN
JAN GRADERT REVISITED

The five men grabbed a quick lunch at the Steel Grill and headed over to the Graderts'. The couple still lived in the house they'd bought back in the early fifties. It was a nicely kept two story brick house located in the historical section of Gering, which backed up to Mitchell Pass.

The spry elderly woman was anxiously awaiting her guests from her living room window. She stepped out the front door and headed toward the sidewalk as she saw two cars pull up to the curb in front of the house.

"Why Doc, look at you! You're as handsome as ever! Who are these nice men?"

After the introductions were made and the small talk subsided, Jan asked the men to join her in the living room. She hadn't talked about her experience in years and now all of a sudden she had five professionals who couldn't wait for her to rehash every second of the ordeal. Why did they have so much interest in her story now?

Doc assured her that this was strictly an informal meeting regarding the events they shared. Although both were considered very strange at the time by the locals, these men wanted to see if maybe there was some connection after all in the two unbelievable stories that happened at the same time in the same vicinity. Time had passed and people moved on. They were there for information; not to dig up demons from the past. He was careful not to give her more data than she needed about their motive. The fewer people involved, the better. Although she didn't tell Doc, that unspoken arrangement worked just fine with Jan.

Nick and George were very observant of the elderly woman. They listened to how she spoke, what she said and her actions. They wanted to know if the woman in front of t h e m was credible and still capable of giving an accurate account of that cold December night in 1959. If she stumbled, lost her concentration or simply forgot where she was going with her story, her narrative could not be used to build their case like they hoped it would.

Luckily she didn't disappoint them. She left no room for doubt of her memory or her mental faculties once she began her story. Her mind was like a steel trap.

Jan sat her cup of tea down on the coffee table in front of the couch and began. "My students had just presented their annual Christmas Playhouse in the auditorium. After the play, I helped the janitor put the chairs away and probably left the schoolhouse around nine that night. It was a very cold night and a light snow began to fall. Luckily it wasn't accumulating too badly on the road when I left Hemingford. I hated driving in snow, especially late at night.

It was more of a swirling snow out on the highway. You know, that mesmerizing kind that makes you snow-blind. I was focusing hard on the road and listening to the radio when I saw this small herd of maybe a dozen jackrabbits dart in front of the car. I'd seen them many times in my years of commuting along that stretch of road, and I actually grew fond of their company.

This night was different. There were more of them. They seemed bigger. My lights were right on them and I got a good look. All of a sudden, I saw a pair of big black eyes turn back at me from one of the rabbit's backs. It suddenly dawned on me that there was some kind of small human-like creature on the back of every rabbit in sight! I could see their tiny legs tucked along the sides of the rabbit, covered in rabbit skin. Their whole body was wrapped in fur that blended in perfectly with their mounts. If one of them hadn't turned around to look back at me from under the hood of his rabbit pelt coat, I probably never would have noticed them.

I can still see those eyes like it happened yesterday. They were much bigger than usual in proportion to the head. Kind of like a fly, you know: big, black, bulging eyes. I saw the facial features also. The mouth and nose seemed very small. The skin had a grayish hue to it. Maybe it was the headlights or the snow distorting the color, but the skin seemed gray and aged. The face looked directly at me and it seemed to be scowling at me, like I was trying to run them over or something.

They didn't ride upright on their rabbits like one would typically ride a horse. These creatures rode horizontally on the back of the rabbit and they blended perfectly as if they were one. They appeared to be about the same length since their small feet rested securely right above the rabbit's large rear haunches. All of them had something like a tube flung over their back.

The brief encounter probably only lasted a matter of seconds, but it's as if time switched to slow motion. Everything seemed so very clear and real to me. Suddenly that warp came back to real time and I lost control of the car. Fear had taken over and I headed for the ditch. I got high centered on a snow bank and my rear wheels couldn't make contact. They just spun. I had hit my head on the steering wheel and I was bleeding. I needed help.

I began walking north in the direction of the Bosworth ranch, several miles back towards Hemingford. I hastily grabbed my boots, flashlight, scarf and hat out of the trunk before I left the car to help keep me warm.

I remembered seeing a faint light just over the small ridge to my right. The crest couldn't have been more than a hundred yards away. I thought that someone would be there who could help me. You know, like a car or truck. I determined that was my best bet. The Bosworth ranch was a couple of miles away compared to what was just over the small embankment on the other side of the fence. If I could get to the top of the ridge, I could see what was below from the tree line. Luckily there was a cow path that led in that

131

direction and I stepped through the fence and followed it to the top. It wasn't more than a three minute hike.

I proceeded very carefully up the hill. I began hearing some unrecognizable noises as I approached the trees. Instead of seeing vehicle lights like I'd anticipated, I saw something that took my breath away.

To my utter astonishment, there were the small creatures I'd seen on the rabbits just minutes earlier. There were about a dozen of them wrapped in their rabbit cloaks. They couldn't have been more than two feet tall.

Several larger figures that were perhaps double that height were also present. These creatures were similar in appearance, but appeared to be robed and very skinny and frail. Their bodies seemed disproportionally different than a human's. The arms and legs seemed longer and the head larger. I don't think they liked being in the elements, but they seemed to be giving the orders.

All of them were standing in front of a glowing saucer-shaped object that was e m i t t i n g a faint blue light from the outer rim of the underbelly. I'm guessing it may have stood no more than ten feet in height and approximately sixty feet around. It just hovered in the air, making a soft, low-pitched whirring hum.

The only other noise came from these creatures. It was a sound that didn't resemble any language I'd ever heard of. It sounded almost like each of them was emitting their own varied harmonic pitches.

The larger creatures appeared to be moving some type of rock from a hole in the side of the ridge bottom effortlessly over to the waiting ship. The differently sized rocks seemed to float between the pointed fingers of these frail creatures. The smaller rabbit men observed from a safe distance behind this floating line of rocks. I must have gotten in on the tail end of the rendezvous, because within minutes the larger shapes got in the hovering object and disappeared in almost the blink of an eye.

One of the rabbit men made a shrill whistle-like noise and suddenly these little men descended into the hillside, pulling a larger rock over their exposed entrance, making it impossible to see. The rabbits grazing in the grass amazingly followed these creatures into the hole, probably upon the same command.

Thank God I managed to make the walk to the Bosworth ranch that night. I was cold and frightened, but I survived. After all the ridicule from the newspaper interview, I decided then and there to just keep quiet about the whole experience. No one believed me anyway. My husband did. The Bosworths did. Sheriff Suske did and of course you, Doc. But that was about it.

Does any of this make sense to you gentlemen? Did I give you any useful information?"

All five of the men avidly concurred. Jan's story was extremely interesting and important to their quest.

Doc asked Jan if she could recall the exact location where the incident had taken place.

"Why yes, of course! I knew that stretch of highway like the back of my hand. I've never had any reason to go back, but I'm sure you could probably still find that gate and cow path that leads up to the tree-lined ridge where I witnessed the whole thing. You two vets know the Bosworth place, right? That gate I'm talking about is maybe two miles south of their lane, right off the highway on the east side. You can't miss it! If you know when you'll be going, I'll call Shar Bosworth and let her know you'll be paying them a visit."

"Tomorrow morning around nine will work fine for us Jan. If you wouldn't mind calling Shar, we'd sure appreciate it," Doc replied.

The whole meeting lasted about an hour. After a warm round of thank you's from everyone, they gradually made their way outside. The small entourage wanted to see where Yollie had been hit while there was still daylight. With daylight savings time, it would be dark around five. They didn't want to waste any time.

"Jake, we'll follow you," said Nick as he and Dr. Souders climbed into their state issued Ford Taurus.

The two cars pulled into the Young driveway about ten minutes later. As usual, Yollie was there to greet them. She'd recovered completely from her ordeal thanks to Dr. Hutton. The well mannered dog greeted her guests with a brief lick on the hand and nudge with her nose, which yielded the anticipated pat on the head from each of them.

Her wagging tail and big brown smiling eyes told all of them, "Hi guys, I'm glad to see you, now pet me some more!"

Yollie sat at attention next to Jake after making another brief round. "Good girl, Yollie, good girl. Sit."

"Anyone need a bathroom break before we begin? The head is just down the hall to the right. If you'd like something to drink, just speak up. If not, I'm ready any time you guys are," announced Jake.

Doc Mino had done about all the walking he wanted to do for the day. His old knees weren't too excited about having to cross over a ditch, crawl over a fence and then meander through a pasture full of cow shit and stickers.

"If you guys don't mind, I'll just wait here. I thought I heard your lovely wife in the kitchen, Jake. I'll go keep her company while you're away. You guys take your time. Judy and I will be just fine!"

Dr. Hutton also decided to stay behind. He'd keep a watchful eye on the old flirt. Besides, his services weren't needed at present anyhow. He sat down at the kitchen table with Doc and Judy and got caught up on all the holiday news both had to offer.

Jake offered to take the Escalade. The breeze was starting to put a chill in the air and their destination was a good mile and a half up the road. Yollie was the first one in, and she immediately hopped in the back.

Jake had marked the spot on the fence line with a red bandana. He'd had a hunch he'd be going back to the spot in the near future and decided to make it easier for them to find, especially if it snowed. He pulled the SUV over on the shoulder of the gravel road and led the other two men to their desired destination, which was about seventy-five yards due west of the fence line. Jake had marked the second spot with one of his walking sticks planted firmly in the ground. A few minutes later, the three stood at their destination.

"Not much to see, guys. Yollie was laying right about here. I found the quiver over there," he said as he started leading the men in a northwest direction, where he'd stuck another stick in the ground next to the badger hole.

Nick commented, "The quiver apparently dropped straight down the hole, far enough that they weren't comfortable retrieving it at the time. It would have put at least one of them, or maybe all of them, in a very vulnerable and precarious situation if the badger surfaced, so they opted to leave it till the next morning."

The two men asked Jake about the rabbits that night. "How often do you see them Jake?"

"Not very often nowadays. The jack population seemed to flourish when I was a kid back in the fifties. I'd see them all the time on the farm or darting across the roads. After returning to Nebraska, after a long work hiatus, I was amazed by how their population had dwindled. Being hunted for the fur took a toll on them. Sometimes they were even poisoned. For some reason, ranchers and farmers don't seem to like them. We do see some on occasion on our walks, more so in the winter than the summer months, but usually Yollie is rousting up a pheasant or quail to chase. Yollie is disappointed if she doesn't get a little hunt in. We usually take our walk before dark when I'm home. This time of year it gets pretty nippy when the sun goes down. Seems like that's the time they may be foraging for food. Food supplies can get rather scarce this time of year and they're forced to look a little harder to stave off starvation."

The two veteran state cops began canvassing the area in different directions, stopping and evaluating everything in range for a brief time and then moving on to another spot, repeating their pattern until they came together. Jake could tell this wasn't their first field investigation together. He was sure they'd both encountered many similar situations over their years trying to solve murders, find missing people and all things in between. Nothing would slip by these two seasoned pros. He stood silently in his spot, watching and appreciating their thoroughness.

After about twenty minutes of looking, the two men headed back towards Jake. "Nothing here. Say Jake, can you see any jacks from your back porch?" asked George. "Maybe we should do a little surveillance work for the next hour or two over some more of that scotch, if you wouldn't mind."

"You know Nick, come to think of it, I do see those pesky wabbits pwetty good from my patio chair, hee, hee, hee!" he chortled as he did his best Elmer Fudd impersonation in a ruddy, slow voice.

It had been a productive day for the men and it was time to sort out their findings over a cocktail and some welcomed fire pit heat. They were encouraged to have a direction to pursue rather than coming up empty-handed, as so many of their investigations had. Jake gave Judy a quick call on his cell from the field to ask her if she had any holiday leftovers she might be able to heat up. After a few seconds of looking in the refrigerator, Judy suggested that they come back to the house and she'd place an order for a couple of p i z z a s from the Gering Pizza Hut. She'd take Yollie and pick them up in about forty-five minutes.

"That would give you guys a chance to talk. I'll start taking drink orders here at the table. I think I've got a couple of thirsty veterinarians sitting in front of me. They might prefer something other than coffee now that it's past five o'clock."

The five men adjourned back to their comfortable chairs from the night before. Jake lit the pit and the propane heaters. After he finished, he turned and made an offer.

"I have a few more cigars left if anyone wants one other than me." Four hands immediate shot up in the air.

"Hey Jake, just out of curiosity, would you happen to own a .22 long rifle?" asked George.

"I sure do. If the opportunity arises, you have my permission to do some hunting on my property. I do believe rabbits are always in season."

Jake excused himself and a few minutes later returned with the scoped semi-automatic rifle.

"I'll set it right over here with the safety on. You guys feel free to use it anytime."

He knew these two men were no strangers around firearms and was quite comfortable in making the offer. With the success they'd already encountered today, maybe they'd get extremely lucky and actually shoot a Jack!

All of the men agreed that Jan's story was very credible. The emotion and detail were still there after all these years. Nick and George strongly concurred. They'd listened to thousands of statements over their careers and they knew an unreliable source when they saw one.

Nick addressed the group. "Now we've got little creatures riding rabbits with weapons. They apparently are in cahoots with aliens and they rendezvous here in the panhandle to cut up cows. Makes perfect sense to me! For years now, the world has c o n t i n u e d t o report more alien sightings, to the point that most people believe in them. We've had an uptick of alien sightings right here in Nebraska. That certainly wasn't the case with Doc and I at that time. We were breaking virgin territory."

"Why Nick, back then we were both breaking a lot of virgin territory," quipped Doc.

After a brief, broad, guilty smile that resembled that of a cat after eating the canary, Nick continued. "No one can give a solid reason as to why they come, but they come.

We now have a link with these so-called Jack People to cattle mutilations. There's nothing in documented history that substantiates this rare species. I have come across several sites on the internet regarding them, but so far they seem to fall into the category of an urban legend or some sort of mythological creature, like a gnome or our own native jackalope.

Can we safely say that there is a connection between these Jack People and aliens? I believe we unequivocally can. Can we tie these small poisoned weapons to initially bringing down the animal? We've already done it. Can we say they're doing the mutilations? I don't think so.

Remember Jan talking about that saucer's ability to hover in place above ground? I think the Jacks bring the animal down and the aliens somehow lift the unconscious animal up into their ship and do their thing in a controlled environment and then drop the animal back to Earth when they're done with it.

So far there have been no tracks of any kind around either carcass. If the animal is removed from the original locale where it was brought down and then dropped down in another area, wouldn't that explain why we haven't found any prints or tracks? I guess there's always a possibility that the carcass could be dropped down into an area that had prior prints in the ground surface, but that's a long shot. A dead animal will attract scavengers that will leave prints, not the other way around.

Guys, I suggest we visit the spot where Jan witnessed her experience. Did you remember hearing her say something about rocks being floated into the ship from a hole in the earth? That's where we need to start first thing in the morning."

Doc interjected, "Say Nick, thinking back, I have two other things I'd like to add. Remember that major newspaper story written by some Lincoln reporter named Gavin Aldama around that time?

In his article, he told of an event that happened back in the late 1800s up around O'Neill, well before Roswell. A rancher supposedly found an alien crash site. The article said that the three unidentified creatures found in the wreckage were buried in a local cemetery.

What would happen if we followed up on that story and paid a visit to the cemetery?   If there was anything that was exposed to any possible radioactive materials from an alien crash and buried there, we should be able to find them with a Geiger counter. They weren't commercially available until around 1928, so by that time no one ever had any desire to go back with one. Some radioactive material can be detected for thousands of years."

The old veterinarian continued.

"Jake's family was from the O'Neill area. They homesteaded around Ewing and Clearwater. He knows the area and the cemetery. It might be worth the trip. His uncle Hank is a retired District Court Judge living in O'Neill. He might be of great assistance in showing us around the area. He knows this part of north central Nebraska like the back of his hand.

Secondly, in that same article, Gavin Aldama included a blurb about an old Sioux living in Alliance. Joe Yellow Bear had probably never seen a flying saucer or cattle mutilation, but he had heard of something that struck Aldama's interest. Yellow Bear's old Indian stories referenced some sort of mythical little people.

The creatures were bad omens to the Native American tribes. I can't recall ever h e a r i n g anything more about them. I don't remember the whole story, but I do have the paper in my files. Maybe we could find some of Yellow Bear's family who might be able to bring his stories back to life. I'll bring that news clipping with me tomorrow. Both stories are referenced in the article and might be worth pursuing."

"Damn Doc! I forgot all about that article. That's a great idea! Guys, we have a lot of ground to cover before Friday. Is everybody in?" Nick excitedly asked.

George Souders would call the sheriff in Alliance first thing in the morning and try to get a contact for Joe Yellow Bear.

Five raised scotch glasses signified their unanimous, silent response.

CHAPTER SEVENTEEN
DOWN THE RABBIT HOLE
WEDNESDAY, DAY THREE

Jake pulled into the U-Rent store parking lot at eight AM the next morning to rent a Geiger counter. He'd called the store the previous afternoon to reserve it for the next four days.

It was a cold, overcast early December morning. Jake turned on the heat and defroster as he drove down the hill towards the Scottsbluff Holiday Inn Express to meet his out of town friends.

The group thought it might be beneficial to include Yollie, since her keen sense of smell might come in handy. It was obvious to the group that she was very well mannered and wouldn't create any problems. Yollie was content to find a spot in the rear area of the large SUV. She was excited to be included as one of the gang.

The men made plans to drive both cars out to the Bosworth ranch early that morning. A call from Jan Gradert to Shar the night before confirmed the Bosworths' permission for the men to access the property.

George got the name and phone number of a Samuel Yellow Bear from the Alliance sheriff. Samuel was now living on the Rosebud Reservation in South Dakota, just four miles north of the little town of Cody, Nebraska. George called the man from his cell on the way to the Bosworth Ranch. Samuel was Joe's grandson. He'd love to meet with them.

Although they couldn't pinpoint the exact time they'd be in the Cody area, Samuel agreed to meet them at the Cody Husker Hub at their convenience. George would call Samuel when they left Chadron, Nebraska and meet him in about an hour from that time.

Just to confirm the reason of their visit, George wasted no time in asking Samuel if he'd ever heard any stories specifically regarding the Jack People from his grandfather. Although Sam hadn't heard the stories in many years, he assured George that he was very familiar with them. He'd heard them many times as a child.

Thursday morning, they'd head for O'Neill to check out the cemetery, and time permitting, try to track down the reported crash sight to see if the Geiger counter might offer any new clues to verify the story. They'd spend the night in O'Neill and part company on Friday. From this point on, the two Lincoln crime lab heads were halfway home. Jake would have his two Gering accomplices back in town by late afternoon.

Jake picked up the delicate instrument and carefully stowed it in the roomy back compartment with a suitcase and his .22 long rifle case next to Yollie. For good measure, he'd also thrown in his twelve gauge semi-automatic Remington shotgun and a .357 S&W nickel-plated revolver.

Jake had learned his lesson of needing a gun and not having one the hard way several years ago in the parking lot of an Albuquerque motel. Two men approached him from behind when he was getting out of his car. They took his watch and billfold and threatened to kill him if he refused. Since that experience, Jake obtained a concealed weapons permit. He never wanted to be put in that helpless position again while traveling.

He pulled into the motel parking lot and quickly found their two adjoining room numbers on the exterior of the building. After a quick stop for gas and five cups of convenience store coffee, the men hit the road. Jake took the lead. His Escalade held three men that knew western Nebraska like old Indian scouts. This was their territory.

Doc had made copies of Aldama's old newspaper article and gave everyone some homework to read on the way. They'd compare notes later tonight at their motel in O'Neill.

The section of fence they were looking for was roughly a thirty-five minute ride. With two old vets in the car, they knew Robb and Shar Bosworth and the rest of their extended family. Both had taken care of the family's livestock for years.

Just as a courtesy, Jake pulled the Escalade into the lane and drove up to the house. Dr. Hutton went to the door to announce their arrival. After a brief conversation with the Bosworths, the men pulled back onto the highway and headed for the cattle gate about two miles back. The men had permission to go wherever they wanted. Jake saw the gate and pulled the SUV over onto the shoulder.

Dr. Mark jumped out of his seat and approached the wire gate. He slid the wire up over the gate post and the two vehicles drove through. Mark quickly shut the gate and rushed back in the car.

"Colder than a well digger's ass out there, boys!" he quipped after an uncontrolled shiver.

"Duly noted, son. I think I'll sit this one out and stay in the car," Doc quickly replied, without hesitation.

The cold morning chill hadn't subsided. The digital temp reading on the dash read eighteen degrees. Not a good day to be out in the elements for any extended period of time, especially when factoring in the blustery wind. The wind chill brought the temperature down to nine degrees.

The tree-lined ridge Jan described lay directly ahead by about one hundred yards. Once they reached the bottom of the draw, they got out of their vehicles and began to look around. Not much to see but a few large rock formations that lined the bluffs and miles of flat, open pasture.

Jake stood back and watched Nick and George begin their initial observations just like they'd done in the field behind his house the day before.

A few minutes into their search, Nick yelled back to the others. He was standing by some larger rocks. "Hey Jake, could you bring that Geiger counter over here, please?"

Jake gladly obliged. With the tool in hand, Nick turned it on. He skimmed the circular flat head around over the tailings that lay in front of the ridge. The meter needle began to move to the right as the clicking sound indicator picked up a signal.

"Sounds like these rocks might hold some radioactive material," Nick noted.

"Probably uranium. There are interspersed mines throughout about a twenty-five mile stretch beginning north of here. Remember Jan's comment about rocks being loaded on to the floating saucer?" replied Mark.

"Can anyone see anything resembling an opening?" George asked.

A few minutes before, Jake's curiosity had gotten the best of him and he'd made the short hike back to the SUV. He had carefully unwrapped the small quiver from its packing box and let Yollie pick up the scent. In less than a minute, she was standing over another pile of rocks just forty yards to the east of where the men were standing.

No sooner had George finished his question than he was given an immediate answer from the dog's loud bark.

The men began to remove the rocks where Yollie stood. After a little probing, George found a small opening. "I've got something here!"

The other four converged on the hole. It was too small of an opening for them to get a good view. Nick pulled out his flashlight and got on his belly to take a look into the dark crevice.

"I can't tell how big this is on the inside. Hey Mark, can you call up to the house and see if Robb could bring his tractor down here? Maybe he can make this opening a little bigger for us to explore a little further."

The local vet obliged, and within fifteen minutes they saw Robb driving the tractor through the gate. He was bundled up like the Michelin Man with his various layers of clothing. The bucket was attached to the front of the tractor for snow removal and could easily do the heavy lifting in seconds, compared to strenuous hours with a pick and shovel.

During the brief wait, the men retreated to their vehicles with the heater blasting, if o n l y for a short reprieve.

The rancher hopped down off the tractor. After the brief introductions, Nick got down to the business at hand.

"Robb, in your years living on this land, have you ever seen anything resembling small caverns or tunnels here in this area?"

"No. I grew up on this ranch. It's been in the family for over one hundred years. If there was a cave, I'd certainly know about it. The only thing that I ever see around this area is jackrabbits. Tons of 'em. They seem to congregate here in this locale. Maybe there's a large jack den buried under the hole you found. Rabbit holes certainly aren't uncommon on the ranch."

The five amazed men looked around at each other in absolute bewilderment. Jackrabbits? What a coincidence!

Robb began to maneuver the larger rocks around the opening with the tractor bucket until the men could get a good view of what they were dealing with. There was a small area beyond the initial opening that seemed to have several different passageways leading further back into the hillside. Again, they were too small

145

to see into. It appeared that Robb might be right. It looked like numerous rabbit footprints covered this initial small inner section that led further back into the hillside.

"Looks like a rabbit den, and a rather large one at that. Could you go back a few more feet to the left and see where this tunnel might lead? We won't go any deeper than that. No sense in tearing up the butte, but if you wouldn't mind," asked George.

Robb obliged. After a few of the larger rocks were removed, Nick looked down into a narrow section of the exposed shaft, about three feet below him, and saw small bones sitting on a raised ledge that lined both sides of the tunnel section.

There were lots of them.   The bones were neatly placed on the ledge, and there were no bones on the floor of the burrow. The men thought that observation was odd.

Without being able to see and reach at the same time, Nick blindly stretched his arm down into the opening and carefully pulled a number of the bones within his grasp up to the surface where he could get a better look. He handed them up to Mark's outstretched hand and reached down for more.

Nick saw something out of the corner of his eye that deserved a second look.

"Hey George, bring me a flashlight and the camera and take a look at this."

Although not fully exposed, both men saw strange hieroglyphics lining the wall directly above the ledge.

"Wow! That's odd. Pretty fancy artwork for some dead rabbits," George said as he knelt down over the small entrance, hovering over Nick's shoulder with his camera. Jake snapped a couple of photos with his cell phone as backup.

Mark carefully spread the bone samples on the flat ground by the rear tractor tire. They were of various sizes and colors, indicating that some might be older than others. Between the two cops and the two vets, they determined that the bones were probably from numerous rabbits that for some reason may have crawled into this section of the tunnel to die.

Either that or a predator was involved, which may have brought the dead animals into this flat area of the tunnel to eat. That was the unlikely case, because it would have to be a pretty neat predator to not drop a single bone on the floor.

It appeared that the tunnel took a sharp dip down and narrowed, making this area the best place for a meal if that was the case. It was an educated guess at this point.

Neither scenario would indicate how the drawings were put on the wall. There was obviously more to this than what met their trained eyes. George made a note to ask one of his colleagues from the State Historical Society, Dr. Norm Overbay, to perhaps bring a team out to the site next spring and do some archaeological research in this vicinity.

George put the bones in a plastic lab bag and placed the bag in his trunk. He'd take the bones and some rock samples back to the Lincoln lab and take a closer look at them.

Nick and Jake snapped a few pictures of the site before they left. The men thanked Robb for his use of the tractor and they were soon back on the road heading to Alliance, thankful to once again be in a warm vehicle and out of the freezing temperatures.

The immediate topic of conversation raised in both cars was how lucky they were to have Yollie pick up a scent off the quiver and find the hidden rabbit den entrance. The men automatically assumed the rabbit scent that Yollie picked up from the quiver led her to the opening. Without the dog, they would have been looking in vain. The three men in the Escalade were sharing their praises with their four-legged friend and Yollie t h o r o u g h l y enjoyed the attention.

Soon their conversation changed to Nebraska football. The Huskers' win over the Thanksgiving weekend earned them a bowl bid to play in the Holiday Bowl against Georgia on New Year's Day. Every Husker football fan in the state was ecstatic with the Big Red victory and upcoming bowl game. The duration of the hour-long drive was consumed by the Big Red.

The Taurus followed a safe distance behind. Their conversation soon headed in a different direction after discussing the excellence of Yollie's tracking ability. The two cops began to dig a little deeper into their good fortune. If Yollie picked up a rabbit scent on the quiver and was following that scent, wouldn't she be confused by all of the rabbit scents that must have been in the area?

Robb said the butte was a rabbit haven and there were probably hundreds of rabbits in that immediate vicinity. What led her directly to that den opening? Maybe she got lucky. Maybe she had an exceptionally keen sense of smell. Maybe it wasn't the rabbit scent she was following. What if she picked up the scent of the critter that was riding the rabbit and that scent led her to the hole instead? Maybe that would explain the drawings on the wall.

These two veteran cops were the best lab experts in the state as well as being exceptionally street savvy detectives. Both men had started their legal careers walking the streets of Lincoln as rookie cops. They looked beyond the obvious and dug beneath the surface. The devil is in the details, and the devil was no stranger to these guys. They saw him almost daily in their line of work.

The bone samples in the trunk looked like rabbit bones on the surface, but their forensic knowledge led them to believe that some of those bones, although roughly the size of a large rabbit, took on some humanistic features as well. The leg bones of a four- legged horizontal rabbit would be a lot different than those of a two-legged, upright human form. Rabbits don't have fingers.

They'd have their two animal doctors take a closer look at them tonight in the warmth of their motel room and get their opinions.

Why were the bones found neatly placed on the raised ledge and not scattered randomly on the ground of the tunnel floor? Perhaps they were placed there together in some sort of a burial ritual. Rabbits wouldn't go to a common burial spot and plunk their dying bodies neatly on the ledge. They'd have to be placed there.

Humans, on the other hand, would and often do have ceremonial burials, but the space was too confining for a human being to have done the intricate artwork from the inside.

Several of the specimens looked extremely old. Until they had a chance to examine them further, they could only speculate about what they might be carrying in their trunk.

They'd curtail their thoughts for the time being and focus on their working vacation. It'd been many years since either of the two Lincoln brass had been out in the Nebraska panhandle.

The landscapes in this neck of the woods were all ranch country consisting of rolling hills, scenic buttes and badlands. Farming was difficult in this part of the state due to the terrain. It had gone relatively unchanged for the past century, whereas eastern Nebraska had been tamed by the plow and was now covered with corn fields. The flat, fertile black soil was ideal for farming and provided some of the top per-bushel yields in the Midwest.

Granted, their investigation was very important, but so was their time together. These two professionals had spent several years working in the state crime lab at the same time, although they hadn't had the opportunity to really work together, especially with Nick's retirement almost fifteen years ago.

George always admired Nick's leadership abilities after becoming head of the department and his keen ability to think outside the box when looking at a difficult challenge. He tried to emulate Nick when he took the top position twelve years later.

   Both men were enjoying the rare chance to spend some time together working on this case, but they were also enjoying the camaraderie with Doc Mino and his panhandle gang. As expected, Nick was having a great time reminiscing with his old friend from their previous investigation conducted over fifty years ago. Since Nick's retirement, he hadn't had the chance to get out in the field and he was relishing every minute. He and George would have plenty of time to talk shop on their long drive home on Friday.

CHAPTER EIGHTEEN
HOLT COUNTY

As planned, George called Samuel Yellow Bear when they arrived in Chadron. A one o'clock meeting was confirmed at the Cody Husker Hub.

The men arrived at the small restaurant and bar and grabbed a table off to the side of the limited dining area. Pat, the owner, took their drink order while they waited.

Samuel arrived promptly at one. He was a tall, slender man in his late forties with a distinguished long, neatly combed black ponytail hanging from under his black Stetson cowboy hat. His long tresses were bound with a colorful braided bead tie which matched his hatband.

He was greeted by the waiting men immediately after entering the front door. The men exchanged some small talk after the introductions were made. After feasting on the house special of fried chicken gizzards, fried dill pickles and beer, the men settled in to hear Samuel Yellow Bear's stories.

His grandfather, Joe Yellow Bear, was adamant about passing the tribal history down t o his children and grandchildren. They were some of his most valued possessions and he took great pride sharing his elders' stories, stories that he'd cherished since his childhood. As the eldest of fourteen grandchildren, Samuel took special interest in the tales, realizing it would be his responsibility to pass them down to his children and future generations. He was an astute listener, just like his grandfather had been many years earlier.

Since his audience wanted to hear about the Jack People, Sam narrowed in on the tribal recollections of their experiences with the nasty little creatures. Although they could be pranksters and bring laughter to the tribe, they were greatly feared for the evil they could also bring. Jacks were to be avoided if at all possible. You never knew what to expect from them when they surfaced.

Joe shared some of their humorous tricks, but soon turned to two of the more brutal ones.

One included a young brave who was inexplicably mutilated while on a scouting party back in the 1870s. His listeners were extremely interested in how the young man was thought to have been taken down by some sort of small, sharp projectile thought to have been a poisonous porcupine quill. A fragment was found lodged in his upper left thigh.

The second story was even more astounding. It involved the murder and rape of a teenage Sioux girl. It sounded eerily similar to the 1959 unsolved murder of Leah Krzycki in a Hastings farm field. The fact that a braided horse tail was found around the same time of all three murders was probably not coincidental. It was becoming obvious there was a connection with these intricately woven tails and someone's impending death.

Nick had one question. Did Samuel have any idea where these deaths may have taken place? They were stunned by the answer.

Joe Yellow Bear had lived in Alliance, Nebraska most of his adult life, but he was raised in the hill country just east of Hemingford. For many years, their tribe controlled a stretch of land that ran from Alliance over into the Agate Fossil Beds another thirty miles west of the small ranching community.

There was a twenty mile stretch of forbidden land next to the buttes scattered around the area that was prohibited because it was known Jack territory. Strange events happened when someone trespassed across the unmarked boundary line and encroached up into the hill country. That's apparently what both of the young victims had done prior to their murder. They were probably killed for knowingly violating Jack territory. They'd been warned repeatedly by the elders since early childhood to avoid it, but as teenagers sometimes do, they chose to ignore it just once to test the theory. Their deaths further substantiated the tribe's belief that the land was truly bad medicine.

Their meeting with Samuel Yellow Bear lasted just short of ninety minutes. After picking up the check and thanking Samuel for his time and invaluable recollections, the men adjourned to the back parking lot of the Hub and stood silently next to their vehicles.

What they'd just heard was incredible. Again, Nick and George found Samuel to be a very sane, credible man. He was a proud Sioux who had no reason to bullshit two top state law officials.

The Jack People were no longer viewed as mythical creatures. They would now have to be considered real with a long history in this very area. The same neck of the woods where the two cattle mutilations took place, the same vicinity where the Bosworth ranch was located and the same locale where Jan Gradert had spotted the flying saucer!

Following a brief moment of silence, Doc finally asked the question, "Gentlemen, could the Jack People still exist in western Nebraska today? Is it at all possible that we may have violated their territory and disrupted one of their sacred burial sites this morning? What exactly are those bones in the trunk?"

The two cars stopped for gas in Valentine and proceeded on Highway 20 for the next two and a half hours to O'Neill. Jake phoned ahead to the Super 8 and made reservations for each of them in separate rooms.

After checking in, all five piled into Jake's Escalade and proceeded to the Town House Restaurant. They were meeting Jake's uncle, Hank Reimer, for dinner. Uncle Hank was a retired District Court Judge who had served for more than thirty years.

Coincidentally, he knew both Nick and George from their state legal careers. Although they'd never worked a case together, they would often run into each other at their annual State Bar Conventions held around the state.

After enjoying a great corn-fed Nebraska steak, the men adjourned to the bar at the back of the restaurant. George could trust the judge, but at the same time didn't want to give him all of the reasons they were so interested in coming up to O'Neill. He certainly didn't want to divulge their findings from earlier in the day. Even a sober judge would have trouble comprehending whatever it was they'd found.

What they did want to know dealt with the old newspaper report that surfaced in Gavin Aldama's article about a possible alien crash that had occurred back in the late 1880s somewhere in the O'Neill vicinity.

"Yes, there was a crash. My grandparents homesteaded in the Ewing area just twenty- five miles southeast of here, back around that time. Their one hundred and sixty acres w e r e on the other side of the Elkhorn River, across from the Stan Lundahl ranch.

It happened in the late spring of 1884. My grandmother used to tell me the story when I came to visit. By that time she was in her late 80s, and of course I was just a child. She gave some of the details of the crash, but over the years she had forgotten a lot of them.

What was written in the article was probably pretty accurate. Unfortunately, I'm unable to offer much more on that subject. As far as the rumor of alien bodies being buried in a cemetery, I'd say it was probably the Ewing Cemetery and not here in O'Neill like the story suggested.

I can, however, share another similar story with you that I'm very familiar with. As a judge that was involved in the case, I can tell you firsthand of the details surrounding it."

The men ordered another round of drinks and the judge proceeded. The story would prove to be icing on the cake.

"Junior Roberts was a well-known rodeo clown from O'Neill. He was born and raised in Holt County, graduated from high school here and got an early start in rodeoing quite by accident.

Our local Lions Club used to sponsor Rodeo Days, an amateur rodeo that coincided with the Holt County Fair held every July. Tom Early, the chapter president, was in charge of the rodeo. He had a last minute cancellation by the scheduled clown and Tom was desperate to find a replacement. Junior was a young, strapping teenager at the time who knew his way around farm livestock. He'd been raised on a ranch about ten miles west of O'Neill. Junior accepted Tom's offer to try his hand in the clowning business as a fill in, and the rest is history.

Junior took to it like a duck to water. Within a matter of just a couple years, he was working all of the major rodeos in Nebraska, South Dakota, Wyoming and Colorado. He got to be so good and well respected that in his later years he'd be asked to participate in some of the national rodeo events held in Texas, Las Vegas or California.

He'd load up his pickup with a miniature covered wagon. That was one prop in his act. The other was a tiny chariot he carried on top of his horse trailer. Both were pulled by one of Junior's three mules, which he rotated in and out of his shows.

He'd intermittently race both the chariot and the wagon around the arena, waving to the fans during the breaks between events or when he wasn't busy protecting the cowboys from wild bulls and broncs with his trusted broom and barrel. Anyways, he'd put the mule in his livestock trailer behind the pickup and away they'd go. He was gone every weekend during the three month summer rodeo season.

It was tough and dangerous work. Junior certainly wasn't a big man, but he was very athletic. He lettered all three years of high school in wrestling and made it to the state finals his senior year. A man in his line of work has to be in excellent shape. The young clown would load everything up before the break of day and drive all day to his destination for a Friday night and Saturday afternoon or evening rodeo. Junior would spend all day Sunday driving home. Oftentimes he wouldn't arrive back at his ranch until the wee hours of morning and then spend another hour or more unloading the truck and taking care of the mules, rain or shine. Next Friday morning it was the same process, except in a different town or state.

People don't realize just how important a good clown is to the safety of those exposed cowboys once they hit the ground. Riders can get killed by the large, mean animals. Rodeo clowns are also known as bull fighters. If a cowboy is hurt, the clown has to spring into immediate action without fear for their own safety to distract the animal so it can't inflict further injury to the downed cowboy or his rescuers. It takes nerves of steel to put your own life in danger to save another, going head to head with a nasty animal. They're bred to be mean and ornery, just like a racehorse is bred to be sleek and fast.

Junior broke a lot of bones over his thirty year career. He paid the price, but it was well worth it to him because he never lost a cowboy or even had one seriously hurt on his watch. He took a lot of pride in that fact.

He certainly didn't do it for the money. Most of his paycheck was spent on gas, repairs and doctor bills."

The waitress appeared to take another drink order. Hank ordered a Bud Light draft and continued after the brief but welcome interruption.

"I'd known Junior and his family for years. He married his high school sweetheart, Esther, and over the years they had two sons of their own, Robert and Marvin. When he wasn't on the

156

circuit, he'd raise cattle and some occasional hogs out on his 720 acres.

Because of the demands at home of feeding livestock and taking care of kids, his wife seldom traveled with Junior. Most of his time was spent behind the wheel of the pickup, and after a while she got bored. Esther would rather stay home.

One weekend, however, back in August of 1987, she accompanied him on a long trip to Pueblo, Colorado for the Colorado State Fair. Junior actually took several days off work and they were able to mix work with a little vacation time in nearby Colorado Springs. The two were driving home on a deserted stretch of Highway 385, just about ten miles north of the little town of Cheyenne Wells, Colorado. It was around nine-thirty on a Sunday night and they had the road to themselves.

All of a sudden, out of nowhere, came a large, bright light coming from some sort of saucer-shaped object hovering just above the hood of his truck. The alien craft stayed with the truck as Junior tried to outrun it. After a few miles, Junior frantically pulled the truck over on the shoulder of the road. The object vanished as fast as it had descended.

'What in the hell was that?' screamed his hysterical wife.

Of course, Junior had no answer. They both just sat in the seat for a minute and tried to gain their composure. Esther soon climbed out of the passenger side door for a much needed potty break.

Junior took a strong snort of the Jim Beam whiskey he had stored under the front seat. Before she could climb back in the truck, the object instantly appeared again out of the black sky, hovering motionless just about thirty feet above them. Both of them were paralyzed in fear.

Within seconds, an extraordinarily thin and bright beam of light surrounded her and slowly drew her upward into the craft. She was screaming hysterically and thrashing her body in the air in an unsuccessful attempt to free herself from its grip. A few seconds later, she vanished into the darkness. That was the last time Junior Roberts saw his wife.

Junior didn't know what to do. He was alone on this deserted Colorado road, sitting in total shock. He'd faced thousands of life threatening, scary situations in his days, but he knew what he was dealing with. Nothing would compare to what had just happened. Could he be having a nightmare? This certainly couldn't happen in real life. Where was Esther?

He got out of the truck and screamed her name while frantically scouring the limited area illuminated by his truck headlights. Nothing. Junior decided to get back in the truck and go back to Cheyenne Wells. Maybe he could get help there or at least use a phone.

The small town of Cheyenne Wells was home to just over 800 residents. Since it was the county seat in rural eastern Colorado, they did have a County Sheriff's Department. Junior quickly reached in the back of his truck and pulled out his red spare gas can and sat it off to the side of the road to mark his location.

He made the twelve mile trip back into town in a matter of minutes. There was nothing open this late at night, so Junior drove down Main Street figuring the Sheriff's Department would be there. He was right.

Junior tried to open the glass door but it was locked, although there were several lights on in the building. He immediately began pounding on the door and yelling, "Please help me! My wife has been abducted! Please, you've got to help!" he pleaded.

When the night duty officer unlocked the door, Junior told him his unbelievable story. Since he was the only officer on duty, he quickly called the sheriff and relayed the story. Fifteen minutes, later Sheriff Bob Frank arrived at the station and he and Junior were soon on the road looking for the gas can.

Sheriff Frank did a preliminary search of the area with his flashlight and found nothing. Esther had vanished into thin air, if there even was an Esther.

The law officer found the story to be rather odd. The man telling them the story was visibly upset with a slight hint of alcohol on his breath, but seemed to be in control of his capacities well enough to vividly recall the incident. Needless to say, it would be a hard report to write.

There was one motel in the small hamlet. Sheriff Frank assured Junior a complete search of the area would be made in the early daylight hours and they'd expand the search statewide if necessary. The two men agreed to meet at the station at seven A.M. the next morning.

The search again revealed nothing. There was no more Junior could do by staying in Cheyenne Wells and hoping Esther would miraculously appear. He decided to continue the eight hour ride home to O'Neill. He had responsibilities at home that needed his attention, and he did have control of them. Staying here drowning in worry was not the best plan. If his gut feeling indicated any ray of hope, he'd stay, but it was telling him otherwise.

Junior knew that fear could paralyze a person and he'd witnessed the tragic results far too often in the rodeo arena. He'd found out more often than not that if he took immediate action to aggressively deal with the fear, he'd end up safely on the other side of it. Inaction and worry reap nothing positive.

The days turned into months. After two years, Junior gave up hope. He'd been investigated and cleared of any wrongdoing in his wife's strange disappearance. It was time to take the required action and get Esther declared legally dead from unknown circumstances.

Junior came to my office in February of 1989 and asked for my help. As I said, I'd known the young man all of his life. O'Neill is a small town and he knew I was the best person to get his request legally authorized by the state for insurance purposes. He had a fifty thousand dollar life insurance policy that would go a long way towards providing for his children's needs. I gladly obliged and waived my fee.

Junior Roberts told me in detail the events that surrounded that unforgettable weekend. To this man, it was like it had happened yesterday. He told me how the weekend started just like they always do prior to shows. He had everything loaded in the pickup and was walking out to the pasture where the mules were kept.

He noticed something unusual about Jezebel as he approached the three animals with their buckets of oats. His mule had a strange braid in his tail. The braid was meticulously woven in a design that Junior couldn't readily identify. He thought it was very peculiar, but wasn't something he had time to deal with at the time. He needed to put Buster in the trailer and get on the road. Pueblo was a good ten hour drive.

With the tragic events that soon followed, Junior forgot all about the mule until he arrived home early Monday morning. With everything racing through his mind, Jezebel's tail certainly wasn't a priority. Over the next couple of weeks, the detail was gone and only a messy ball of twisted tail hair remained. Junior thought nothing of it and eventually cut out the matted clump.

He hadn't told anyone about the event except when relating the entire story to me. Like a veteran cop, a judge has a sixth sense when it comes to liars. Junior was telling the honest to God truth regarding his wife's strange disappearance.

It's certainly the most baffling case I'd ever been involved with, and it haunts me to this day.

I still see Junior occasionally at the courthouse or the cattle auctions. He's moved on with his life. He re-married. He was nearly killed in the last rodeo of the season seven years ago over in Norfolk. A bull stepped on his head and fractured a good portion of his left outer skull. He lost all hearing in his left ear and it left him blind in the left eye. He wears a metal plate in his head as a reminder. That was the end of Junior's career. It had been a good ride, but it was time for him to hang it up.

He'd been elected Holt County Clerk about twenty years prior and serving two masters during rodeo season was taking its toll. He's near retirement now and turned over a lot of his ranching responsibilities to his nephew. Junior Roberts is a good man, but he's sure had his share of hard knocks. His strong will and belief in God carried him through."

Nick and George were familiar with Hank's story, but since the case crossed state lines, the investigation was turned over to the Colorado authorities. They had forgotten that Junior Roberts was from O'Neill. Now Hank dumped it squarely back into their laps. This incredible story they'd just heard from the judge played right into their current investigation.

Another braided tail connected with an unexpected death? Another female alien abduction? There was little doubt that Esther's body had eventually been dumped somewhere out in the rugged Rocky Mountains, never to be found.

The night was getting late and the out of town visitors had a long day ahead of them. The Ewing Cemetery would be their first stop in the morning.

Before departing the Town House parking lot, Nick asked Hank to step over to the Taurus. He wanted to show him a picture that he might be interested in seeing. He reached into his briefcase in the trunk and pulled out the picture of the braided tail that Chief Tews had taken out at the Krzycki farm in Hastings roughly fifty-five years ago.

161

"Junior's mule probably had something similar to this tied in his tail."

Hank studied the photo under the dim parking lot light and shook his head in disbelief, but realized this was horse country. After a slight hesitation, the judge turned to Nick and said, "Nick, you need to realize a number of horse owners around the country take a lot of time and pride in plaiting their horse tails. There are two ladies here in O'Neill that enter their braided tails and manes every year at the State Fair in Grand Island. A lot of people, especially women, love to take the time to do this extraordinarily time consuming hobby. Actually, Terry Jo Peterson and her husband, Kent, are good friends of ours. She's one of the ladies I just mentioned. I've seen some of her work. According to her, plaiting was believed to have originated from several possibilities. Gypsies were thought to be the first to practice the procedure. Others say that Satanists or even the Supernatural originated the practice. The Mexicans believed it was El Duende, horse loving dwarves that lived deep in the canyons and desolate valleys who started the whole braid thing. My point is, it is not uncommon and certainly not new. It's been done for many, many years. Maybe we should show these pictures to them and get their opinion before we jump to conclusions."

After a moment of silence Nick spoke. "Judge, we're on official business up here and we could sure use your help. It's not just the braided tail. There's more. I can fill you in on the details tomorrow if you're interested."

This was his turf and he knew practically everyone in the county. He could be very valuable if a permit or even a warrant was needed on the spot. The judge was glad to oblige.

The Escalade made the short drive back to the motel. Just as the vehicle pulled into the parking lot, Yollie instantly sprang to full alert in the back window and gave out a low growl.

162

The startled men got a brief glimpse of the cause of her alarm. Eight large jackrabbits were sitting motionless in an empty dirt parking lot across the street from the motel entrance, about twenty yards away. Standing beside them were eight small Jack People, staring them directly in the eye. They wanted to be seen briefly in the bright headlights before disappearing into the total darkness.

A loud and harmonious "HOLY SHIT LOOK AT THAT!!" reverberated out into the night's freezing silence.

CHAPTER NINETEEN
THE SAVANT'S WARNING
THURSDAY, DAY FOUR

Nick and Doc had been working this case for over fifty years. They'd heard a lot of very credible testimonials regarding some very unbelievable events, yet they had believed them. Seeing the unthinkable, finally after all these years, with their own eyes brought a very strange sense of closure to the seasoned veterans. The case hadn't been solved yet, but it gave all of them newfound hope that they were certainly going in the right direction. The evidence they'd heard and now seen firsthand in just the last two days was overwhelming.

After a continental breakfast in the motel lobby, the caravan picked up Hank and proceeded to Ewing in their two vehicles. Doc read the Gavin Aldama newspaper story regarding the crash again just to bring the judge up to snuff.

Hank led the small procession on a tour of the barren rural landscape surrounding Clearwater, Nebraska. After driving for what seemed to be an eternity out in the middle of nowhere, Hank told Jake to turn off the road to the barbed wire gate coming up on the right and stop the car. He quickly got out to open the gate and let the two cars proceed before closing it behind them. A few minutes later, the cars stopped.

"This is the place where the crash reportedly happened. It's hard to recognize and appreciate this spot with all of the prairie covered in snow and tall prairie grass, but as you can see, this particular spot right here has nothing growing on it; not even a weed. It's like this year-round.

The Lundahl family, who owned the property at the time, are all long gone. It's changed ownership a number of times over the last one hundred and some odd years. Terry Harpster, the current owner, probably doesn't even know of the story that happened right here on his place. I wanted to show you exactly how remote the land is out here."

"Just for giggles, let's see if the spot is radioactive. Jake, can you please get the Geiger counter?"

As suspected, the counter went off the charts.

"It's simply amazing how long this stuff lasts! If there are any aliens in the cemetery, this machine should sing like a canary!" exclaimed Nick.

"Hopefully the son of a bitch will just sing and not fall over dead," quipped Doc, giving his trademark mischievous wink.

Thirty minutes later, they were at the front gate of the Ewing cemetery, located several miles south of the small town. Both Hank and Jake had several generations of relatives buried there and they were very familiar with it.

The judge got out of the car and led the men down the center dirt road that divided the little community graveyard. He pointed out a number of interesting graves as they enjoyed the serenity the hallowed ground had to offer.

"This fella here, Carl Pierce, was my great uncle. He was helping a neighbor move a house with a team of horses and a wagon just around the turn of the century. A corner of the house got hung up on a tree branch. The branch didn't break, but when it cleared itself of the house, it whipped loose like an over-wound spring and caught Uncle Carl in the head. Killed him instantly. I was told it almost took his head off.

Probably half of my relatives in here were killed in similar instances. This was a tough and dangerous place to be back in those days. If the severe weather or a serious illness didn't get you, a runaway team of horses could. Bill Ralston, my second cousin on

Mom's side, buried over here, can attest to a team of horses. He was run over right down on Main Street back around the turn of the century. Bill was only twenty-three and left a young bride and two small children. They're buried here next to him."

Rural Nebraska served up another cold December morning on a frost-covered platter. Everything for miles around was covered in a glistening white glaze as the sun slowly rose over the frozen tundra.

Their breath billowed out a temporarily visible cloud of warm air that soon evaporated back into space.

The trip so far was throwing them a lot of unexpected, unimaginable clues and it was nice to enjoy the frozen solitude, even if they were walking through a cemetery. It was a very peaceful, serene walk.

Yollie, on the other hand, was scurrying all around the grounds. As a matter of fact, she'd probably made her rounds several times by now and was enjoying every new sniff available to her keen sense of smell.

Hank stopped in the middle of the graveyard. "The old section of the cemetery is back over there in the far northeast corner. There are a few unmarked paupers' graves next to the back fence. I suggest we start there."

Jake led the group towards the back corner with rented Geiger counter in hand, although a golf club or shotgun would have seemed more appropriate with this motley group. He scoured every grave in the section as the others watched and listened to Uncle Hank's family history in this area. After a twenty minute search, he shut the instrument off.

"Sorry guys, looks like we're out of luck."

Cold and dejected, the six-some stood in silence. They had been hoping to strike the mother lode here, but instead they were coming up empty-handed. It was exciting to think of the possibility of uncovering something that had never been seen before, except for m a y b e a limited few gathered deep in the bowels of Area 51 some seventy years ago, after the Roswell incident.

It certainly was fun to dream of the men standing next to the proof that aliens actually do exist and have their pictures posted on the front page of every newspaper in the world. A line would have to be drawn to the TV appearances they'd make and exactly how much of their story could be revealed. What's the going rate these days for Oprah's guests? Could they stay in the Lincoln room when visiting the White House? Their names had better be spelled right in the history books. Speaking of books, there certainly would be substantial advances handed out to each of them for their printed story. Jake had his i Phone digital camera in his left coat pocket just for the occasion. Think of just the p i c t u r e royalties!

Each individual offered up a fresh serving of *What if?* What if there was no crash and it was just a hoax? What if it did happen, but they were looking in the wrong spot? What if the bodies were buried in the nearby private Reimer Wulf cemetery further up the road another eight miles? What if the bodies weren't radioactive? What if the aliens w e r e buried somewhere else like in O'Neill, Emmet, Clearwater or Neligh? Maybe they should go to the little ghost town of Venus, located twelve miles east of O'Neill. Why was it named Venus anyhow? What if predators dug up the unmarked shallow graves and ate the evidence? What if the alien craft was powered by something the Geiger counter wouldn't pick up? What if someone beat them to the punch many years ago before mass media and their find went to the grave with them? What if the remains were handed out as special mementos?

What if, what if, what if. For a brief few minutes their constant chatter could compete with any teenaged girl's slumber party.

Suddenly Hank silenced the silly cycle. "What if the aliens were buried *outside* the cemetery? After all, this is sacred ground to those that are buried here. The Christian families would not want something not of Earth to be buried here among their loved ones, would they? I think we're looking in the wrong spot."

The judge carefully crawled through the barbed wire fence and turned to ask Jake for the Geiger counter.

"Let's try **this** side of the fence line."

Hank wandered around the open field that neighbored the cemetery. It took him a little over an hour to get the long rod with the saucer on the end singing like the little canary they hoped it was. He was getting a reading.

"Let's start digging here, guys."

A quick question was posed to the judge by George. "Don't we need a warrant to exhume a body, Hank?"

"Nope, not in this case. There is no legal documentation of a recorded burial here and secondly, this is outside the cemetery boundary. For all we know we could be digging up a dead coyote. We're good!"

If a District Court judge said they're good, there was no need for further discussion.

Jake handed a shovel to his uncle and kept one for himself. The two slowly and carefully began turning up the frozen black soil. About three feet down, a piece of rotted wood exposed itself with the turn of Jake's shovel. Nick got down on his knees and began some detailed excavating with his gloved hand.

There wasn't much left of the wood box. It could have been an old packing crate someone used as a makeshift casket.

With a little more dirt removal, Nick began uncovering the remains they were searching for. George and Jake snapped some

168

pictures to document their find. Nick carefully began picking the few remaining bones out of the decayed boards and handing them up to Doc. He delicately placed them in the bottom of a cardboard box Jake had stored in the trunk.

Most of the fragile bones had charred marks indicating they'd been exposed to severe heat at one point. Many of them were cracked or broken. They may have been damaged from the crash or by just the weight of the decaying box and dirt caving in on them. It was difficult to determine exactly what part of the skeleton they came from or how many skeletons there might be.

This would be have to be sorted out later in the Lincoln lab. No one had ever seen an alien skeleton before, and they had no clue as to how these pieces might fit together.

Their find was certainly not as they'd expected. A dozen small, broken and charred bones do not necessarily prove beyond a doubt they were alien bones. No skulls or larger, intact bones were found. If they existed, they were probably taken by those that found them in the first place as a souvenir.

Although their findings at this point were purely speculation, they were confident of what their lab findings might later prove to be true. The few bones they did manage to retrieve did light up the Geiger counter. This wouldn't be the case with regular animal bones.

By now it was past noon and hunger began to overtake their excitement. Nick placed the box in the trunk of the Taurus. To make sure the bones from the Bosworth ranch weren't left in Jake's Escalade, Nick shouted "Hey Jake, can I get those bones from yesterday? I don't want to forget them. While you're there, why don't you hand me the quiver? I promise I'll personally return it to you after we get the labwork completed."

Jake obliged and closed the rear hatch door.

Since their restaurant options were slim in Ewing, the decision on where to eat was easy. Hank made the only choice. "Gentlemen, let me buy you lunch at DW's Pub. Drinks are on the house!"

Parking was always readily accessible in downtown Ewing. If you couldn't pull into a curb spot, you could just park in the center of the exceptionally wide Main Street. Two open spots in front of the little town pub were waiting to be filled. After a quick bathroom rush, the group congregated at an unoccupied front table by the large antique Wurlitzer jukebox close to the front window overlooking Main Street.

Since DW's was the only bar and eating establishment in town, the place always drew a crowd at meal time. Their food was good and reasonably priced. Coffee was the preferred drink of the locals at this time of day. The out of town guests broke rank and ordered two pitchers of Bud Light and six frosted mugs. Food orders were promptly delivered by a friendly barmaid who doubled as bartender.

From past experience, he knew this little bar was a friendly and trusting place. Several years ago Hank stopped in for a beer around three in the afternoon. The place was e m p t y , except for the bar owner.

"Mister, I've got to go pick up my kids at school. I'll be back in twenty minutes. If someone else comes in or you need another beer just help yourself. We'll settle up when I get back," she politely stated.

Hank was impressed with her complete trust. Not only for the drinks and liquor inventory, but the cash register itself. You'd never have any bar in the city do that. It gave him renewed faith in his fellow man and it felt extremely good coming from the judge's point of view. Hank thought maybe he was being too kind and maybe she recognized him as the District Court Judge. A lot of people knew him, but he might not know them.

"That must be the case," he thought. "Very nice gesture all the same."

The excitement level was high, but professional discretion prevailed. George again asked Hank of any legal ramifications that might surface later. The judge gave the same answer he'd given them out at the cemetery.

Nick reminded his friends that their finding was an indirect result of an informal pending murder investigation. He gave the two vets and Jake a brief lesson on what that meant. There would be no discussion of their findings with anyone outside of this table. That wasn't just from this morning at the cemetery, this was for everything that was being disclosed during the week. Until Nick and George could conclusively prove their findings, they had nothing other than a wild imagination. George and Hank concurred with the legal advice.

As he had promised Hank last night before leaving the Town House, Nick came clean with the judge about what brought them to Holt County. This was his jurisdiction and he c o u l d obviously be trusted.

Now that some bones were found, he was also a witness in the investigation. The *whole* investigation. Nick and George took the next hour to bring the judge up to speed on the long-standing mystery. No doubt about it, their findings so far in the week were extraordinary.

That brought up the last and most important topic that they must all agree upon. The case was like no other case in modern times. How much of it needed to be divulged? Would it be in the public's best interest to do so?

Jack People, cattle mutilations and now aliens might set off mass hysteria. Were they somehow connected or were they just a coincidence? Where should the line be drawn?

The men sitting around the table would be excellent choices to make that preliminary decision. The Feds would get involved. Could they face repercussions for breaching some national security laws? This was a serious matter and would not be taken lightly. For all they knew, they could end up dead if their secret was considered classified by an uppity government bureaucrat.

Some very important decisions needed to be made in the very near future if their findings tested out to be what they thought they were.

A final decision could be made when the verification was official, but some preparation might be in order. The challenge gave them all something very important to think about with little time to come up with a concrete plan.

The men watched out the front window as a dirty Nissan Maxima pulled into an open parking spot in front of DW's. A woman and a young boy got out of the car and hurried into the restaurant. The two took a table next to theirs.

Jake decided to change the subject and talk about the pending Husker Florida Citrus Bowl game on New Year's Day against Georgia. The others immediately followed the lead and opinions began flying. There were many years of loyal Nebraska fans sitting around the table, and for that matter, the whole bar. The conversation bounced from present players and how they stacked up against the many talented athletes that had come through the revered system.

Doc asked the table a trivia question. "Say fellas, who is Nebraska's all-time leading rusher?"

The guys thought for a minute. There were so many names to choose from over the years. Which one of the greats held this honor? Could it be Roger Craig, Jarvis Redwine, Bobby Reynolds, Johnny Rogers, Lawrence Phillips, Ahman Green? All were tossed at the Doc, but not the right answer he was looking for.

Suddenly the young boy sitting at the next table blurted out in his high pitched voice, "It was Mike Rosier. 2,148 yards and 29 touchdowns. He played for the Huskers from 1981 to 1983. The second leading rusher is Lawrence Phillips, who would have been number one if wasn't for a five game suspension in his junior year. He ran for 165 yards in the 1996 Fiesta Bowl against #2 Florida to lead the Huskers to a second back-to-back National Championship. The Huskers have won five national championships, second only to Alabama with eight."

The five men quizzically looked back to see the lad who had just answered Doc's question and more. The small-statured boy remained sitting in his chair with his back towards them.

"Why, young man, that was very impressive. If you'd care to join us on another question, we'd be glad to pay for your meal if you answer it right," Doc excitedly replied.

This kid was the break they all needed to unwind after unearthing their cemetery treasure.

The youth stood up and turned to the men. They were immediately drawn to his lack of size, disproportionate head and piercing black eyes. The frail young boy exposed his long, slender fingers as he fidgeted with his hands while he stood before them, anxiously waiting for the question.

"How many Outland Trophy winners has Nebraska produced for the Defensive Player of the Year Award?" Doc politely asked.

"Mister, that's easy. The award originated in 1946. Since that time, nine Huskers have won the award, but there were ten winners total from Nebraska. Dave Rimington won it twice in 1981 and 1982. Ndamukong Suh, a defensive tackle, was the last Husker recipient in 2009. The first was Larry Jacobson in 1971, followed by Rich Glover in 1972, Dave Rimington, Dean

Steinkuhler in 1983, Will Shields in 1992, Zack Wiegert in 1994 and Aaron Taylor in 1997."

"Heisman Trophy winners?" George blurted.

Without batting an eye, the boy calmly replied without hesitation, "Johnny Rogers in 1972, Mike Rozier in 1983 and Eric Crouch in 2001."

"What year did Bob Devaney die?" fired Jake.

"He died May 9, 1997 at age 82 in Lincoln of unspecified causes, but probably due to a heart attack. He coached the Huskers from 1962 to 1972. His record was 101-20-2 and h e was inducted to the College Football Hall of Fame in 1981. His Husker teams of '70 and '71 won back to back National Championships," came the response, all in the same breath.

"Speaking of coaches, where is Tom Osborne from?" Jake asked again.

"That's so easy! He's from Hastings. Graduated from high school in 1955 and played quarterback for Hastings College before being drafted by the Washington Redskins in 1959."

The table began applauding this little walking Husker encyclopedia, as did the rest of the patrons in the restaurant.

"Son, that is truly amazing! What's your name?" asked Nick. "My name is Egon Harrasser." Nick shook young Egon's hand and followed up with the next question. "Egon, how old are you?"

The boy stared Nick straight in the eyes, defiantly crossed his arms and refused to answer the question.

His mother politely interrupted. "Sir, Egon isn't being rude. He has what is known as Savant Syndrome. You can ask any question related to Nebraska football and he'll give you the correct answer in a heartbeat. Ask him simple questions like his age and he's clueless. Been that way since birth. He's lucky to be alive. There were many complications. To answer your question though, he's seven years old."

Egon sat back down at the table and picked up his cheeseburger from his plate and took another bite while his shy mother cautiously continued the small talk with the six curious admirers at the table across from them.

Before their impromptu conversation, Egon's mother had been sitting silently, eating her meal, not even taking the time to look up at the men. The woman was also small in stature and very timid. She made a token attempt to acknowledge her son's new admirers.

"Are you folks from the Ewing area?" asked Mark.

"No sir, we're just passing through. We're from around Hemingford and on our way home," was her soft, almost inaudible response.

The woman spoke with an accent, but due to the fact that her voice was difficult to hear, George couldn't identify the origin. If he had to guess, it may have been German. She obviously wasn't interested in engaging in any lengthy conversation.

Mark had Nebraska season tickets for the past twenty years and never missed a game. "Mrs. Harrasser, if you wouldn't mind, I'd like to get your address. It would be my honor to have you and your son attend a game with me and my wife. I'm a responsible person and here, I'll give you my card that explains who I am. I certainly can be trusted and I'd love for you and Egon to actually attend a game. I'd gladly pay all expenses. It would be my treat."

The woman quickly scribbled on the back of Mark's card:

Egon Harrasser
905 Elm St.
Hemingford, NE
308-779-3349

Mark took the card with the information, shook the mother's hand and placed another one of his cards into it. He turned and grabbed the check from their table and patted Egon on the back.

"You won the bet son. Congratulations! You sure know your Nebraska football! You folks be careful on the way home," Mark politely warned.

Before he could turn and leave, the fragile boy quickly looked up with his piercing cold eyes, grabbed the veterinarian's hand with a firm grip and softly sneered. "Better be careful yourself, mister fancy-pants veterinarian."

Mark pulled his hand away and continued towards the bar register to pay the tab, with his entourage tailing close behind.

Once outside, he turned to his boisterous friends and asked, "Did you guys hear that?"

All five men nodded their heads. "I wonder just what the hell the kid meant? How did he know I was a veterinarian; he certainly didn't see my card."

"Aw, forget it Mark. He probably thought you were hitting on his mother. By the way, were you?" Doc teased. "As you can see, the boy isn't quite right in the head. If it doesn't pertain to the Huskers, you can't believe anything he's saying or even understand him. He has a strange accent, just like his mother."

By now the snow was falling and the late afternoon sky was covered in an ominous gray blanket of gloom. Hank hopped in the passenger seat of the Escalade with Jake while the four others climbed into the Taurus for their half hour ride back to O'Neill. Jake planned to spend some time with his aunt and uncle back at the house over dinner, so they'd ride together. He'd see the guys in the lobby around eight tomorrow morning for breakfast.

As the two cars slowly approached the outskirts of Ewing, the men saw several buckskin horses huddled near the highway fence line. Hank loved horses and wanted a closer look at the beauties. This was a good time for Yollie to stretch her legs after being cooped up in the car for the last two hours. Besides, Jake had bought a hamburger for her and didn't want her eating it in the car. He slowly pulled the Escalade over to the shoulder.

The Taurus pulled up on his driver side and Jake lowered his window. "You guys go on ahead. We'll be along shortly. I'll see you down in the lobby around eight in the morning." he shouted.

Jake and his uncle got out of the car and walked over to the horses through the accumulating snowfall. The three horses were huddling close to each other for warmth. As the two men and dog approached the fence, the horses cautiously broke rank and separated.

Jake immediately picked up on what stood before him in the fading shadows of light that remained. One of the horses had a braided tail! The immaculately tied but unrecognizable pattern had been woven with great detail.

"Holy shit, Uncle Hank, will you look at that!"

Jake hurriedly reached for his cell phone to call for the others to turn around and witness their strange, but very relevant find. Total silence. He had never experienced any signal outages in his previous trips to O'Neill. His battery indicator showed a full charge. Maybe it was the snowy weather or maybe it was some unforeseen force at work, but the call could not be completed. All he heard was the frightening silence, which sent an instant chill up his spine and dissipated in an unexpected shudder. Jake had an ominous feeling in his gut. Something was wrong.

177

"Never mind Hank. I'll take a picture and show it to them in the morning.

CHAPTER TWENTY

ABDUCTED

The last ray of fading daylight disappeared over the frozen horizon as the Taurus tracked north on Highway 20 towards O'Neill. The snow covered headlights dimly radiating on the ice-packed road looked like a narrow, dull stretch of pale gray ribbon being threaded through the desolate, barren black eye of the foreboding needle that   lingered in the distance.

The snowy darkness made the night seem even colder. Nick, George, Mark and Doc were looking forward to their warm, comfortable motel rooms and a little private down time from their long, grueling day. By the same token, it had been a very exciting day that none of the men would ever forget.

Their idle chitchat was suddenly interrupted when a large, bright and shining saucer- shaped object incredibly appeared and started hovering just ten feet above the hood of the car. The startled men froze in fear.

"Slow down and pull over, George!" yelled Nick. "Let's see if it keeps going!"

George slowly applied the brakes on the snow swirled road, dropping their speed down to forty miles an hour. The craft immediately responded and maintained its position.

Doc suggested they maintain their current speed and continue on to O'Neill. This intimidating, menacing object had definitely gotten their undivided attention, but other than scaring the crap out of them, it hadn't yet posed any physical threat.

"Just focus on the road and hopefully it'll vanish when we get closer to town," the old vet exclaimed. "Maybe we'll meet an oncoming car that will bear witness to these monkeys, or even scare them away!"

Since their options were slim and none, George took Doc's advice. All eyes were alternating from the dark road ahead up to the massive and unrecognizable bright light above, hoping to see it disappear into the night just as fast as it had appeared.

After proceeding another five terrifying miles along the deserted road, it was evident that their plan wasn't working. Whatever it was obviously wasn't going anywhere.

A sudden, loud bang resonated inside the car as the Taurus was instantaneously plucked up off the road. George no longer had control of the car. The stunned men looked at each other in total shock.

Their pale, panic stricken faces silently screamed, *What in the hell is going on!*

The car was now methodically being raised upward off the road. Within a matter of seconds, the Taurus was literally swallowed up into the belly of the beast. The four occupants were cast into total darkness, and a sudden burst of incredible forward thrust of G force snapped their seatbelted bodies backward into an immediate blackout.

Nick painfully began to regain consciousness. His head was throbbing, his vision was blurred and his entire body ached. He had no recollection of what had transpired or how long he'd been out. His normal thought process was impaired, probably with some s o r t o f sedative that would hopefully wear off soon.

As he slowly became more cognizant of his surroundings, he frantically tried to focus his scrambled thoughts toward his friends. A dim blue light hung over his head, but it gave him no clues to differentiate reality from the surreal. He tried to move his body but he felt nothing. His limited awareness and visual range did indicate he was strapped to some sort of hard surface, lying on his back. He tried to yell for help, but no sound came out. He was being held prisoner in the confines of a very active room.

His position suddenly began changing from horizontal to vertical, and the reality of his situation began to drain back into his thought process. This was no dream. As his head began to clear, his thought process filled with escalating horror, like the slow but constant flow of tap water about to fill a bucket. He was staring at an extended wrap-around control panel which sat directly in front of a narrow window that contoured the exterior of the room.

Although visibility was poor, he sensed he was in the air, hovering above the Earth's surface. Some of the strange, unrecognizable markings he'd seen etched in the quiver and braided into the horse tail were now in front of him, illuminated in various sizes and colors on the large control panel. He could differentiate a magnitude of stars above and a few scattered ground lights below. He was somewhere in the middle of nowhere.

Standing before him were four, frail-looking creatures with large black eyes bulging from large elongated heads that were disproportionate in size to their four-foot frames. Their noses and mouths were also out of proportion. Their facial features were exactly the same with no clues to differentiate them from one another. They were hairless, with a pallid gray skin tone, and they were clothed in long robe-like garments.

At their side was a much smaller creature with similar features, but it certainly was not identical in appearance. He had drooping eyelids over his large, bulging black eyes and his large head featured a distinct, slanted forehead. He stood less than two feet tall and wore what looked to be a rabbit skin robe, which covered his entire body from head to toe.

The two very distinguishable features he possessed over the others were the ornately marked quiver draped over his shoulder and Nick's own recognizable Nebraska State Patrol badge pinned on the front of his rabbit hide coat.

This creature stepped forward, approached Nick and spoke directly to him in perfect, high pitched English.

"My name is We-Ota-Wichasha. I believe you have something of ours and we're here to reclaim them but first, I want to show you something. You've earned the privilege."

Nick was unable to speak. He wanted to tell that furry little prick to give him back his badge and gun, but it felt like his vocal chords were somehow immobilized, assuming they hadn't been removed.

Maybe what he had to say had been heard too many times before, and it was becoming very predictable, predictable to the point that these beings didn't want to hear what any human had to say. The cocky little shit could probably just read his thoughts anyway if he really wanted to know what he was thinking. It was obvious to Nick he didn't.

With a simple gesture of his hand, the restraints holding Nick were released. He began to get some feeling back in his appendages, although they were greatly limited. He could move, but very slowly. The thought of overpowering these much smaller and weaker beings that seemed to be unarmed briefly crossed his mind, but his body could not cooperate. Besides, where would he go? Jumping out the window of a flying saucer was not a good option. Whatever they'd put in his system was still there, and he was totally at their mercy.

Another simple motion opened a sliding metal door into a confined area flooded in light. The initial sight was so repugnant that Nick fell to his knees and tried, once again in vain, to scream.

The high, voice-recording type sound from his captor was heard once again. "Get up now, or I will get you up."

Nick regained his posture as his group of captors escorted him down what resembled some sort of sickening human assembly line. In front of them were three separate surgical tables holding the bodies of his buddies. Presiding over each table were two of the taller creatures. Their intent was very obvious to Nick now. His friends were being dissected in different stages, right in front of him. Doc was on the closest table, then George and lastly, Mark. They were being filleted like trout.

Three distinct robotic arms attached above the table would instantly yet meticulously spring into motion as they were needed.

The first arm would mechanically float over the body and spray a purplish gel over the cadaver for sterilization and to chemically dissolve a minute strip of unwanted fur or hair directly in front of the desired area for a more precise cut. After the process, it would automatically kick back to position out of the operator's way. A second arm would immediately follow. Several probes were injected into various points of the carotid and femoral arteries and a powerful vacuum attachment would forcefully suck out every drop of fluid. The same process was repeated in the body cavity to remove any liquids in the internal organs. The arm also kicked up out of the way after completing its process.

The third arm had two large grips on each side of what appeared to be some sort of a laser. It could be easily guided by the operator to remove the desired body part with extreme precision. The removed flesh and bone would be rinsed in some sort of chemical bath before being placed in a pan and given to the other attending creature. The freshly harvested organs or body parts were taken away.

A complete set of new replacement parts would soon be brought back on a large tray and then meticulously and precisely reinserted into an adjacent clone by the second alien on another line, directly behind and running parallel to the first.

It was obvious to Nick that both creatures had two distinct jobs. One would control the cutting and removing of parts from the corpse while the other was responsible for replacing and reinstalling the freshly, genetically altered parts back into the prefabricated clone shell. The flawless system of taking out parts and putting new ones in looked like they were playing with Legos.

Nick closed his eyes and wept in silence as he was led through the room. The sickening stench was partially removed by a powerful but very quiet exhaust.

Beyond the three tables holding his friends were four more tables, two of which held cattle cadavers. A similar process was being done with the cattle parts, but these parts would go through another cycle. The freshly removed animal parts would be taken away and replaced with fresh, genetically altered parts compatible with a human clone that lay just a few feet away.

We-Ota-Wichasha took the time at each of the stations to explain exactly what his prisoner was seeing.

"We, or what you refer to as the Jack People, are a dying race. We can no longer compete in today's complicated world. We now depend on the human race for our altered future survival. I'm sure you've heard the term *if you can't lick em, join em*. That's what we've been doing now for the past fifty years.

I've been keeping tabs on your relentless interest in our species. As you can obviously see, I have help in my simple mining operation here in Nebraska. This species of extraterrestrials has visited your Earth many, many times and left indelible marks that y o u still have no explanation for.

My people are direct descendants, left here on Earth to find fuel, food and information on this planet and its inhabitants. At one time, our numbers around the planet were many, but we're now the last of a dying breed. We were able to adapt to this harsh terrain in small numbers to accomplish the tasks requested in simpler times. Your world has become more complex and by doing so, you are making my people extinct. It's time for us to take the next step in our conquest over the humans that have slowly been taking our limited and shrinking territory.

We prefer to take Angus or Hereford cattle now for our needs, although we still depend on a smaller number of humans to reproduce. We use the female for breeding and the male for parts. We're using more cattle, however, since their DNA closely resembles that of humans in the cloning process.

It depends on which purpose we desire to fill. If we just want to infiltrate the masses and spread our own programmed, desirable characteristics through future human generations, we'll go with the clones. They're sloppy, but do what they're told. At this stage of the process, they're relatively fast and easy to produce. For the most part the clone's sole purpose is to breed. If necessary, they will fight and brutally kill on command. They don't have to think, work or otherwise contribute to your race. They're simply a number and are easily replaceable or reprogrammed. Sometimes they fit into your society and sometimes they don't. We don't care. Most end up in your prisons for a multitude of reasons, but they all reproduce.

If we need looks, intelligence, personality, charm, wit or any other beneficial human characteristic that suits a specific need in your society such as a movie star, college professor or politician, we can program one of our successfully inbred human offspring for the task.

Unlike your popular beliefs, not all of these seemingly important humans have to be good looking. Remember Peter Lorre, Jack Palance or Henry Waxman? They're all one of us.

These highly desirable half-humans are somewhat capable of love and emotions when it benefits them, but are merciless when it comes to benefiting mankind. They have ulterior motives that work in our favor. I'll introduce you to a few of them later.

Your concept of common sense, fairness, compassion and religion does not exist in this species. Some make it to higher levels than others, but all leave their mark in some way on your society and its values. Their sole purpose is to lower the values

185

and morals of the human race, not raise them. If we can destroy you from within your own societal norms, we win. War is passé. We've had patience over the past several centuries, but they're now being pushed. Your recent deployment of atomic weapons and their growing numbers have hastened the process.

This takes time and involves human interaction. Hundreds of thousands of people go missing worldwide every year. You blame kidnappers, runaways and serial killers for most of the disappearances, but it seems no one is putting any of the blame on where most of it should fall, and that would be on us.

We find it strange that at least half of humanity believes in the possibility of extraterrestrial life, yet when something out of the ordinary happens like the pyramids or the Bermuda Triangle, you don't give us aliens any of the credit. You humans, in your need for an immediate explanation, come up with some way to steal our show.

Your race is rather naive regarding our existence and purpose. We find it rather amusing, but it's actually better for us to go unrecognized on your planet as the small, fragile alien forms you see around the ship. As you can see, we are a rather frail bunch. Our customized half-breeds which harbor your desirable human characteristics can compensate for us quite nicely. I must say, we've put out some astonishingly beautiful clones. Unfortunately, we've created some monsters in the process.

All of the missing women we successfully breed do return to raise our offspring, but never in the same community from where they were abducted. There are too many questions that put too much pressure on the woman and her baby. They'll never see their families again. We'll make sure the odds of successfully raising our offspring in another part of the world where they both will thrive are in their favor. We see to their needs so they can survive nicely in their new surroundings.

The mother has no recollection of her experience here with us. She takes the infant as her own and accepts any physical or mental issues it might have. Once our descendant is grown and acclimated into your society, they can move around the world to where they're needed."

As We-Ota-Wichasha rounded the last table, he spoke in a soft, but stern voice. "Let us continue."

As they reached the end of the assembly line, the corpses were thoroughly cleaned with a high power wash. A body tray underneath each cadaver was stored in a designated rack that lined the left side wall of the room. They would be dropped back to Earth at various locations for the desired effect.

When not riding his jackrabbit steed across the western Nebraska plains, We-Ota-Wichasha took an active part in this decision-making when it pertained to the people he'd selected for pick up and where to dispose. Otherwise, a panel of three would make the final choice about where to drop a body to achieve the biggest bang for the buck.

Sometimes they would be immediately returned to their original site or in close proximity of their abduction. In other instances, they'd be dumped thousands of miles away. The horrifying response was the same regardless of where these cadavers, either human or animal, were found. Who could have done this and why?

Nick was led into another separate room that contained six tiny holding cells. Five human females were currently being held captive. They were being kept alive in a semi- comatose state, waiting for their optimum gestation cycle. The need for constant food or water, unnecessary bathroom breaks or loud screaming and pleading had been eliminated in the process. Their tormented faces showed they were cognizant of their horrific situation, and although screaming hysterically in agony, the room was completely silent. Human emotions were never a factor in the process.

The sixth woman was lying flat on a table and positioned as if she was taking a gynecological exam. Her captor was in the act of artificially inseminating the hysterical young woman.

If the pregnancy failed after a month, they'd repeat the process. If three attempts failed to produce a healthy embryo, the female would be dropped to Earth.

It was a very eerie sight, to say the least, and Nick was quietly screaming with her over what he was witnessing.

The last room Nick entered was the retaining area. If the insemination process worked, this room held twelve impregnated women who were in a pure comatose state while going through the five month gestation period.

Most fetuses would not survive this stage. Others would be too deformed at delivery and not be kept alive.

If the human female had initial success of getting pregnant but didn't produce an acceptable, live offspring, she'd be taken to the holding cell and impregnated once more. The three strike rule applied here also. There was an ample source of childbearing females to choose from, and repeated failure would not be tolerated.

The discarded bodies that were dropped to Earth stirred up quite a commotion when they were found. The odds of them not being found far outweighed the odds of the other scenario. More times than not, the dead bodies would never be discovered. They'd fall in water, in remote rural areas or rugged terrain. Overexposure to any one area would draw suspicion and create undesired pandemonium over the possibilities of alien existence. Real fear spread out over the globe was the desired end. Widespread panic in a designated region due to excessive drops was not. There was a fine line that had to be tread carefully. Precision drops, however were a necessity to keep the fear of the unknown alive.

If one was found in a populated area, humans would tag the death on some crazed serial killer. Earthlings had no idea why or how these strange deaths occurred. They did, however, know that it scared the hell out of them when a mutilated corpse was found with no logical explanation. Humans were too analytical; they needed an immediate answer for everything. If one wasn't readily available, they could be counted on to try and make one up. To the aliens and Jacks, this could be very amusing.

As the motley entourage ended their tour, We-Ota-Wichasha spoke to Nick one last time.

"You're an intellectual trained in solving mysteries. As you might guess, this is what we call a slave ship. You've just witnessed its sole purpose. We need you for our survival. Your friends are dead. The quiver and its contents, pictures and bones are now back in our possession. We have no further need for you, but we are going to spare you. You have been a determined, yet honorable adversary."

CHAPTER TWENTY-ONE
SOMEBODY CALL THE COPS
FRIDAY, DAY FIVE

Aunt Marge was an excellent cook and she'd spent the afternoon in the kitchen. She was pulling a homemade pan of lasagna out of the oven when the men arrived home from Ewing.

The three sat in front of the fireplace and enjoyed a glass of wine while the men filled her in on the day's events. It had been a long time since they'd had an opportunity to do some reminiscing. Jake thoroughly enjoyed every opportunity to spend time with Aunt Marge and Uncle Hank.

Jake Young was born in 1949 and lived his early childhood years in O'Neill. The predominantly Irish Catholic town was home to a little over 3,000 people nestled in the remote sand hills of north central Nebraska. His family relocated to Hastings in the early sixties.

Jake's grandfather was the Holt County Judge for many years. The courthouse was directly across the street from the schoolhouse. Since both of his parents worked, Jake would go over to grandpa's office for two hours every day after school.

Grandpa Reimer was a busy man. He was often in the courtroom, at his bench trying cases or in the adjoining law library reviewing them. If Jake behaved himself, he would sometimes get to sit on his grandfather's knee and take in the whole courtroom proceedings from the bench. That was on a good day.

If Jake was being a little unruly, Mrs. Sessions, Grandpa's secretary, would escort Jake up to the third floor, four-cell jail and lock him up for a nap. That only happened when the jail was empty, which it usually was. O'Neill was a pretty peaceful, law-abiding little town.

Sometimes he'd go up to the fourth floor residence of Sheriff Leo Tomjack and play with his son, Terry. It was all good to Jake. He looked forward to whatever it was the afternoons had in store for him.

There was always something to do with his cousins. Marge and Hank had five children: three boys and two girls. They'd play football or baseball in the back yard. They'd ride their bikes all over town. They'd play all day in what they called the jungle, which was an undeveloped block filled with trees and over growth directly across the street. An abandoned storm cellar made an excellent cave and hiding place when playing hide and seek in the jungle.

Little League baseball was Jake's favorite summer pastime, followed closely by swimming lessons at the community pool.

Jake loved going out to the family farm with his dad and grandpa to feed the livestock every night. He'd take his BB gun and hunt for birds. He'd ride his horse, Cinnamon. He'd climb to the top of the windmill. Sometimes he'd get to sit on grandpa's lap and drive the tractor or old 1949 Chevy pickup. He'd play in the haystacks.

Sometimes they'd take the fishing poles and go down to the river. Grandpa carried a shovel in the back of the truck, and within a few minutes they'd have a dozen worms for bait. They'd sit on the banks and patiently watch for the bobber to be dragged under the water by a catfish, blue gill or crappie.

In the wintertime when the river was frozen, they'd chop the ice with an ax and drop their lines in the hole. Grandpa had a joke about ice fishing that he shared with everyone every time they went ice fishing.

"Know how to ice fish? Cut a hole in the ice and put peas around the hole. When a fish comes up to take a pee, you club him!"

It was funny at first, but it did wear thin when overly repeated to various cousins, brothers, sisters, nieces, nephews, grandchildren, in-laws and other assorted friends and family. Jake still enjoyed hearing grandpa tell the joke with the same enthusiasm as if it was the first time. Since grandpa was also a lawyer, he'd take the liberty to drag the story out a little bit in places, depending on his audience. The man was in his final act, so they all c u t him some slack when it came to repeating jokes and stories. Anyone else would have been unmercifully silenced.

The warm days would be capped off with a cool swim in the Elkhorn River. There was always a new adventure waiting when he was with his grandpa.

When snow covered the pasture, his dad would tie a saucer sled to the back bumper o f the car with a long rope and drive around in the pasture, going in varied patterns and speeds, whipping Jake around on the ground at an amazing clip. Dad would watch out of the rear view mirror and laugh heartily when he saw Jake flying five feet up in the air after being launched by a frozen cow patty or prairie dog hole.

Jake was about seven when the Davy Crockett movie hit the big screen at the Royal Theater in O'Neill. For a quarter, Jake could see the movie plus get a box of Black Crows and a Hire's Root Beer.

Jake and his three male cousins loved Davy Crockett. That Christmas, all four of the boys received a real coon skin hat, a fringed leather jacket, a flintlock play rifle, boots and a rubber Bowie knife complete with a plastic sheath. They were Davy Crockett!

One day Jake, Warren, Dewey and Jerome were playing cowboys and Indians.   Dewey was pulling his big brother Jerome down an alley in Jake's Radio Flyer red w a g o n . They pretended Jerome had been severely wounded and needed a ride. Jake and Warren scouted out all of the fifty-five gallon drums that were used to burn trash, which lined both sides of the dirt-rutted alley. The boys were constantly on the lookout for pop bottles that were worth two cents each and easily redeemed up at Janosek's Grocery. The boys would eventually end up there later in the afternoon to trade the empty bottle booty for some Top's baseball cards and bubble gum. Maybe today would be the day they'd get a cherished Mickey Mantle, Stan Musial or Ted Williams.

Jake noticed something of interest that might be a valuable prop on their imaginary cavalry excursion in one of the unburned barrels. He didn't know exactly what it was, but whatever it was would look good on Jerome's forehead. The wounded soldier needed to look the part if he was to continue his wagon ride home.

Unbeknownst to the youths, a used sanitary napkin probably wasn't the best choice of props. But, since they didn't know what it was, on it went.

This was too good not to share. The small militia of cousins decided to show Aunt Marge the wounded soldier. Surely she'd be impressed with their creativity and reward them with milk and cookies after a hard day of protecting defenseless women and children who ventured beyond the fort walls.

Jake went running up to the front door and frantically pounded on the door. "Aunt Marge! Aunt Marge! Please come quick! Jerome's been hit bad by those renegade Indians!"

Aunt Marge came to the front door all right. Within seconds, she went right on through it yelling "Jerome Reimer, you get that thing off your head right now and get in this house! You boys get in here this instant! Jake, you go right home mister. I'm calling your mother!"

Jake sauntered down the street, pulling his empty wagon, wondering what the heck had just happened. Everything was going so good a couple of minutes ago when milk and cookies danced in his head, and now he was being sent home to face the music. Apparently Aunt Marge didn't have much of a sense of humor after all. The boys gave her far more credit than she deserved.

Jake walked begrudgingly through the front door and sat down on the couch, still in full uniform. His mom was waiting for him and he expected the worst. Instead, Mom was pretty cool so far. She simply told him not to dig those things out of the trash anymore. It had something to do with a sanitary napkin that wasn't so sanitary and a napkin that wasn't really a napkin. She could tell by Jake's expression he wasn't following her explanation.

"Jake, we'll wait until your father gets home. Hopefully he will explain it better than I did."

Sure enough, later that afternoon, the minute Dad walked into the house, Mom grabbed his hand and pulled him back to their bedroom and shut the door. Their brief conversation was followed by long and hearty laughter. Dad attempted to maintain his composure and give Jake the serious, fatherly look.

His advice was very simple and easily understood. "Son, just don't do it again."

Jake got the point and so did his cousins. Expecting far worse, the boys considered themselves lucky with an attempted explanation of their misdoing.

His grandparents, aunts, uncles, cousins and extended family lived in the surrounding area, so he always found a reason to return. Now that most of the family was gone, his visits to O'Neill were less frequent, especially since he'd relocated out of state with his career moves. It was fun to get back to the old stomping grounds and spend some time now that he was living back in Nebraska.

Jake left the house around nine-thirty that night and drove back to the Super 8. It had been a long day and he was looking forward to calling Judy and perhaps watch a little TV before turning in.

Friday morning came quickly. Jake took Yollie for a short walk across the street to t h e deserted lot where they'd seen the Jacks before meeting with his friends for breakfast. He had the picture he'd taken last night of the horse tail that he anxiously wanted to share. There would be a recap of the week's activities and they'd talk about the next step once all of the lab results were in. Extensive testing of their findings would surely be the first thing Nick and George would do together next Monday morning back at the Lincoln lab.

He figured both parties would be on the road by noon. His trio would arrive back in Scottsbluff by early evening for a steak dinner with Judy.

The morning was cold and overcast with a fifty percent change of flurries. The men would depart earlier if it started to snow. Since Christmas was just around the corner, he and Judy were looking forward to a quiet weekend shopping for presents and watching the Broncos play the Houston Texans on Sunday. Jake had his fingers crossed they wouldn't run into any real bad weather along the way.

Doc's wife, Janet, had passed away about ten years ago, so there wouldn't be anyone waiting at home for the spry old veterinarian. He was all alone except for a housekeeper who dropped in twice a week to prepare some easy, re-heatable meals and clean the house.

Mark's wife, Martha, was visiting her sister in Cheyenne for the weekend so he was batching it.

The trip had been good for all of these guys to get out of town for awhile but like Jake, they'd all be glad to spend the night back in their own bed.

Jake waited patiently in the lobby until ten after eight. He was surprised that none of the guys had joined him. They were usually very punctual. He dialed Doc's room from the lobby phone. No one answered. He must be on his way down. Jake tried Nick's room and again got no answer. Okay, they're coming down together. Their rooms were next to each other. He'd give them a few more minutes.

Another ten minutes passed and still no one showed up. Jake was really getting concerned. Maybe the Taurus needed gas and somehow got delayed at the station. Yeah, that was probably it, but why would they all go? Wouldn't at least one of them meet Jake in the lobby as planned? Wouldn't they call him on his cell if they were running late? He decided to take Yollie for a stroll around the parking lot and look for the car.

The white Taurus with Nebraska government plates was nowhere in the lot. Where in the hell could they be?

Jake tried all four cell phones. No answer from any of them. Instead of being directed into the usual answering mode, the phones were all silent. D e a d s i l e n t . Not even the customary dial tone was heard. Surely all four phones didn't run out of power at the same time. For the second time in the last twelve hours, the silenced phones raised a big red flag that something was terribly wrong.

Jake's concern now turned to desperation. Where could his friends be and why wasn't the car there? Maybe they took a wrong turn home last night and got stuck. He was running out of possibilities. He'd call Uncle Hank and enlist his help to find his missing friends.

Hank met Jake in the lobby fifteen minutes later. After a brief discussion, Hank decided to call his friend, Holt County Sheriff

Carl Arness. The sheriff joined the men in the lobby after the short phone conversation.

Arness radioed his two on duty officers with an APB to begin looking for the state- issued Taurus. Since the initial call was requested by a District Court Judge and involved two top state law enforcement officers, the usual twenty-four hour time restraint to file a missing persons report did not apply. This was a matter of immediate concern and Arness wasted no time in calling the Nebraska State Highway Patrol for their assistance as well. As in any missing person case, time was of the essence.

Sheriff Arness assured the two men that everything that could be done to locate the four men was being done. He'd call Hank when he received any further information. They'd done all they could do for now, so he excused himself and left the men standing inside the front entrance.

Jake and Hank decided to retrace their steps from yesterday. It beat sitting around waiting for the phone to ring. They'd covered some remote rural roads and maybe, for whatever reason, the men went back for something. Maybe one of them had lost a billfold, glasses or keys. The chance was remote, but worth the time. Why hadn't they called if they were lost or stuck? Nick and George would know what to do in any situation. They were seasoned cops, not a couple of amateur high school kids. Whatever the reason was for their disappearance, it had to be an extraordinary one.

The men made the short trip down to Ewing. They drove out to the cemetery and on out past the Lundahl ranch. Every inch of road they'd covered yesterday was covered again this morning. Before heading back to O'Neill, the two decided to have an early lunch at BK's Pub.

They sat down at the bar and looked briefly at the menu. Hank's phone began ringing. "Hello Judge. Carl Arness here. No sign of the men or the car so far. A state patrol plane out of Norfolk has been requested in the search. Weather permitting, if the car is still in the area, they'll spot it. In the meantime, sit tight. I'll get back to you with an update by mid-afternoon, if not sooner."

After lunch the two decided to go home and wait for any news in the comfort of a cozy living room and a warm fireplace. Right before two o'clock the phone rang. It was the sheriff again.

Low visibility had curtailed the air search for today. Authorities would resume again first thing in the morning, weather permitting. The forecast for tomorrow called for clear skies with a slight chance of precipitation. A severe cold front would settle in on Sunday afternoon with the possibility of up to five inches of snow. If Jake wanted to beat the bad weather, tomorrow or early Sunday should be a good travel day. The sheriff assured them that if the men were found safe, a state plane would gladly make the flight to Lincoln and out to Scottsbluff to personally deliver everyone safely home.

Just around ten on Saturday morning, Hank got the call they'd been waiting for. The plane had spotted what appeared to be a mangled car in a pasture just five miles southwest of Clearwater. Sheriff Arness was heading that way and invited Hank and Jake to join him. He'd be at the house within minutes.

Several Nebraska Highway Patrol vehicles sat out in the pasture next to the car when they arrived. As the men got out of the SUV one of Arness's deputies approached them.

"Sorry boss, it doesn't appear that the missing men are in the car. Judging by the state issued plates, this is definitely the vehicle we're looking for. There are no other vehicles involved or tire tracks of any kind in the snow. The car wasn't driven to this location. It appears to have just fallen out of the sky."

Jake pulled his uncle off to the side. "Uncle Hank, remember Nick asking me for the box of bones I had in the back of the

198

Escalade? Let's check the trunk for bones, briefcases and the quiver."

The badly damaged car was lying with the wheels up in the air. It looked like it had been run through a car crusher at the junkyard. That was certainly not the case, judging by the crater the car had made in the dirt and snow upon impact. Hank asked the sheriff if they could possibly flip the car over to get a closer look at the interior and the trunk.

Jake and Hank couldn't rule out the possibility that bodies weren't still in the car just because of the lack of blood until the car was upright. Arness pulled out the steel c a b l e from his front wench located on the bumper of the Dodge Ram and secured it to the far frame rail. With a little push from the men, the crushed auto flopped over upright with a loud thud.

One of the State Troopers grabbed the Jaws of Life tool from his vehicle and several fellow officers assisted him in ripping the flattened roof back from the pancaked Taurus. Sheriff Arness's deputy was probably right in his assumption, but the officers needed to verify that no bodies were in the car. If there were four bodies in this twisted heap of metal, they certainly weren't bleeding. There weren't any of the usual telltale signs of four badly traumatized fatalities.

As suspected, the car was empty. One of the officers managed to pull the registration from the glove box to verify that it was a state issued vehicle belonging to the State Crime Lab.

A thorough inspection of the car and its contents, including the trunk, revealed nothing. No suitcases, brief cases, box of bones or quiver. It had been picked clean.

Jake and Hank gave their statements to the presiding highway patrol officer outlining when the car went missing and the four men that presumably were in the car. The two men were careful not to divulge too much information regarding their connections with the missing men. Both had the sense to simply say they were all old friends who decided to rendezvous in O'Neill for some great pheasant hunting. That certainly would draw no suspicion that would require any further detailed explanation. Besides, who was going to press the District Court Judge with any allegations he was somehow withholding the truth?

Within an hour they were back in the Sheriff's SUV heading for O'Neill.

CHAPTER TWENTY-TWO
THE LONG RIDE HOME
SATURDAY, DAY SIX

There was nothing more Jake could do in O'Neill except worry. He could do that at home. Hank would notify him if any new information came in. Later in the afternoon, Jake and Yollie hopped into the Escalade and motored west on Highway 20 towards Scottsbluff. He wanted to get home before the expected storm hit. The last forty-eight hours had been an exhausting postlude to an otherwise exciting week. If his friends were found safe, they were guaranteed an immediate flight home by a Nebraska Highway Patrol plane.

Jake couldn't help but worry. He had really enjoyed the companionship of his old and new friends over the past five days. The week had flown by so fast. He appreciated the opportunity to be part of the informal investigation and be trusted with the information and evidence they'd managed to collect. It was just a couple of weeks ago, when Yollie was taken into Dr. Mark's clinic, which had set the whole wild experience into action.

The late afternoon overcast sky painted a dreary shroud of darkening depression over the two lane deserted highway. Traffic was sparse other than an occasional rancher in his pickup making the short trip home after tending to the cattle. Jake turned on his headlights and put a CD into the player. Radio reception in this part of the state was very limited, especially at night.

Instead, he chose to put on some Firefall. The band had formed in Boulder back in the seventies and Jake knew their songs well from his Denver days. He'd seen them in concert several times over the years and tonight they were like old friends, which is exactly what he needed. *Strange Way* seemed appropriate for the moment.

Yollie had the entire back seat to herself and she was taking advantage of it to catch another nap. As the sky grew darker, a slight flurry of blowing snow began to fall. Jake was glad to have four wheel drive and all terrain tires for times like this. Nebraska weather is very unpredictable and many a motorist has ended up in the ditch or worse on such a night. Jake took out a Punch cigar from the glove box and cranked the music up. He had a long drive ahead of him and it was time to try and relax the rest of the trip. All the worrying in the world wouldn't help find his friends any faster. The situation was out of his hands now. He'd just have to play the excruciating game of wait and see.

Approximately ten miles south of Bassett, his cell phone rang. It was Dr. Hutton's wife Martha and she was concerned about Mark. She hadn't heard from him over the last forty-eight hours, which was very unlike her husband. He hadn't answered his phone all day and as a last resort, she was calling Jake. He pulled the SUV over on the shoulder to take the call. This was a conversation he'd rather not be having right now. It was going to be awhile before he got back on the road.

Before he began, Jake opened the back door for Yollie to let her stretch her legs. Might as well kill two birds with one stone since they had many more miles to go. She wouldn't go far.

Jake shared the bad news with Martha. No use sugar coating it. The car had been mysteriously found out in a pasture far from any main road. There were no occupants in the wreckage. No one had the slightest clue of their whereabouts. He assured her that both Mark and Doc were in good company with Nick and George, assuming they were all together. With their credentials in state law enforcement, a thorough search would be conducted and they would be found. It was a just a matter of time. He assured Martha that once the men were located, they would be flown home. If he heard any recent news from his uncle Hank, he'd call her with the latest update.

She wanted his assurance they could meet tomorrow afternoon in person. Martha had been in touch with Doc's two daughters. They were driving into town tomorrow and wanted to be included when they got together. The meeting time was set for three o'clock.

Jake ended the twenty minute call and decided to take a brief stroll around the car to get some fresh air himself. A cold, blustering gale does wonders to clear the head and invigorate the senses on a long, boring drive.

After a few minutes of staring blankly out at the dark night sky and asking God for some help in finding his friends, Jake called out to Yollie. It was time to get back on the road and he felt a little better asking for some divine intervention to his dilemma.

Jake repeated his calls to the dog. He gave the "get your butt back here right now" whistle several times.

Jake jumped back into the SUV and quickly gave a long, loud blast from the horn that pierced the quiet darkness. Yollie finally emerged from the darkness and met Jake with the "Sorry I'm late dad, but I'm here," smiling pant. Jake opened the back door and the big dog lunged into the seat and resumed her prone position. They were once again on the road with another five hours of driving ahead of them.

The Escalade made another brief stop in Valentine, Nebraska to get some fuel and a quick deli sandwich and a few other essentials that might come in handy at the adjacent Scottie's Ranchland Foods. Jake knew he was stretching it when he asked the young female cashier if they sold any nicer quality cigars.

"Sorry sir. Swisher Sweets is about the extent of our cigar selection."

In his college days, Jake would have gladly settled for the sweet, fast burning excuse for a cigar, but over the years his tastes had become considerably more refined.

"Thanks anyhow, I'll pass. Never hurts to ask," he replied in a somewhat disappointed tone.

A good cigar has a way of making a long road trip just a little more enjoyable. It gives a guy something to do and think about while focusing on the dull white lines that dot the endless road ahead. He did have one Punch remaining, so replenishments weren't yet a dire necessity.

The digital dashboard clock was approaching eleven when they arrived in Chadron. Jake could count the cars on one hand that shared the road with him as he drove through the small college town of seven thousand residents. By now the light snow had stopped and a cloudy, dark night would blanket him on the rest of his two hour drive home through the black, rolling hills south of town.

As he drove by the city limit sign, he thought back to a happier time earlier in the week when the men were just starting their trip. He missed the conversations about their findings and the excitement they shared as they continued to uncover new clues at every stop along the way.

Nick and Doc had lived most their lives wondering about Jack People, cattle mutilations and aliens. They had come so close to solving the fifty year old case. With just a little lab verification, these two would have been the most famous guys on Earth, at least for a while. It was a real pleasure to have been asked to accompany them along the final leg of their journey. They certainly didn't have to include him, but that's the kind of guys they were. All four men were down to Earth, unassuming professionals who Jake had grown very fond of. He truly valued their short friendship and enjoyed the constant ribbing Nick and Doc would dish out to each other in a kind but humorous way.

Jake had heard the term, kindred spirits, but he'd seen very few in his lifetime. These two fit the bill in Jake's book.

Jake had built a strong bond with George and Mark also. Both were strong family men that brought a lot to the table. George was an incredibly talented law officer, criminologist and scientist. Jake would call Mary Souders tomorrow out of respect for George and have a similar conversation with her, like he'd just done over the phone with Martha. George would appreciate the compassionate gesture.

The missing men had only disappeared forty-eight hours ago. Was he being overly premature thinking the worst? Yes, the possibility still existed that they still could be found safe and sound. Although Jake had always considered himself an optimist, he had that strong aching in his gut that was telling him differently.

None of his friends were answering their phones. In fact, none of their phones were in service, which in itself was quite perplexing. He at least expected an automated voice to tell him that the party he's trying to reach is unavailable at the time and try placing a call later. Hell, static would have even sounded good compared to the silence. It's like answering a phone call and no one speaks on the other end when you say hello. You have a strong hunch someone is there, but rather than speaking, they're engaging in a sick game with you that only one party wants to play.

The crushed car with no trace of the men's possessions was very puzzling. An accident on the highway was one thing, but to find the mangled car out in a field with no logical explanation for how it got there was too bizarre for Jake to comprehend. The car scenario certainly didn't shed a positive light on the debacle. The thought of Junior Roberts' unexpected experience with an alien craft on a deserted highway raced through his mind and he quickly drew a possible comparison.

The most disturbing thought that put the heavy curtain of doubt over the disappearance was the sight of the Jacks standing in the field across from the Super 8. The men were dealing with the unknown until they showed their faces. The Jack People do exist and in all probability, so do their alien friends. Jan Gradert had convinced them of that fact just several days ago. No one doubted her story then, so why should Jake doubt it now? These forces may have superior capabilities to unleash their torment on all mankind if they chose. The fact that they're dealing with six mortal men would be of little concern to them. They hold the upper hand that few men on Earth have ever witnessed, at least any still alive.

The brief encounter with young Egon Harrasser and the braided horse tail sent shivers through his body. The gut feeling was back now, in full force.

It was so difficult and only natural for Jake not to wonder if the men were dead or alive. Finding the bodies and having a funeral would bring some finality and closure to their grief, even as painful as it might be. Without that final closure, torturing questions would haunt all of them every waking minute for the rest of their lives.

Are they alive? Where are they? Why can't they come home? Why can't they notify us? Will we ever see them again? were just a few of questions that raced through his mind and would not go away.

He thought of each of the men and what they'd accomplished in their careers and what brought them together so unexpectedly. It was such an incredible mystery that would have certainly made worldwide headlines, assuming the government wouldn't use their slanted media cronies to bury it in a short column on page seven, a story that would be forgotten about in days.

As they approached the Chadron State Park entrance, Jake decided to pull off the deserted road for a brief few minutes for a pee break for both man and dog.

Jake stood in the parking lot looking up at the night sky and again said a prayer for his comrades. He needed all the strength he could muster when he would meet with the worried families tomorrow in person. There was still a ray of hope, and that's what he would focus on. He'd always been a positive person and he needed to share that energy with them. It would be a fine line he had to walk to not spread false hope.

This was a very disturbing case, even to seasoned law enforcement. The next few days would hopefully offer some closure to this raw, gaping uncertainty everyone was feeling now. It had only been forty-eight hours since he'd last seen the four friends. It was far too early to give up hope.

The short pit stop gave Yollie another opportunity to stretch her legs again. As Jake pondered his situation, the dog took advantage to do some brief exploring around the dense pine growth that surrounded them. She was having fun and a few minutes more would do them both some good.

Jake slid back behind the wheel of the still running SUV, shut the door and watched his trusted friend wander around in the distance. The headlights barely hit the focused animal as she sniffed around each tree for whatever fresh scents they might offer.

Jake's cell phone suddenly started to chirp. It was from Uncle Hank. He'd just received news from Sheriff Arness.

"Hi Jake, a brief update. Nick Jensen has just been brought to the Norfolk Hospital. One of Sheriff Arness' deputies found him staggering down a snow-packed dirt road around five miles from the car. He appears to be in stable condition physically. That's the good news.

Unfortunately, he is in another world mentally. The emergency room doctor told me that he's not responding to our voices. He has no focus; his eyes are happily smiling and staring upwards to somewhere in the past as if he's gone back to happier times. He doesn't speak; at best he might occasionally babble and point up in the air. He has no memory; hell, he can't remember his name, where he lives or if he's married. The poor man can't even count to three!

The doctor is keeping him stable until a Nebraska Highway Patrol plane transports him back to Lincoln sometime, probably in the next half hour. He'll be taken to St. Elizabeth's Hospital and a professional crew will give him a complete examination.

I was told that over time there's a chance he might eventually recover, but that is being optimistic. He's been through a very harrowing ordeal of some sort to end up in this condition. It doesn't bode well for the others.

I'm sorry I have to tell you this sad news. I knew you'd grown very fond of the man. I didn't know him very well, but everything I'd ever heard about Nick through colleagues was nothing short of admirable. He really was a very classy man. It's sad to see him like this and again, my condolences. The press will issue a news release first thing in the morning. I'm so sorry."

It was certainly not the news Jake had hoped for. Considering the circumstances, the news was even worse than death for Nick. If this had happened two weeks ago, his rapid, unstable and uncertain condition might have been blamed on a naturally occurring m a l a d y like a stroke and better understood.

Although in his seventies, the man was mentally sharp and physically fit. Jake had seen the man hiking, jogging, crawling, jumping, eating, drinking and intelligently engaged in life at its fullest all week. Nick was having one of the last great adventures of his active life and capturing every second of it. He was less than forty-eight hours away from putting the final piece of the fifty-year-old puzzle in its rightful place.

Jake replied, "Thanks for calling Uncle Hank. I'm glad you were there for me on this one and had a chance to get to know Nick and the other guys. It's been a little difficult to look back over the past week and imagine something like this happening, but under the circumstances, it's certainly possible. We're dealing with something most men have never been faced with. I agree with you and have no reason to offer up much hope.

Just thinking out loud here, but we're the only two that have not gone missing or mysteriously brainwashed. That has me concerned. Very concerned. Three missing men and a vegetable don't tell stories. We can. I'll be home in probably two hours. I'll take it very cautiously and I hope you do the same. I'll call you in the morning to let you know I made it home safely. It certainly is a shocker.

We weren't carrying the evidence of their existence. The Taurus had been picked clean and hopefully they got what they wanted. At this point, our story to the authorities wouldn't sound much different than what they could expect from Nick.

Remember, there will be a lot of questions coming soon about this incident. The FBI might even get involved if some answers don't surface in the next couple of weeks. We'll certainly be questioned again about our involvement. I suggest we corroborate our story and stick with the pheasant hunt."

Hank hesitated with his answer. Without all of the facts in yet and not knowing what direction the story may turn, he remained silent. He knew the best approach in handling the questions that would come. Being a judge, he certainly didn't want to perjure himself or tarnish his outstanding reputation by intentionally giving misinformation to the authorities, but with his years on the bench he knew how to persuade the prosecution.

"Jake, we're mostly on the same page here. We can discuss the subject again after we know more about the direction we're going. There's still that possibility. Keep your fingers crossed. I'll know the best way to present our case as more of the facts surface.

Unfortunately, there are too many nagging, unexplained events that a hunting alibi won't answer. With the people involved and the facts surrounding them, there will be more questions. For now, you don't talk to anyone without first notifying me. Be careful what you tell Judy. There's no reason to burden her with more than she already knows," Uncle Hank said and ended their conversation.

Jake had been playing with the unknown all week and didn't truly comprehend the extent of the possible threat. This week wasn't an Easter egg hunt or a college fraternity scavenger stunt, this was a potentially dangerous situation the men may not have fully understood, and it may have come back to bite them. If he'd known the severity beforehand, he may have had serious second thoughts about joining the merry troupe. It wasn't supposed to end like this, and unfortunately the end was not in sight.

Jake was so focused on the safety of his friends that he'd overlooked his own situation. Here he was, alone on a deserted highway, late at night. If the opposition wanted him, he certainly was an easy target. The negative thoughts motivated him to get home a little sooner. It was time to put a sense of urgency into the last leg of his long trip back to Scottsbluff for his own survival.

The phrase *not if, but when* would probably haunt him the rest of his life. The trip had instantly changed his life with Judy and their family in a catastrophic way. He was finding out rather unexpectedly that grief and fear are both formidable opponents to deal with individually, but the combination of the two was devastating. He had no idea whom or what he was dealing with here, and that thought invoked raging, primal fear.

Who could he talk to who would believe his story, other than his uncle? Should he e v e n tell the entire truth to Judy, especially about the Jacks and the braid? This would be an incredible cross to bear for both of them. No one would ever see this coming in their wildest dreams. It appeared to be very clear to Jake with every passing minute that the nightmare was real. He'd have to tell Judy something regarding the tragedy, along with the other families, but perhaps a white lie might be justifiable in this case. He'd tell them all just enough of what they needed to know without putting that increased burden of fear he was shouldering over onto them. This might be the one secret he'd take to his grave to spare the others.

Jake's continued strategy was to use the hunting trip rationale for the men's week long excursion, but what had his friends told their families? Were they chasing fifty-year-old ghosts? Were they on official or unofficial business? Other than Mark, did any of them like to hunt and use it as a credible reason for being in O'Neill when they went to Scottsbluff? Could they continue to support that line or would others blow a big hole in the story? Jake needed to get some answers by asking unassuming questions to offer credence to their alibi before they proceeded any further in that direction. The old adage of *hope for the best, but prepare for the worst* came to mind.

As he gathered his thoughts and began to focus on the present, he was suddenly jerked back into reality by the sight of Yollie in the distant light about fifty yards ahead. The dog had given chase to a number of jackrabbits running full speed down the deserted highway.

Jake was overcome by a strange sensation that this was not an ordinary herd of rabbits and immediately threw his SUV in gear and joined in the chase. Because of the snow pack still on the road, he was limited on his speed. The overwhelming number of rabbits had Yollie somewhat confused about where to focus. They seemed to stay together in a cluster, but when their pursuer got too close to one, they'd split off individually and break her concentration. Strength in numbers was always a good strategy in confusing the enemy.

The chase now veered off the road ahead as Jake narrowed the gap. Before they disappeared from sight, two of the large rabbits bringing up the rear confirmed Jake's instincts. Both small riders held back to glance at the oncoming vehicle in unison. He was

211

startled to see the large eyes, partially covered under their hoods, staring back at him!

This was no coincidence. Both Jacks deliberately pulled the small collars of their robes out straight, giving Jake a good look at a shining silver law enforcement badge pinned on the garments. These brazen Jacks seemed to be toying with Jake as they suddenly disappeared into the darkness, continuing in this frivolous game of cat and mouse with Yollie somewhere out in the cold and eerie Nebraska night

CHAPTER TWENTY-THREE
THE ELEVENTH HOUR

Jake spent the next half hour driving up and down the road where he'd last seen the Jacks veer off the road into the trees. The furry little bastards had obviously gotten his attention for a reason, and he was sure they'd be back. There was some unfinished business that had been festering most of the week on both sides, and this was the time and place to finish it.

The persistent nagging of Jake's fear was now accompanied by a new emotion of anger. Both jockeyed for position in Jake's head as he frantically looked for his dog.

The two emotions took turns spinning around and fighting to control his immediate thought processes. He was very afraid of being in this horrifying position all alone on a deserted road late at night. Jake knew he was up against a very worthy opponent that lived for centuries on cunning and stealth. The badge was proof that his friends had the unfortunate experience of being in a similar position just two days ago, and it was obvious what that outcome was.

Fear maintained the lead.

On the other hand, Jake felt a strong obligation to retaliate for his friends and now his dog. They'd inflicted enough pain on too many people and it was time to put these little sons of a bitches on the shelf in their little rabbit hole graves. If vengeance was to prevail, now was the time. Jake figured he had one chance to get it right, or he'd be joining his friends, wherever they might be.

Until now, they'd mostly been something out of western Nebraska mythology. They'd been imagined. They'd been ignored. They'd won most of their respect through fear and intimidation; not necessarily through their actions. How tough could these little light weight midgets be with a full bag of porcupine quills for weapons? The thought almost made him laugh. Instead, it gave him an instant burst of renewed confidence.

Rabbits do have natural enemies, and man is close to the top of the list. Thousands of rabbits get shot or run over every day, no matter how fast or agile they seem to be. They can't outrun a bullet or a car, and he had both. Jake had his rifle, shotgun and a .357 revolver, plus plenty of ammunition. Hell, if he had to, he could even throw snowballs! They couldn't hurt him if he stayed out of their limited range and they had no extraterrestrial help. Like it or not, they'd laid out a direct challenge and Jake's life was on the line.

Anger and the desire to fight now took the reins of Jake's emotions. If he ran, he'd be running forever.

He took a long look at the darkness that surrounded him. No shooting stars. No bright, shiny objects hanging overhead. No beams of light pulling him up into the night sky.

Without their alien accomplices, the Jacks should be at a big disadvantage. If Jake stood any chance at all, he hoped it would stay that way. He wanted to minimize his chances of being targeted from thin air. He imagined how a rabbit must feel when it was unexpectedly plucked out of nowhere by a hovering eagle hunting its prey.

Jake had little time to plan his strategy. He was at a major disadvantage in not knowing how or when his adversaries would reappear and what situation he'd be placed in when they did. Jake didn't like his odds playing defense. Too many negative options. He'd have to turn the table and play a red zone offense. If the Jacks did call for reinforcements, they'd be there lickety-split and he'd be a goner. The two minute drill clock began.

Jake was a moving target driving up and down the road with his lights on. He'd have to get out of the SUV and use it as a decoy. If something were to come along and hoist it up into the air, he certainly didn't want to be inside. He'd seen those results.

The landscape around Chadron State Park was heavily wooded and hilly. Jake located a large bluff about twenty yards from the highway. The high, flat and rocky surface would protect his back. No one could get behind or on top of him, which was a big plus. He pulled the Escalade off to the shoulder of the road and turned off the ignition. Thirty seconds later, the timed headlights also shut off. He needed the darkness to work to his advantage.

Jake crawled between the front seats and reached for his weapons, shells and the Geiger counter located in the back seat and quickly assumed his new position over in the passenger's seat. He grabbed his garment bag hanging from the right back seat door and pulled out an extra shirt, hanger and ball cap. He put the twelve gauge pump shotgun and the rifle in front of the passenger seat for easy access. The Smith and Wesson revolver was tucked securely in his zippered coat pocket.

After locating the necessary props, he assembled a makeshift dummy in front of the steering wheel. He propped the Geiger counter between the seat and the wheel, hung the hangered shirt on the handle and stuck the hat on top. From a distance, this strange- looking contraption should resemble a driver behind the wheel.

He managed to cover all of the interior lights that would ordinarily go on when he opened the door with some duct tape he had in an emergency kit. He quietly opened the door and swiftly exited the vehicle, softly closing the door behind him.

Jake wasted little precious time finding a strategic position in front of the rock wall. He lay on his stomach, holding the rifle in the at-ready position underneath some dense brush cover. It would be next to impossible for a dart to hit him from a distance from any direction without striking multiple branches first. His enemy would have to get real close to inflict any real damage. From this location, he still had an unobstructed view of the parked vehicle directly ahead of him as well as from both sides.

He lay patiently in this protective cover and waited for the Jacks to make their next move. Jake had spent the last half hour driving up and down the highway looking for them. It was their turn to find him. Jake was confident they'd present themselves when the time was right. He uttered a silent prayer they'd come alone and soon.

Another twenty minutes passed until Jake saw something appear on the road in front o f the SUV. Standing about fifteen yards ahead were eight mounted Jacks surrounding Yollie. The dog was obviously securely tied, offering no threat to her captors. Eight long narrow ropes were tied to her four legs and each Jack held the other end. Her mouth had been tied shut with more rope. A narrow strip of rabbit fur covered her eyes. They wanted the dog on her feet to prove the dog was still alive. If Yollie was sedated, the task would be harder to do.

Two of the Jacks cautiously drew their mounts nearer to the metal monster that could easily crush them if they got too close. Both sported law enforcement badges on the exterior of their rabbit skin robes. The other six mounted Jacks held their position in the distance.

Jake had them where he wanted them, but they were spread out. One shot might take out one, but the rest would scatter and probably kill Yollie in the process. It would be j u s t a matter of time before they found his hiding spot and killed or kidnapped him. He needed to draw them all together in a tight-knit group to inflict any serious damage. Only one option came to mind, and he immediately acted on it.

It had been a cold and snowy winter thus far across the panhandle Nebraska. This time of year, under these conditions, the only source of food for the jackrabbits was to forage through the ice and snow for plant roots, twigs and tree bark. Since trees in this part of the country were scarce and the rabbits competed with a large deer population, food was in short supply.

These Jack People and their rabbit mounts had been called away on special assignment from their usual comfort zone where they had ample food supplies hidden in their caves and tunnels. Both were suffering the consequences of hunger and lack of shelter. They would take refuge in a rabbit burrow when one presented itself, but most nights they would hunker down somewhere on the frozen prairie and snuggle tightly together to maintain body heat.

Only one man and a useless dog. We-Ota-Wichasha made a vow to personally take down this last threat on his own. He liked his odds and his warriors were always up for a challenge. The chief would not need reinforcements tonight. The Jacks had the prized dog in captivity and dangled the restrained animal as bait. After all, nothing could stand between a man and his dog. They had the vehicle stopped on the shoulder of the road. The SUV was dark and the engine off. It posed no immediate threat.

We-Ota-Wichasha knew that as long as his Jacks were spread out, he held the upper hand. The jackrabbit bucks react with lightning speed. The vehicle or even a weapon couldn't take them all out simultaneously, let alone individually. The lone occupant would have to exit the inoperative vehicle in order to retrieve the dog and he probably would be armed. It was still eight against one and he liked the odds. That was their plan.

Jake had a plan of his own. As We-Ota-Wichasha and his second-in-command drew nearer to the vehicle, he hit the auto start button on his key fob. When the engine started, the headlights came on. He hoped his dummy behind the wheel cooperated in the plan. All eight of the Jacks were now drawn out of the shadows and into the light, but at a heightened sense of readiness, focusing totally on the car.

Several of the warriors aimed their long blowguns at the Escalade and blew a vast array of stones into the windshield to taunt their lone opponent. If the dummy behind the wheel would only get out of the vehicle to come and get his dog, they'd show him some real showmanship with their shooting abilities. They'd dealt with plenty of humans over the last two hundred years and this guy was nothing to them but another notch on one of their quivers. The coward behind the wheel probably started the metal monster to make a rapid retreat.

Once they were all spotted, Jake reached into both of his deep coat pockets and pulled out two large plastic bags filled with fresh carrots, leafy heads of lettuce, bright red and plump radishes and tasty celery with some apples thrown in for good measure, in case these furry bastards preferred fruit.

He quickly began strategically throwing the assortment out on the closest shoulder of the road from his hiding place. The mixed greens hit the ground to the side of the SUV so his targets wouldn't be threatened with being suddenly run over. The lights of the Escalade lit up the smorgasbord like it was the featured salad bar at the Cornhusker Radisson on game day!

Since the food was on the side of the SUV, they risked no chance of getting run over. The engine was running, so the driver would probably use this opportunity to skedaddle and run. The Jacks still had Yollie. They might not get the guy behind the wheel tonight, but they had his beloved pet, thus inflicting another dose of pain onto the poor sap. Let him go. We-Ota-Wichasha and his clansmen certainly knew where he lived.

The pleasant and unexpected sight of fresh food was too much for the starving enemy. They all raced to the life-sustaining mix like their lives literally depended on it. Luckily, the little shits were starving.

The expected chaos was just what Jake hoped for. The unmounted Jacks were sitting ducks without the speed of their trusted rides under them. As his distracted prey ravenously tore into the food, Jake determinedly sprang to his feet with his twelve gauge semi-automatic shotgun in hand and rapidly approached the starving cluster, emptying all six .006 shells from a distance of less than fifteen feet. The Jacks never saw him coming out of the brush. He pulled out his revolver to finish any wounded leftovers.

Within a matter of seconds it was over. Nothing on the road was left alive. With his heart still racing and the adrenaline flowing, Jake carefully walked through the bloody carnage and plucked the two glistening badges from the mangled Jack bodies, wiped them off with his handkerchief and placed them in his pocket.

He thought for a fleeting moment of taking some pictures of what was left of these mythological creatures lying before him, although there wasn't much left to see. He wanted nothing more to do with them and opted to close the book forever. It was best they stayed a myth. Any proof of their existence might come back to haunt him later through their accomplices, so the decision was easily made. All traces of their violent ending would soon be wiped clean by the coyotes howling for their supper in the near distance.

He turned and approached Yollie, still standing blindfolded in the middle of the deserted highway with the now dangling ropes still tied around her four legs. He could tell by her eyes when he removed the bindings and blindfold she was glad to see him. She gave him a big lick of assurance that he was forgiven for getting her into this mess, again.

Jake opened the back passenger door for Yollie then quickly cleared the makeshift dummy props over to the empty passenger seat.

Once settled comfortably back behind the wheel, Jake put the Escalade in gear. If the little bastards hadn't called in their air support by now, they probably weren't coming. It was time to make the final leg home without any further interruptions.

CHAPTER TWENTY-FOUR

HOME AGAIN
SUNDAY, DAY SEVEN

Jake pulled into the garage around one o'clock Sunday morning. He made his way into the living room and found Judy sleeping on the couch, awaiting his late arrival. He gently nudged her as he kissed her forehead.

"Hi honey, I'm home!" he softly whispered.

Judy immediately sat up and wrapped her arms around her husband. After a long embrace she adjourned to the kitchen to pour two glasses of wine. She wanted to hear all about the trip, especially what had just transpired over the last fourteen hours since their last phone conversation.

The two sat up for the next hour getting caught up on the events of the past week. Judy sat intently on the couch, listening to Jake rehash most of the highlights with Yollie lying comfortably at her feet. Even though she'd only known Jake's traveling partners a short time, she'd formed a bond with them and sympathized with her husband's sudden and unaccountable loss of his new friends.

Jake chose his words carefully. A good night's sleep would give him time to gather his thoughts and determine the best way to tell the story without causing great alarm or raise suspicion about his recollection of the past week's true activities. He would divulge more of the truth to his wife than he would the others, but he didn't want to share his concern for their safety and create any need to worry about any future repercussions. He certainly was not going to bring up his recent massacre on the highway of the little rabbit people and their cute little rabbits.

After hearing the watered down recap, she asked, "My God Jake, is there any hope that Doc Mino and Mark Hutton could still be found alive? Just because you found two badges by the crushed car doesn't mean that George is dead. Maybe Nick will eventually recover. Maybe those badges aren't even theirs."

"I'm tired of thinking about it now. It's been a tough twenty-four hours and I'm beat. I'm just glad to be home and sleeping in my own bed with my wife! I'll call Uncle Hank first thing in the morning to see if there's any more news. He can verify the badge numbers, but I've got a strong gut feeling what the answer will be."

Jake woke up around seven the next morning. The adrenaline rush from the night before had made sleep difficult. There was too much racing through his mind, and he wanted to take care of a very important phone call to Uncle Hank before Judy awoke. He'd let her sleep in a couple more hours. He preferred not to involve her in the conversation because that would trigger a round of questions that Jake would like to avoid at this point. There were some very important strategic discussions between he and his uncle that needed to take place first before too much was said to anyone. It was very difficult for Jake to have to take this approach with his wife, but telling her the whole truth would put the fear o f God in her forever. She was visibility shaken by what she already knew, and there was no point in totally overloading her with too much information.

Freshly fallen snow covered the landscape in a clean coat of white.

To avoid any chance of Judy interrupting the conversation, Jake took the cordless phone from the kitchen and settled into one of the patio chairs outside where he could be assured of privacy. It was a little chilly, but the three patio walls offered some protection from the elements.

"Good morning, Uncle Hank. Just so you know, I'm trying to keep this conversation between you and me. If I change the subject suddenly, you'll know why. If that's the case, I'll call you back at a better time. I don't know what you've shared with Aunt Marge, but I'll understand if you do likewise. We'll both need to determine what needs to be shared.

I made it home last night and have a rather bizarre story to relay to you but first, is there any news on your end?"

Hank solemnly responded. "Unfortunately, there is Jake. Chief Arness was summoned to a house on the outskirts of Ewing last night. The residents reported a body was found lying in a ditch across the road just a short distance from their mailbox. It w a s pretty mangled and officials are trying to determine the identity of the victim as we speak. No identification was found. The officer's initial report indicated the victim may have been badly mutilated, similar to the cattle incidents we're both aware of. This might be another personal message being directed to us.

The authorities are making this a top priority, but not much will happen on a Sunday with a major storm threatening the state. I have a strong suspicion that the individual is one of our missing friends. Human mutilations are rare, but they do happen.

By the way, I asked the investigators to provide me with Nick's next of kin. According to them, Nick has one son named Alex Jensen living in Omaha. They'll let me know once they've located him.

So what do you have to report?" asked his uncle.

After a lengthy conversation of Jake's harrowing trip home, the two men hung up the phone. Hank promised to call as soon as the body was positively identified. Jake gave the two badge numbers to his uncle for verification. Again, there was little doubt. Unfortunately, most of the investigation would have to wait until Monday. A sense of urgency is nonexistent on a snowy, Sunday football afternoon in any branch of government, including the State Crime Lab. A skeleton crew might be doing some preliminaries, but the big dogs that held the keys wouldn't be in till the start of the work week.

Neither of the men held little hope regarding who the dead man was or who the badges belonged to. Jake was disappointed that he couldn't provide current information to all of those concerned family members he'd be meeting with this afternoon. He hoped to give them the latest information available at their three o'clock gathering, but it would more than likely have to wait until at least sometime tomorrow.

The state authorities had notified all three families late Saturday afternoon in their official capacity of the missing men. At this point, they couldn't give any specifics of the investigation other than that it was a top priority and they would be notified of any further information as it came in. Jake knew that their loved ones and close friends would be looking to Jake to provide them with something more.

He called both residences to confirm their appointment time.

Jake thought now would be a good time to call George Souders' wife, Mary, at their Lincoln residence. He politely introduced himself and after a lengthy conversation followed by sincere condolences, Jake promised to keep her informed when he received any official news from his uncle.

Jake was concerned about what George might have told her about his purpose for spending a week in the western part of Nebraska. With some careful, indirect questioning, he learned her husband simply told her he had some unofficial business to handle with his old work associate Nick Jensen on a cold case file, but didn't give any specifics. In George's line of work, Mary preferred not to hear the details anyway. She trusted her husband implicitly and generalities worked great in their discussions on work-related issues.

Jake didn't reveal his direct involvement or knowledge of their purpose in Scottsbluff, but he did want to plant a very strong seed. He had been invited by Doc Mino to join his former work associate and his two Lincoln friends to do some last minute pheasant hunting on their return trip home. The retired vet knew that Jake and his uncle Hank had some great private land privileges up around O'Neill, one of the premier hunting areas in the state. The two men had discussed making such a trip several times over the past year at their Thursday morning Lions Club meetings. After their business was finished earlier than anticipated, Doc Mino had called him to see if he would be so kind to arrange the hunt and perhaps join them. At Doc's urging, the two law enforcement officers decided t o take in some pheasant hunting on their drive back to Lincoln after getting a welcomed confirmation from Jake, their gracious guide, and his uncle. It took just one phone call from Hank and the men had access to any number of fields. It was a little out of the way, but the men had the time and desire to take a few well deserved leisurely days to enjoy some great hunting with their friends.

It was perfectly understandable to her that her husband decided to take an extra couple of days on the way home and spend some additional time to hunt with people he enjoyed being with. George very seldom took any personal time for himself and frankly, she never gave it a second thought. She was glad to see him do it.

Jake arrived at the Hutton residence promptly at three o'clock. After exchanging pleasantries and deep condolences with everyone, they adjourned to the living room. It was time to try and give these hurting souls some much needed comfort and answers.

Jake was elated with Mary Souders' reaction to the pheasant hunting rationale. He was encouraged to stick to that initial approach and wanted to reinforce their planned story again. After all, none of the family members were in town last week and they, like Mary, hopefully wouldn't have any reason to question that decision.

His hunch proved to be correct. No one thought it was out of the ordinary. Not a single comment or question to the contrary was raised. Jake knew the hunting story was not the end-all, but for now it would buy some valuable time. He needed every precious minute he could garner until the enemy played their full hand and showed the full aftermath.

Even though they didn't know Jake, his reassuring and comforting demeanor won them over easily. They could understand how their loved ones enjoyed his company. He was very helpful in their time of need. Jake put them at peace, telling them of the last several days he'd spent with them and their fun times and the discussions they shared. His genuine compassion was very soothing.

He obviously didn't go into the hidden agenda of Jack People, cattle mutilations and aliens with anyone he talked to. No one needed to know their true intent. These very questionable oddities would detract from their need to put some closure to the untimely deaths, and it could possibly turn this tragedy into a three ring circus if any one of these three topics got a life of their own in the news media. There was absolutely no reason to go down that path.

The family members certainly didn't question the caliber of the people who the missing men had spent their last week with. No lingering questions of what brought the men together ever surfaced. They were all highly respected professionals and stalwarts in their communities. Jake reassured the families that all of the men were having a great time together on their last minute, impromptu excursion.

The kindred spirits association came up a lot when talking about their newly formed circle. From an outsider's viewpoint, it would appear that all of the men had been good friends for a very long time.

None of the family members had any reason to blame anyone for the strange circumstances surrounding their disappearance, especially not Jake. After all, he and his uncle were in separate cars, miles away from where the car was found and they were just as much at a loss as the families were.

It was an unexpected, inexplicable tragedy similar to the thousands that occur every day, everywhere around the world. Along with the many tears that flowed, tears of laughter often followed with the stories shared.

Speculation from any law enforcement family would certainly center around some sort of retaliation from a past criminal case. Two of the men in the car were Nebraska's finest, and they had been together. If someone wanted to retaliate, they could take out two top cops with one horrible act. Because of that fact, they were sure that every effort would be made, above and beyond the call of duty, by state and local officials to bring those responsible to justice.

Unfortunately, there just happened to be two highly respected veterinarians in the car when the deed took place.

This was the assumption on everyone's part, and Jake wanted to let a sleeping dog lie.

The fact that the car was found crushed and abandoned in a remote field was a bitter pill for all to swallow. Nick's situation was also very puzzling. At least he was alive, and that offered them some hope. They simply had no possible answers. Jake assured them that both questions were critical to the lead investigators also. Until they heard otherwise, he suggested they all hold positive thoughts for Doc, Mark and George's safe return. It did remain a possibility.

Jake didn't share the fact that an unidentified body had recently been found. It would only create more anxiety and fear. They'd all find out soon enough tomorrow.

He returned home shortly after five that evening, emotionally and physically drained. All family members had questions that Jake himself pondered and certainly didn't have an answer to. They all hoped for the best but expected the worst. They were playing the *what if* and *why* game with themselves, and it was not winnable for anyone.

It was a true pleasure to meet with the family members, but he certainly wished the circumstances were different.

After a two hour nap on the couch, Judy woke him for a late supper. They talked about how the visitation went and what they might expect next, which didn't take long. Jake beat her to the punch and divulged some of the general conversation he'd had with Hank earlier in the day while she was still in bed.

Everyone's suspicions proved to be true with a call from Hank just before noon on Monday. The body found in Ewing was confirmed to be that of Dr. Mark Hutton. Both conversations were brief. The badges, as expected, belonged to Nick Jensen and George Souders.

The state authorities had notified the family just minutes prior to their call to the judge.

Shortly after twelve, the phone rang again. This time it was a very distraught Martha Hutton. "Jake, I'm sure by now that you've been notified of the news about Mark. I was wondering if you'd be so kind to come by the house again around two this afternoon and discuss our arrangement options now that we know for sure.

We'll have Mark cremated and we'd like to have a memorial service later. The Mino family would like to join us. Both families feel a joint service at a later date would be very proper under the circumstances once we know a little more. It's been a while since either family has last dealt with funeral arrangements, and we thought it only appropriate if you could offer your professional suggestions before we meet with the funeral home Monday morning. We're certainly not abandoning hope for Doc's return, but with Mark's confirmed death, it does shed a rather gloomy light. We'd like to be prepared. We won't have the memorial service until after the holidays, and that will give the authorities a little more time to determine Doc's status.

We'll also have to release a statement to the media soon, since this story regarding the missing men has been on all of the local channels statewide. We could certainly use your expertise and we'd be most appreciative. I know from our meeting yesterday you thought highly of both of them."

Jake graciously accepted their request. It would be his honor to help in any way he could.

CHAPTER TWENTY-FIVE
JUDGE HANK'S STRATEGY

The holidays took their toll on everyone. The last two weeks of 2013 were emotionally draining for those involved in the unexpected tragedy.

Since Jake and Judy had hosted Thanksgiving, the extended family decided to do get together for Christmas somewhere other than Scottsbluff. Jake made a call to his friends who owned the High Plains Homestead, located out on the prairie sixteen miles north of Crawford, Nebraska. It was centrally located for most of the attendees. Jake had the pleasure of meeting Mike and Linda Kessler about a year ago, and he'd stayed at their fun resort several times while in the area on business.

The Homestead was usually closed for business over Christmas, but the Kessler's would be home for the holidays. When they heard that Jake would like to bring fifteen family members out to their unique lodge, they graciously accepted.

The High Plains Homestead is an authentic replication of a late 1800s Nebraska prairie town, complete with jail, mercantile, saloon, schoolhouse, Main Street, houses, blacksmith shop, bunkhouse, cook shack and cabins. It's a popular tourist spot in the summer months, but closes down in the late fall; there is, however, an exception when you know the owners.

Jake and Judy were looking to get away for a three day holiday. Jake's sister Barb and his nephews Alex, Skip and Gunther lived just a short distance away. It wasn't more t h a n a three hour drive for any family members who made their reservations. Since Christmas fell on Wednesday, Uncle Hank and Aunt Marge would arrive Tuesday morning. The two men had plenty to discuss and this was their opportunity. The Homestead offered numerous hideouts to escape to for complete privacy. They had the complete run of the otherwise empty facility.

Mark Hutton had been confirmed dead just ten days earlier. Because of the holidays and their previous statements, Jake and Hank hadn't been questioned since the initial start of the investigation out in the field where the car was found.

Law officials from around the state were very familiar with Judge Henry Reimer's credibility, integrity and professionalism for his many years of admirable service on the bench. His word was gold, but state law officials needed to get sworn statements from both of them. There had been no new progress in their investigation, and talking to the last men to have been involved in the case might uncover some overlooked clues.

A holiday rendezvous was just what they needed to corroborate their statements. Hank was very aware about what was at stake with his testimony. So was Jake. Since the judge was the expert, he'd decide the best strategy to take during the questioning. There was no way Hank could be officially tied to anything but arranging a hunting outing. He'd only had contact with the men for around twenty-four hours. The others all checked in to the Super 8 motel. They'd all been seen together at DW's talking football. He'd made a call to Junior Roberts to obtain permission to hunt on his property. H i s testimony regarding times and dates, if requested, would go unquestioned. The judge was not on trial nor was his word.

Jake's, however, needed a little work. Although he certainly wasn't implicated as a suspect in the case, he carried more of a history with the men, albeit a brief one. The story by now was all over the state news outlets. Media coverage was taking advantage of the totally bizarre story and had been using it as their lead since the morbid death of Dr. Hutton and the strange case that Nick Jensen offered over a week ago. There were still two men missing, and then there was Jake. He was becoming a very valuable link in the investigation.

State authorities were asking anyone with any information to come forward. Key figures such as Jan Gradert, Robb and Shar Bosworth and Samuel Yellow Bear all had given their statements to law enforcement officials. The U-Rent Store in Gering verified a Geiger counter rental to Jake Young for the week of the disappearances.

The pheasant hunt was becoming a little more scrutinized, and authorities sensed a v o i d in the initial story. It would appear on the surface that what Jake had told authorities initially made sense, but it also seemed like there may be more to the story that perhaps h e hadn't been totally forthright about. It was just a matter of time before Jake would be put under the microscope.

Hank didn't want to directly represent Jake legally since he was also involved in the case, although in a smaller capacity. He had to excuse himself because of their relationship. Hank's grandson, Joel Reimer, could. Joel graduated from University of Nebraska Law School and had practiced law for the past five years in Omaha. Joel and his wife Rita would be arriving at the Homestead later in the afternoon. Both Hank and Joel would attend any informal questioning. Since Jake was not a suspect and only being asked for information, there would be no conflict of interest if grandson and grandfather attended the unofficial inquisition as legal counsel. Hank would preside over the hearing and Joel would represent Jake.

Joel, Rita and their two sons, Henry and Louis, arrived around four Saturday afternoon. It was about an eight hour drive from Omaha, and they were the last to arrive. The now complete family spent a couple of hours partaking in festivities at the bunkhouse which acted as command central when the family all got together. The separate building next to the cabins had an ample living room with plenty of room for everyone to be comfortable.

A little after eight-thirty that night, after Joel put the boys to bed, the three men retreated over to the Dirty Creek Saloon, just a few minutes' walk from the bunkhouse. Jake got Mike's permission earlier in the day to open the building and the liquor cabinet.

Hank spent an hour presenting the more detailed, unexposed pieces of the case to Joel. The young Omaha attorney, like everyone else in the state, had been riveted to the story, especially since there was family involved. Jake was more than glad to let the two lawyers do the talking. He sat in absolute silence as the two lawyers reviewed his situation.

After concluding with the briefing, Hank offered his best legal advice to the two on how to approach the questioning. He'd had considerable time to think about how to handle Jake's delicate situation.

"Honesty is always the best policy. I've lived my life by the law and I'm not going to change that philosophy. We have absolutely nothing to lose by giving the facts on this fifty-year-old murder case. I think we'd be doing Nick and Doc a major injustice if we didn't. They came so close to solving it. The truth, however, will be difficult to tell to the many skeptics that will appear before us. This testimonial will be given, more than once, to many levels of the bureaucracy. Get used to it. We have the truth in our favor and we'll use it, but only to those that need to know. This doesn't mean we run out to the press and tell our story. That's not what I mean. The media couldn't handle the truth and would make a mockery of the entire incident. None of us wants that to happen. We'll be very selective about who we share the truth with, and once placed in their hands, they can determine what they want to do with it.

I believe the best defense is a good offense. Instead of waiting for the officials to make a formal request for Jake to appear for questioning, I suggest we offer Jake's testimonial to the proper authorities' right after the holidays. I'll make out the appropriate list of people I want present in the informal hearing. It'll be a small, select group, but they'll be the right men to present our unbelievable story to. I do have some credibility with these men and I know they'll honor my request."

Hank returned to O'Neill the following Monday after Christmas and drafted a letter to the Attorney General of Nebraska. He didn't put any specifics in writing. He did ask for their presence regarding Jake Young's full testimony in the unsolved case and set the date for Friday, January 10, 2014. The informal meeting would be held in the Nebraska Attorney General's office, room 2115 in the State Capital Building at nine A.M. At this point he did not want to get the Feds involved. They might complicate things.

As requested, several state attorneys were present at the capital on the tenth. Since the Honorable Judge Henry Reimer asked for the meeting, he presided over it. Although the small panel was interested in what Jake Young had to say, Hank did most of the talking for both of them. There would be plenty of opportunities for Joel and Jake to give additional testimony of the events that transpired earlier in the week and answer any questions, but the judge wanted to be in charge of giving out the important details he'd been directly involved in at the time of their disappearance. The judge was an excellent orator, while Jake was a novice in this type of setting. After all, that's why these men were here sitting before him. He wasted no time in the proceedings.

In his opening statement, he prepared those in attendance for an unbelievable chain of events that transpired in early December, merely a month ago. He gave an overview of what brought these men together in both their official and unofficial capacities. Although all the files that contained the original documentation and several pieces of key evidence had strangely disappeared, Hank gave testimony to what was included in the initial presentation that December morning at the clinic office.

The statements given by the others coincided with what was presented in their earlier testimonials. All of the men present had the opportunity to review them prior to that morning's meeting.

Jake had a chance to give a complete recount of the events leading up to the Thursday night disappearance coming home from O'Neill.

The two men told their incredible story in two hours and then opened the session up for questions. Uncle Hank admitted that the pheasant hunting story was not exactly the end result, but now that the truth had been exposed in its entirety, he no qualms about leading with the story until he had a chance to set the record straight with today's proceedings. He wasn't trying to hide the facts; he was trying to buy time to decide exactly who should be told the facts. This was a major security issue that was extremely sensitive in subject matter, and he didn't want to start rumors or a massive wave of worldwide hysteria.

In closing, Jake presented a full blown picture of the buckskin's unexplained braid, t h e cemetery bones and the rabbit tunnel hieroglyphics. This was the only visible evidence they had to show other than the two badges belonging to Nick Jensen and George Souders. Everything else had been either picked clean by the aliens or left for the coyotes to clean up on a lone Nebraska highway.

The select group of men in attendance were stunned by what was presented. In their various capacities, they'd been exposed to stories relating to alien sightings and cattle mutilations. Judge Reimer added some very credible evidence of their existence, a l t h o u g h he provided little proof. None of the men had ever heard of the Jack People, but at this point in the presentation, nothing would surprise them.

Archer Pugh, the lead attorney representing the Nebraska Attorney General's Office, gave a closing statement after thanking Hank and Jake for coming forward with the truth to this baffling mystery. It was still unsolved, but at least all of the facts were now on the table.

In conclusion, Pugh first made a motion to absolve both men of any wrongdoing by withholding evidence. Those in attendance would talk next week via a secured conference call to decide how to proceed with the information given them. They'd have the weekend to determine their best approach to try and appease the general public without giving them all the details. They all understood the delicate predicament Jake and Hank had been in the past month, because it was now in their lap. They'd have to determine what to do with it. For now, the story was assigned a top security classification and would not be discussed with anyone without the proper credentials.

CHAPTER TWENTY-SIX

DEAD SILENCE

The two families decided to hold a memorial on Mark's birthday, January 21. With Jake's help, they planned a beautiful service at St. Francis Episcopal Church. There was no sign of Doc Mino, now in his eighties, and it had become obvious to his family and community that Doctor L.H. Mino was probably not returning.

The church held over four hundred people and the chapel was overflowing out into the vestibule. Dr. Mark and Doc Mino had made a lot of friends over their combined 70-year careers tending area livestock, pets and their community. Jake and Judy, along with U n c l e Hank and Aunt Marge, sat towards the front with the Hutton family, just across the aisle from Doc Mino's daughters and their families.

Two generations of respected veterinarians, business partners and friends gone forever. The entire Scottsbluff and Gering communities suffered the loss, in addition to the many friends and associates across the western panhandle of Nebraska and eastern Colorado and Wyoming.

Doc founded a Seeing Eye Dog program in the community back in the late 1970s and volunteered a lot of his time working with these specially trained K9s in training, adoption and seeing to their overall health needs throughout his later career. When Mark took over the practice, he also became involved in the beloved project. Six of these magnificent animals sat stoically in front of their seated owners at the front of the chapel, behind the pulpit. They served as honor guards for their former trainers who'd worked with them since they were pups. Amazingly, the dogs had a keen sense of who was missing from this large, somber crowd. The unexplained loss was reflected in their sad eyes.

Several area ranchers who'd dealt with both men for many years spoke of the dedication the two men had shown the community. A number of funny stories were told by those that had the opportunity to work alongside of them. It was tough for any of the speakers to speak about one without oftentimes referring to the other. They worked together and now, in all likelihood, died together.

Since Jake had befriended both men on a professional and personal level, and was the last to see them both alive, he had the honor of speaking last. He emphasized the quality traits the two doctors possessed and how they applied them to their families and community. He gave a very warm eulogy that was heartfelt and well received by the grieving congregation.

Jake spoke of their dedication to their families and their profession. He'd had a lot of time over the last several weeks to learn what was important to them by driving close to three hundred miles on the back roads of rural Nebraska together. He wanted to take this time to celebrate their lives with uplifting stories instead of dwelling on the sadness of their deaths.

He again focused on the pheasant hunting slant they'd told the authorities and the families. By this time, people knew Jake wasn't there when the men vanished, so they couldn't really expect him to elaborate about the empty crushed car found in the middle of the field and the fate of its former occupants, a mystery which still remained unsolved.

Many rumors had surfaced around the state, but Jake believed that discretion was the better part of valor. It was not up to Jake or Hank to fuel any speculation on this unbelievable story. They'd told the truth almost two weeks ago in a closed session meeting with the top legal officials in the state. The incident was under investigation and that would have to suffice until an official report was released by officials if and when that time ever came.

Jake and Hank certainly weren't seeking the short celebrity status followed by the ridicule people would find for exposing their story. After recently spending a week with two experts who had been down that route for the past fifty years, they knew it was an effort in futility that would only bring added scorn and humiliation. The reputations of all six men meant far more. They knew the truth and that was good enough for them.

Those in attendance were longtime friends and members of the community, and they were looking for an answer. Doc and Jan Gradert had given them the truth years ago and they were laughed at. As he addressed the audience who were now wearing their serious faces, he knew if he gave them any ammunition, the minute they left the church the chastising would begin.

Jake took the opportunity to share the story of Egon Harrasser, the young savant they'd befriended while sharing a lunch at DW's in Ewing. Doc had been very impressed at the young boy's knowledge of Nebraska football, which was near and dear to all in attendance. Mark even extended the offer to take the boy and his mother to a Husker game.

The story was met with many happy tears in the congregation. They could all visualize the story taking place as Jake warmly told it. That was Doc Mino and Dr. Mark Hutton.

He shared the following story in closing. "One day Doc and Mark were working together vaccinating cattle. They took a lunch break up at the ranch house. The wife put together a nice warm meal for them. Her seventeen-year-old son had made some homemade vanilla ice cream the night before for the two guests as a special treat.

Their youngest daughter, who was just ten at the time, was asked to prepare the dessert for the two vets.

Instead of grabbing the plastic Tupperware two gallon tub of ice cream, the little girl mistakenly grabbed a tub of lard which was stored in the back porch freezer next to the ice cream. The lard, looking much like the ice cream with pretty much the same consistency, was also stored in an identical, used plastic ice cream tub. Because of her short stature, she had to jump up and balance her stomach on the edge of the horizontal freezer and stretch down to the bottom to reach the tub while trying desperately not to fall in.

She inadvertently grabbed the wrong container and proceeded to serve her guests the lard, topped heavily with Hershey's chocolate syrup. The gleaming young hostess anxiously awaited their approval before serving the others at the table.

Both Doc and Mark took a large spoonful in their mouths at the same time. After a few agonizing initial chews, there was an immediate gag reflex that only the frozen, chocolate-drenched fat could elicit. Being the polite guests they were and trying to not hurt the little girl's feelings, they nonchalantly and indiscriminately turned to remove the foul substance into their napkins without missing a beat. They graced their little host with a big smile without saying a word, shaking their heads politely, indicating she should proceed serving her family. It didn't take them long to realize their daughter's mistake, and she was soon apologizing profusely to their guests for the mix up. Her apology was accepted after a good long belly laugh by all at the table."

As the congregation wound down their shared laughter of Jake's story, he stepped from behind the pulpit and made his way back to the end of the pew next to the outer row of windows. Once seated, he briefly glanced out through the glass at the dark clouds rolling in over the ominous gray landscape.

As Dan Heleniak, the Dean of St. Francis Episcopal Church, closed the service with a prayer, Jake froze instantly with horror. Out of the corner of his eye he caught a glimpse of a lone Jack standing to the side of his mount under a barren oak tree across the street. Once it made several seconds of piercing eye contact with Jake, the critter disappeared from sight.

Jake's immediate reaction was, *Oh shit, here we go again. It's not over.*

The unexpected vision left him speechless as he stood up to make the exit with his wife, aunt and uncle from the front of the church. It was a quiet ride home as Jake's mind raced in anticipation of his future. Did he actually see the Jack or was his mind imagining the unthinkable?

He didn't mention the incident to Hank, Aunt Marge or Judy. Perhaps with a little time they all could put this daunting experience behind them. They certainly didn't want to worry themselves to death over the all-consuming question of what if. This new aberration certainly wouldn't help their healing process.

The foursome stopped at the Runza Hut in Gering for lunch after the service. After eating, Marge and Hank wound their way back to O'Neill as Jake and Judy made the ten minute drive home.

As usual for this time of year, a light snow began to fall. Just after turning off the main highway onto the dirt road that eventually led to the house, Jake intentionally but unsuspectingly slowed the Escalade down to take a long, careful look at the handful of horses gathered next to the pasture fence located on the southwest corner of the rural intersection.

He took a particular interest in their tails. He was immediately gratified to not see the ominous and strange braiding on any of the animals.

What about the next time and the time after that and the time after that? he thought.

Maybe they would be an early indicator in predicting his future, if he wasn't first driven to insanity in the process.

Once home, Jake changed out of his suit into his comfortable clothes and adjourned to his den recliner. He stared out over the distant back landscape where his life had changed less than two months ago. Would he constantly be on the lookout for jackrabbits every time he sat here? Would Yollie involve him in another confrontation every time the dog went outside?

The fear of an almost certain retaliation did haunt him, although he tried very hard to suppress it. Could the Jacks still be out there? He was certain that their alien cousins were. The thought of these two uncommon but deadly foes dominated his thoughts.

People were seeing them in record numbers worldwide by now. Maybe the Jack People and their alien friends would leave Jake and his uncle alone. They certainly weren't bringing any attention to the situation, which might raise a red flag for another visit.

Besides, the stories were so commonplace now, regularly on the front page of the tabloids sold in the grocery store checkout lanes, and no one gave them much thought.

This experience would haunt both men to their graves, just as it had the other four men who didn't make the trip home. It was like a curse. The method of mental punishment h a d been a tried and proven approach that seemed to fit the pattern of any alien a b d u c t i o n s or interactions that hit the headlines over the past thirty years.

Flying saucers and aliens were widely accepted worldwide by now and over half of the populace believed in their existence, but what about the countless victims who either reported them or had also become their victims, and the lives that were destroyed?

Another incredible story might not put the fear of God in people the way it did back when Orson Wells first read his *War of the Worlds* broadcast back on Halloween night of 1938, but Jake's incredible experience certainly put the fear of God in him. Maybe with some serious discussions, God could get it out.

As Jake sat pondering these intimidating questions, his thoughts were interrupted by the sudden ring of the telephone. After two rings, he picked it up and held the receiver next to his ear. There was nothing but that deafening, dead silence on the other end that Jake had learned to fear the most.

Fifteen seconds later, Jake slowly put the phone down, visibly shaking and now enveloped in unfathomable fear. After a few minutes of staring blankly out on the falling snow and trying his best to regain his composure, he slowly got up from his chair and walked back to the bedroom to get his revolver. His head and chest pounded like a bass drum with every step down the dim log hallway. It was now twilight and the storm was in full force gale.

Acknowledgements:

I would also like to thank my family and friends, both old and new, who I had the pleasure to see while doing a month-long book tour of Nebraska in September of 2013. It truly was an incredible experience!

Thanks for letting me stay with you along my journey!

Barb, Nick, Alex, Linda, Warren, Karen, Rita, Jan, Jerome, Dewey, Walt, Diana, Karen, Ronda, Jackie, Jake, George, Neal, Mrs. Bonar, Mr. Johnson, Dan, Phil, Audrey, Lynda, Kevin, Dennis, Lael, Dusty, Pam, Russ, Shawna, Rusty, Curt, Michelle, Lois, Vivian, Jerome, Mike, Terry, Stew, Carol, Shar, Robb, Taylor, Abby, Marc, Jenny, Lilli, Lainie, Lauren, Henry, Susie, Gavin, AJ, Zack, Dick, Joyce, Joe, Joyce, George, Mary, Mark, Martha, Lance, Fran, Diane, Gary, Mike, Kurt, Debby, Tom, Laurie, Redding Breakfast Lions Club, Halo Publishing, Lisa, Hot Springs Star, Diane at the Crawford Clipper, Scottsbluff Star Herald, Linda, KNEB, Chadron Record, Ranch House Restaurant, Larry, Ron, Janet, Tom, Ft. Robinson, Prairie Bookstore, Chili's, KCNB, Hastings Daily Tribune, the Zoo Bar, the Wrecker Bar, DW's, Steel Grill, Redding Record Searchlight, Carl Bott at KCNR, Mrs. Lashley, Black Hills Books and Treasures, Second Street Slammer, Scott, Shellie, Wally, Barrel Bar, High Plains Homestead, Richard, Dottie, Junior Young, Gary, Phyllis Eitemiller, O'Neill Public Library, Holt County Independent and Adams Transmission just to name a few of the many.

Thanks to grandson Taylor for helping with my computer needs!